# Don't Tell Me How It Ends

# Don't Tell Me How It Ends

A Novel

Adrienne Thurman

THE DIAL PRESS
New York

The Dial Press
An imprint of Random House
A division of Penguin Random House LLC
1745 Broadway, New York, NY 10019
randomhousebooks.com
penguinrandomhouse.com

A Dial Press Trade Paperback Original



This book contains an excerpt from the forthcoming book *Better in Real Life* by Adrienne Thurman. This excerpt has been set for this edition only and may not reflect the final content of the forthcoming edition.

Library of Congress Cataloging-in-Publication Data
Names: Thurman, Adrienne, author
Title: Don't tell me how it ends: a novel / Adrienne Thurman.
Description: New York: The Dial Press, 2026.
Identifiers: LCCN 2025037566 (print) | LCCN 2025037567 (ebook) |
ISBN 9780593978986 paperback | ISBN 9780593978993 ebook
Subjects: LCGFT: Romance fiction | Novels | Fiction
Classification: LCC PS3620.H875 D66 2026 (print) | LCC PS3620.H875 (ebook)
LC record available at https://lccn.loc.gov/2025037566
LC ebook record available at https://lccn.loc.gov/2025037567

Printed in the United States of America

2nd Printing

Book Team: Production editor: Cindy Berman • Managing editor: Rebecca Berlant • Production manager: Chanler Harris • Copy editor: Laurie McGee • Proofreaders: Kate Hertzog, Barbara Greenberg, Barbara Jatkola

The authorized representative in the EU for product safety and compliance is Penguin Random House Ireland, Morrison Chambers, 32 Nassau Street, Dublin D02 YH68, Ireland. https://eu-contact.penguin.ie.

*For Lyra—everything, always.*
*And for all the women whose love and laughter are the true heartbeat of it all.*

# Don't Tell Me How It Ends

# 1

ANY OTHER NIGHT, UPON HEARING MY VIBRATOR'S GARbled last gasp, I'd give myself a mental lecture on personal responsibility and shimmy back into my underwear. It's my own fault for having organizational practices that are more feral than feng shui. That charger could be anywhere. But I'd been depending on the familiar distraction—battery operated as it may be—to ward off my mental crisis—existential as *it* may be.

I swap out the lifeless pink silicone in my hand for the phone, but somewhere between the lock screen and my six emotional support streaming accounts, an errant swipe pulls up the hours-old notification that sent me rummaging through my nightstand in the first place. There's nothing for my landlord and me to discuss; he knows I can't afford the lease renewal alone. *I* know I can't afford the lease renewal alone. We just disagree as to whether or not that warrants a phone call.

I kick free of the bedsheets. No comfort watch is going to be enough to turn my brain off tonight. I'm still in need of an out-of-my-head *full body* comfort of sorts. So, biting back the bitter taste of preemptive regret, I swan dive into the seventh circle of hell, unpausing my *in case of emergency* dating apps. If silencing this mounting quarter-life dread doesn't constitute an emergency, I don't know what does.

The bars on Mass Ave. close in thirty minutes, so there's no time for discretion. I've got to be quick if I want to get in on the desperate apocalypse now Tinder scramble that's already underway out there. So, bomb fishing it is—swiping right on anyone in this half-empty college town who looks like they might be up-to-date on their shots.

A flurry of new messages signals my success—a word I'm using *extremely* loosely at the moment.

Peter (28) comments on one of my mirror selfies: "*Wife!*" With a few heart emojis for good measure. No doubt it's meant to be a compliment, but with that hairline, the word reads more like a threat. Godspeed, Peter.

"*Hey!*" writes J (34). "*You're absolutely stunning. Would love to take you out and get to know you.*" Sorry, J, but if you're only giving up one letter, I'd bet there's one word to describe your actual relationship status: married. Send my regards to the Mrs.

Carlos (32) wants to know, "*Do you enjoy cooking? Do you like to dance? Do you enjoy a good film? Do you vote? What's the last book you read? Do you hope to own a house one day?*" And without even pausing to confirm that I'm present and accounted for, or at the very least, human, he continues waving his red flags high. "*I'm looking for my soulmate. Marriage, kids. Let's make sure we're on the same page.*"

Not even on my darkest day, Carlos.

"*We're all energetic beings,*" says Marcus (30). "*All matter's made up of atoms, with charged particles, that vibrate at a certain frequency, also known as energy.*" Damn. It's always the cute ones.

And Lawrence (25) can't even spare the thumb dexterity required to tap a question mark when he asks, "*Wyd*"

He's perfect.

**Me:** How fast can you get Downtown?

•

I've watched enough *Dateline* over the years to know that giving Lawrence my home address may very well have just set the stage for my own one-hour special. Which is why I also know I have to do this next thing:

**2:34am**

**Me:** Hey, just in case

I send the text along with a screenshot of Lawrence's profile and my location (or last known whereabouts, should things end poorly).

If I'd known Zola was up, I would've texted one of the other ten million or so infinitely less judgmental people in the world. My sister's been reliably knocked out by sundown since that little pink plus on a stick changed everything, but I must've caught her mid-bathroom run or in the throes of a WebMD doom spiral, self-diagnosing rare birth anomalies.

Even the *ping* my phone makes when she responds sounds unusually shrill.

**2:36am**

**Zola:** Jesus Kai. You of all people know how dangerous this is.

She's not wrong.

I may have slightly understated my true crime–viewing habits. It's not just that "I've watched enough *Dateline.*" It's that I've memorized entire seasons of crime scene evidence, could rank my top fifty episodes chronologically, and in addition to recognizing the actors in various dramatizations, I can also recite their past credits as jilted lovers, handsome bartenders, or hiker #3.

But I'm not trying to get into all that while I speed-shave in the bathroom sink.

**Zola:** me and Eliza use your "dates" as a scare tactic in client meetings now

Her text doesn't achieve its maximum impact since I could've scripted the exchange myself. Nothing in this world gives Zo more joy than talking shit on other people's life choices, and in Eliza, she found a boss who promised to reward her for it. I still can't believe professional matchmaking is actually a thing, but apparently Manhattan's elite are just lonely enough to liquidate retirement accounts for their shot at *happily ever after.*

**Me:** Shouldn't I have to sign a waiver for that?

**Zola:** Says the woman inviting strange men over without one.

**Me:** Valid.

**Zola:** if leveraging your dating fails gets me one step closer to a promotion, it's your sisterly duty to support that. I bet Eliza does it at my review this week when she hears what I'm working on next.

Of course, I support her, I just can't get excited about the same mythical promotion Zo's been chasing since I left for school four years ago. Being loyal to a job for this long without any upward movement is the saddest sort of *pick me* behavior. Zola stays pressed, professionally. I'm sure she has her reasons, but since none of those reasons are reflected in her paycheck, I don't ask.

Dating fails? I type instead. Who's dating?

**Zola:** Precisely.

This bravado is exactly why you shouldn't be allowed to stay with your high school sweetheart beyond high school. Zola's never been out in these streets, dodging the litter and oncoming traffic that is *men*. Picking a forever guy off the class roster in homeroom doesn't exactly constitute expertise.

At least, he was *supposed* to be forever. Smith comma Jason played us all. And after more than a decade together, his parting gift to Zola is a lifetime spent picking up the pieces of the thing he blew up from the inside.

**Me:** How's my favorite nephew doing in there?

**Zola:** Already using the baby to get yourself out of trouble?

**Me:** is it working?

The next *ping* to my phone is accompanied by Zola's latest ultrasound images. I send a flood of *heart eyes,* with the hope Zo's maternal instincts will override the hating big sister ones.

**Me:** Ah! He has my nose.

**Zola:** His face is currently smashed against my pelvis.

**Me:** His face is perfect and so is he. I thought you were gonna facetime me into the 3D one! can't believe I missed it.

**Zola:** You weren't the only one.

Her text bubbles have my full attention as they repeatedly appear and vanish, until finally Zola's face, not her words, fills the screen.

Before my phone completes its first ring, I'm already answering the incoming call.

"You okay?"

"Damn," she says through a laugh that's noticeably humorless. "Who's got you all eager in the middle of the night?"

"Right now, you," I say, attempting to sound as earnest as one possibly can with a heel slung over a porcelain sink. "I can't remember the last time you were up past dusk, and now you're calling at"—I pull the phone from my ear long enough to check the time and ignore the OMW text from Lawrence. "Almost three A.M."

I briefly consider, and promptly decide against, dry-shaving my bikini line. I'm working way too hard for a guy who communicates exclusively in three-letter shorthand.

"What's going on?" I ask, plodding over to my underwear drawer.

"It's nothing. I'm being dumb."

But I already know she's not. *Dumb* has never been Zola's style.

"It's just that scan," she says. "It was the one thing I really didn't wanna do alone. And Jason knew it. I set it for the '*only time*' that worked for him. Had to call outta work and everything. But, of course, he still canceled. Who knew you could be a single mom before becoming a mom at all?"

Her words stop me in my tracks. Zo was never supposed to be a single mother. It's not the kind of thing anyone plans on, but Zola didn't just doodle boys' names in the back of her notebooks, she brainstormed LLC's. Her vision board didn't end with "*I do.*" That's where it began. But no matter how meticulous her five- and ten-year plans, Jason was Zola's *X* factor. The one thing she couldn't control for. And because his shit didn't add up, Zola's now the thing she swore she'd never become.

Before I can metaphorically cock back to light his deadbeat daddy-to-be ass up, Zola rushes on.

"And Mom's being newly ghosted by some guy with terrible plugs and transition lenses who failed to mention he's *un*ethically nonmonogamous, and not looking for anything serious. So, of course, that's her entire personality now."

And I know *that*—not the Jason stuff—is where Zola wants

the conversation to remain. It's why she's led me to our forever favorite rabbit hole: Mom.

We've all got that friend who's more committed to her chronic fuckboy drama than anything else in the world, certain the key to her very happiness is singular and man shaped. She's got her breakup script down to a tear-filled monologue about how she's going to die alone, and you have to be all, "*He never deserved you. Ain't nobody checkin' for him.*"

*That's* our mom. At least that's who she's been since my freshman year of high school, when Dad ran off with his associate professor. Just another woman, walking blindly into the rip current of every *next guy's* empty promises. It's the same every time; she lets them pull her further and further from solid ground—from me, Zola . . . herself—until their dizzying tide breaks, and she's spit back out at our feet, waiting for us to fish her out and bring her back to life.

The only thing more inevitable than the breakups themselves has always been their aftermath. Mom's recovery process is a science. *Stage 1: fetal position. Stage 2: CIA level recon.*

She wouldn't exactly win any parenting awards for it, but Zo and I used to love when she'd put us on the case. We'd all stay up late, cracking passwords and monitoring credit card statements as husband number two flew his new white girl around for seedy hookups in three-star corporate hotels. And once we had irrefutable proof of what Mom had probably known all along, we'd listen to her rewrite a romantic history that never was and lament a romantic future that never would be.

But we didn't mind, because it meant we'd survived another *stage one.* That Mom had scraped herself up off the kitchen floor enough to get to work—even if the work was wildly inappropriate peewee reconnaissance. It still meant she could see us again, that she needed us. And that's all we ever really wanted.

Unfortunately, no matter how much time we spent playing

full-time therapists and part-time detectives, it wasn't enough. Mom would eventually find her way back, but she'd do it hand in hand with another guy joking about her teenage girls calling him *Daddy.* In the end, *he'd* be the only thing worth coming back for.

Then, one day, Zo and I grew up. And that meant realizing we should've been charging Mom by the hour all along.

"God, she's exhausting," I offer, teeing Zola up for our usual go-round.

"And I'm pregnant. I'm already exhausted! I don't know why I thought Mom would take care of *me* for once."

Our familiar cadence changes when she says it. Because *this* isn't our usual go-round. Not anymore.

I start cautiously. "Zo. I remember what it feels like to try to resurrect her alone. Those few years after you left for school were heavy. You shouldn't have to do this on your own."

The gentle suggestion that Zola may not be able to handle something erases all signs of her physical and emotional fatigue. Or perhaps it's the intrusive buzz from my intercom that does it.

"Maybe instead of worrying about us, you should help yourself first," she says, sounding like my big sister again. "The world doesn't need another missing Black girl."

I smile at her righteous superiority, knowing that at least for tonight, balance in Zola's world has been restored. Hopefully enough that now, she'll sleep.

"Don't worry," I tell her. "I'll keep my Taser under the pillow."

I practically hear her eyes roll. "You don't get points for saving your life, if you're the one risking it in the first place. Just keep your location on. We can fight about the rest tomorrow."

I buzz Lawrence up without verbal confirmation that it's him. No use feigning regard for personal safety now.

"If you still need me later, I should be free in like an hour."

"Ew," is all she says.

"You're the one growing a penis inside you," I say, laughing as I end the call and open the door to meet my next great decision.

The best thing about having sex with men you'll never see again is that you don't have to wonder if it's good for them. The worst part is that it goes both ways.

Lawrence, I realize too late, is the kind of guy who has sex *at* you. I know he's not up there reenacting his favorite porn scene right now for *my* benefit—at least I seriously hope not. A singular focus on his own sexual experience? That, I can respect. Him living a quarter century under the impression that this rabbit pounding has anything to do with pleasing a woman is a prospect too grim to consider.

To stave off an outburst about how the patriarchy is to blame for the strategic vilification and ultimate disregard of female pleasure, I allow myself the briefest moment of dissociation—mentally restructuring my budget to delay having to sell a kidney, or worse yet, start another roommate search.

"I never do this," Lawrence grunts as he thrusts into me again with so much force, I wonder if my vagina has wronged him somehow.

The movement is enough to bring me back to my body and Lawrence's blond curls tickling my ankles wrapped around his thick neck. He's got the neck of a linebacker. Everything about this guy screams *athlete.* Though between his age and the fluff at his midsection, his glory days are likely a thing of the past.

Still, as a former athlete of sorts, I'm willing to bet Lawrence *does* "do this." And if that's not evidence enough, there's always the fact that he's been at my place a full eighteen minutes, and inside me now for at least three and a half of them.

I don't mean to laugh, but I don't exactly try to stop myself either.

"Says the guy who probably has a Costco-size variety pack of flavored condoms on his nightstand."

Lawrence stills, and the tightness that had begun to coil around my belly subsides.

Confusion twists his dense brows and decently attractive face. "Huh?"

I don't know if he's offended or just trying to sort out how I know he buys in bulk, but I need his head back in the game.

I toy with my nipple while my free hand digs into his hip, urging him to regain his momentum.

"Nothing," I say, my voice purposefully breathy and wanting. "I never do this either. It's my first time."

Who's to say if he takes it to mean it's my first time on the apps or my *first time* first time? Either way, I'm lying and he likes it.

"Shit," he groans, finding his rhythm once more.

Lawrence pulls out of me abruptly, before expertly flipping us over, so I'm on all fours with him at my back. He enters from behind and a smirk plays at my lips. Real comfortable tossing me around for someone who *never does this.*

By my second failed attempt to coax his hand between my legs, it's clear that tonight it's every man for themselves.

I back into him to stay fuller a bit longer as my fingers get to work. The familiarity of my own touch is a welcome departure from the night's series of disappointments. Focused only on tending to my own budding tremors, it doesn't take long to find release. It's guttural, and primal, and probably nothing like the girlish sighs Lawrence is used to from his video girls.

With all my senses fully spent, my brain is finally blissfully quiet. So quiet, in fact, that I could almost forget I'm not alone in the room if not for the "Oh fuck" my final pulses draw from Lawrence as he finishes too.

He collapses back onto the far side of the mattress to catch his breath and gently rolls the condom down before tossing it indelicately onto the hardwood.

I don't read the new Tinder notifications on my lock screen when I grab my phone, but I do open the app just long enough to pause my account again before texting myself one simple reminder: *buy spare charger.*

**10:37am**

**Zola:** And then what happened??

As I finish recapping the night for Zo, the promise of leftover lo mein propels me through the half-empty apartment. For years, this place felt like it was *mine,* but when the sleeper sofa and both roommates were carted off after graduation, I finally saw it for what it's always been: temporary.

**Me:** He asked if it was lame to invite me to breakfast.

**Zola:** Wait, that's actually cute.

**Me:** Don't squint too hard trying to see what's not there. I'm not paying for your professional delusion.

**Zola:** Even if you wanted to, you couldn't afford me.

An incoming call interrupts our conversation, and I drop the phone like my landlord can see me through it. I can't believe I let it come to this.

I should've been planning for this ending all along—it had all been right there in the University of Kansas brochure: four years. That's what they promised and that's what I got. I just thought by the time they handed me my degree in early education, I'd be transformed into someone new. Someone with a job, a 401(k), and a clue what they were supposed to do next.

All I've got is cold Chinese takeout and the acute awareness that I'd rather do almost anything but teach.

When the ringing stops, I come back into view of the phone and Zo's text.

**Zola:** I'm afraid to ask if there's more.

**Me:** He wanted my number, but I said I'd rather keep things on the app til we know each other better.

**Zola:** this is what you said AFTER you fucked him?

**Me:** correct. Then I closed the door and promptly unmatched.

**Zola:** How romantic.

I mindlessly clear the voicemail notification from my screen, as if that alone negates the inevitability of whatever my landlord's been trying to tell me for days.

**Zola:** You shouldn't be allowed to do life without adult supervision. If you were my client, I wouldn't let you out of my sight.

**Me:** if I was pathetic enough to use a matchmaker, I'd deserve whatever I got.

Zola doesn't spend as much time as usual reading me for filth or defending the virtue of her professional pursuits. She's more focused on discussing the depths of Mom's latest depressive episode.

It briefly feels like cause for celebration that I hadn't been forced to learn another new guy's name till he was already past tense, but when I hear the strain in Zola's voice, the thirteen-hundred-mile buffer I've built myself suddenly feels all wrong. If anyone deserves to fall apart right now, it's Zo, but she's on her own out there. Pretending to have *her* shit together so Mom can lose hers.

My phone rings again, but this time when I see the number on the screen, I pick up.

"Hey, girl!" Jess says, wielding the word like a weapon. I already know what's coming next.

"Hi, Jess."

"Girl—"

I bristle, wondering what Reddit post advised her to talk to her Black employees this way. Like I'll be so disarmed by her forced familiarity that I won't notice she's a career bartender turned manager, who's never successfully worked a full shift in her life. Like I'll forget she's never helped me when I needed coverage. Like I'll forget I'm her begrudging employee—and not her *girl* at all.

"What's up, *girl*?" I say, entertaining myself.

"Girl, are you busy today? I am trying not to stay here till four."

I'm currently alone. Taking this call in my vacant living room. Where the coffee beside me is tepid, and the floor below me is digging into my ass. I'm in a bra and sweats, with no plans of showering, and my curls are still matted from being smothered beneath Lawrence earlier this morning. But am I too busy to pick up a daytime bartending shift for a boss I can't stand, on the first weekend of summer that everyone's off campus? I want to say I am.

I'm about to drop my next sarcastic *girl,* when my phone pings in my ear. I check it reflexively.

**Rich:** Hi Kaia. Been trying to get a hold of you. As you know, the renewal window on your lease has passed. I haven't heard

> back about scheduling time for our prospective tenants to see the unit. But the twenty-four-hour notice of entry window has also now passed, so please consider this final notice that we'll be on site to show the apartment at 2pm. Thanks.

Homelessness has now officially been added to my growing list of grievances. Fuck.

"Hellllo?" Jess calls, through the speaker impatiently.

"Ya know what?" I start, a decision forming on my lips along with the words. "I actually can't. I'm getting ready to head back to Connecticut for a while."

"Um. Did you submit for this time off? Because I don't recall approving anything and you're on the schedule in two days." Curiously Jess is all business now.

"I know, *girl*," I say, buoyed by the escape plan taking shape. "But family duty calls."

I don't listen for Jess's response before hanging up, and I don't check one-way flight prices before texting Zola, who must be closer to her breaking point than she'd let on, because she doesn't poke a single hole or demand every granular detail I don't have.

She simply says: YES!!!

# 2

MY FINGERNAILS TAP OUT A FRANTIC RHYTHM ON THE window of Zola's black Volvo when I find her in LaGuardia's pickup line. It's only been a little over a month since she and Mom came out for graduation, but Zola's always quick to match my airport energy regardless.

I yank open the passenger door, expecting to be all ta-da!, but what comes instead are tears. A rush of them, which hit with so much force, it seems to catch us both off guard. These aren't your typical *reunited and it feels so good* tears. These are *it was self-defense, he had it coming, help me hide the body* sobs of urgency.

And they're coming from my sister.

"Shit, Zo!" I say, ignoring my bag and the swarm of cars not so patiently waiting to take our spot.

As far as I can see, there's no blood coming from anywhere and she doesn't look hurt. But I haven't heard even a whimper from Zola in years—not when our dad left, not when she found out she was pregnant, not even when her garbage can of an ex declared a baby wasn't what he "signed up for."

"Is it the baby? Are you hurt? Is it Jason? Is it Mom?"

I pepper her with questions. Panic mounting as each goes

unanswered. The violence of the sobs racking her body makes me fear the worst, but still, she doesn't respond—she can't. She's all screams and snot, doubled over beneath the weight of whatever's happening. I may not know what it is, but I know my sister well enough to know it's bad.

Zola sucks in a breath so jagged and desperate, the effort of refilling her lungs must cause physical pain.

And then she finally speaks. Or tries to.

"I got—" She chokes on another sob and I feel the sting of tears in my own eyes now too. I'd offer her the air from my own lungs if I could.

"Zo, what the fuck, I'm freaking out."

I don't even remember reaching for her, but both my hands are now intertwined with one of Zola's. Her other hand hasn't left her belly.

She tries again. "I just got . . . (*GASP*) . . . fucking . . . (*GASP*) . . . fired!!!"

"What the fuck?!"

I pluck a wad of old paper towels from the cupholder so Zola can address her leaking face. Other than that single movement, the car's deathly still—a stark contrast to the relentless activity right outside.

Her wail gradually calms to a feeble sniffle or fifty, before being snuffed out completely.

Zola removes her hand from mine and uses it to shield her face. I wait for fresh tears to fall, but instead it's laughter that bubbles out.

"What the fuck?" she says through grim giggles. "I mean, Kai, what the fuuuuck?!"

"I didn't even think a pregnant person could *be* fired," I say, having no actual knowledge of discrimination law.

Zola scoffs and shakes her head. "It's a recession out there, haven't you heard?"

"Shit," I say, eloquently.

"That job was all I had left. And she wouldn't even listen to my next pitch."

She says it in a whisper. Staring off into nothing—eyes glazed, wheels turning.

I don't know what she's working on up there, but I'm down for whatever Zo needs, including, but not limited to, elaborate smear campaigns, bank heists, or just sitting in this arrivals lane for the rest of our lives.

Well, maybe not that last one if I have a choice.

"You want me to drive?"

She shakes her head but makes no move for the steering wheel—both hands still firmly clutching her belly.

She's done that constantly since she found out she was pregnant. I haven't been brave enough yet to ask if Zola's offering the baby comfort or if it's the other way around.

I put my full focus into avoiding eye contact with the airport security guy approaching us and try again. "You want to keep talking about it?"

She shakes her head once more, and I think that might be all I'll get for now.

But then she speaks. "Not without ice cream." And the ghost of a smile crosses her lips.

This is more than a flimsy attempt at comedic relief. It's Zola harnessing her unwavering strength, even as she sits in the eye of the storm. And that's exactly what this year's been for her—one inescapable, unrelenting shitstorm.

She deserves a break. She needs it.

"Snack run?" I ask, considering the limited vices a pregnant woman can indulge in. "Binge some shitty movies?"

Zola sniffs just once, wipes her nose with the back of her hand, and nods weakly before shifting into gear, dryly parroting my words: "Snack run. Shitty movies."

•

"Okay, don't kill me," I say, pushing the cart while my pitiful sister trails behind me. "Is there any way this could actually be a *good* thing?"

I warn off the Whole Foods employee beaming at us from the far end of the freezer section with a subtle shake of my head. If he so much as smiles at Zola's belly or asks how far along she is, it will end in murder.

Ironically though, it's Zola who cracks a smile first—and another sarcastic laugh I hardly recognize as hers.

"Oh yeah," she says, the grating pitch of her voice another clue that I've misstepped. "Pregnant, single, living with my mother, *and* unemployed. Now there's nothing stopping me from descending into complete and utter ruin. Thanks for the silver lining!"

She tosses a pint of Half Baked into the cart with so much hostility, I actually flinch.

But because I'm a masochist, I press on. "But you didn't *really* wanna be a matchmaker forever. Spending the rest of your life convincing sad singles that fairy tales come with a money-back guarantee? The whole thing feels made-up."

If a look could be described as a *prebludgeoning,* that's what Zo gives me.

I walk my comment back just enough to make it out of here alive. "Fine. But I know you weren't completely happy with *that* job. And Eliza was never gonna let your promotion happen."

"You don't know that," Zola says, defending the woman whose demise I'd been plotting for our entire ninety-minute drive.

"Uh, I think we kinda do know that now."

Regardless of the intention, I take Zola's momentary hesitation as permission to speak freely.

"How often did you bring her ideas that she chopped and screwed and called her own? How many times did she let you do the groundwork on leads, and then, *oops,* conveniently leave you out of the meetings where contracts were signed under *her* name?"

Zola bristles and reaches for her emotional support belly.

I soften my approach. A little.

"I know you wanted her to be this mogul mentor who put your name on the door right beside hers. But sometimes lady boomers are no better than the old, rich, white guys we've always known were the problem."

I lead us down the savory snack aisle, indiscriminately grabbing preservative-laden, salty goodness from the shelves. Days like this call for gluttony.

"You might've learned the business from her," I continue, "but you gave her access to youth and culture. You gave her your perspective. And fuck her if she can't see the value in that. Because now you get to go build your own fucking door to put your name on."

Something sparks in Zola's eyes before she blinks it away, stepping in to take control of the cart and the conversation. I relinquish both.

"It's not that easy," she decides, steering us toward the registers. "In case you haven't noticed, life is getting incredibly real incredibly fast. And I'm alone. Like *alone* alone. My life's a fucking mess and I'm about to be somebody's *mother.*"

She says it like it's a dirty word.

"Nobody's coming to save me from this, Kai. I'm the one who's supposed to do the saving now."

Her voice breaks when she says it and I know if Zo let herself cry again, it wouldn't be for the baby or the job. Not this time. She'd be crying for all the times she just wanted to be taken care of and all the ways she wasn't. I know because I feel it too.

But as quickly as the emotion is there, she swallows it and continues. "I don't need a door with my name on it. I need a paycheck. I need childcare. *That's* real life."

Zola leaves the unspoken implication hanging—the stakes for her are real, where I, as she's explained many, many times, am still just playing Adult™. Like it's the latest Mattel drop.

But she's in no condition to go round for round, so I don't take the bait. Instead, I stare into my only lifeline out of this conversation and this familiar dynamic where I'm perpetually sixteen.

I'm so busy scrolling my phone, I don't notice it's our turn to check out.

"I guess I'll get this," Zola says, making a show of unloading the cart.

You'd think there were anvils in that bag instead of plantain chips. Sometimes a sister needs a shoulder to cry on, other times she needs a punching bag. *Welcome back, Zo. Happy to be of service.*

"We got like ten things," I say, waving my phone toward the conveyor belt. "Not exactly a two-man job."

Zola relaxes a bit when I hand over my card for the snack haul. She *is* unemployed after all—though, as of a few days ago, so am I. But I'm not saving for two.

"Mom?" Zola guesses, when my focus shifts back to my phone.

"It's like the exact opposite of Mom," I say, laughing at the joke meant purely for my own enjoyment.

Zola quirks a brow in confusion.

Without explanation or warning, I twist my hand to share the absolute poetry on my screen.

"*You tryna fuck?*" she reads aloud. "God. Can't you swipe left or something?"

"I could," I tell her, deleting the first message that snuck through before I repaused my Tinder account. "But then I'm left with these."

I hand my phone to Zola and watch as her face flashes from *intrigue* . . . to *confusion* . . . and *concern* . . . before landing squarely at *horror.* Like one of those little flip-books from when we were kids. The modern-day dating experience in thirty gruesome seconds or less.

She holds my phone out between her thumb and pointer before dropping it into my hand like it's radioactive. "I feel like I should go to the clinic after reading those."

"Little late for that," I say, nodding toward her stomach as I carry our bags out of the store.

We make our way through the lot as Zola physically shakes off the messages that I'm sure will haunt her for years to come.

"Why are you even on there?" she asks once we reach the car. "Those guys are the stuff local news stories are made of. And look at you."

"Oh relax. Great women have been having mediocre sex with terrible men since the dawn of time." *Probably.* "There's nothing wrong with soliciting a consensual dick pic every now and then."

"There is if you're doing it to avoid actual conversations with men who don't speak in innuendos and eggplant emojis. Real-life, grown men who understand that the word *hello* must precede a request that you sit on their face."

After loading the back seat with what would appear to be the take from a grocery heist committed by a couple of six-year-olds, I join Zola up front.

"I know too much about *grown men* to want to have conversations with them. This way it's like visiting monkeys at the zoo—fun, but from a safe distance, so there's minimal risk of them flinging shit in your face and then ripping it clean off."

Her black-brown eyes roll so far into her head that for a moment, they're all whites and spider lashes. That's when you know she's *all the way* over you.

"You're better than this," she says, pulling out of her parking space.

I tear a donut in half, handing Zola the smaller piece. "I promise you I'm not."

"How long has it been since you went out with someone?"

"I—"

She holds up her donut to stop me. "In real life, in public, with your clothes on."

I shrink back into my seat. "Oh. Well, yeah, that's different."

I open my mouth to continue pleading my case, but Zola interrupts me again. "Shit, hold that thought. I gotta pee."

She spins the wheel back toward the store's entrance, ignoring my protests—*we're only a few minutes from home, can't you hold it, etc.*—and mumbles something about baby heads and bladders, before hopping out.

I start my Netflix search while I wait for Zo to return. Her movie night viewing habits demand that I make our selection before she gets a chance to weigh in—lest I spend the next several hours stuck in a raspy Kate Hudson, smiley Julia Roberts rom-com haze. But a tap on the window distracts me from my perusal.

The man waves, as if he's expecting me to return the gesture. I don't.

"Do you need something?" I say, from behind the closed window. Despite the fact that it's the middle of the day and there are countless people passing in and out of the overpriced grocery store beside me, I still double-check the car door locks. *Ways Not to Die 101.*

He smiles at the realization that we'll be doing this at full volume. I don't return that gesture either.

"You can't park here," he says, still blinding me with teeth so white they're glowing.

My eyes drop to his chest, in search of a green grocery apron, police badge, or something else to explain his presence, but he's got on a simple gray T-shirt and blue jeans. The relaxed outfit offsets his square chin and prominent cheekbones in a way that screams, *Sure I'm a model, but look—I'm just like the rest of you mortals.*

Admittedly the clothing choice is working for him. Accentuating a physique that's very likely *not* the result of afternoon car donuts. It feels like a personal attack that he looks that good in such a haphazard outfit while I currently look like the *before* on a transformation post. And can someone please explain why nature wastes perfectly curled lashes and flawless skin on Black men while the rest of us go broke on mascara and concealer, trying to keep up?

He mistakes my inaction for confusion.

"You're in front of the hydrant," he explains further. "You can't be parked here."

He's right that I'm confused, but not about the intricacies of local parking ordinances.

"Do you work here?" I ask, through the still closed window.

He leans his entire six-foot-something self onto the passenger door of Zola's SUV, like we're old friends, catching up. Like maybe he'll stay awhile.

The casual nature of his posture momentarily stuns me, but his single-syllable response ("*Nah*") ignites a new spark of determination. "Are you some sort of plainclothes parking attendant?"

His face cracks into a near smile that he suppresses with the flick of his tongue before catching his bottom lip between his teeth. "Nope."

"So, you're here to—" I pause, unable to come up with an insult that sufficiently conveys my disbelief at the exchange. "I'm sorry, explain to me why we're having this conversation?"

"They stay towing cars out here," he says, the tone of his muffled voice alternating between indifference and amusement. "But if you're really trying to park here—"

"I'm not even parked," I bark back, exhausted by the utter maleness of this chastisement.

The crease of his brow activates the slightest flare of his nostril. "You're not parked?"

"My hazards are on," I tell him, and I don't even care that I'm not making sense. *He's* not making sense.

At that, he has the audacity to laugh. Out loud. In my face. A head tipped, gaping mouth *laugh*.

He recovers, and—to my great disappointment—continues. "So, your car's in . . . which gear?"

*That's it. We're done here.*

I roll down the window just enough that I won't have to say this next part on a yell, but not so much that he can take my purse or my person—or my donut.

"Look, I can appreciate that you've lived with a certain expectation that everyone's just dying to hear your big, strong, alpha-male opinion, so this isn't entirely your fault. And as Fairfield's self-appointed parking authority, I understand you feel a certain obligation to—"

"Oh, now I'm an alpha for trying to save you a tow." He's playful when he says it—mischievous, like a cat batting at a mouse. Too bad I refuse to play dead.

"Ah," I say, raising a finger. "See, I think that's our disconnect. I didn't actually order saving today. Must've gotten the wrong car."

He pulls himself off the car, extending to his full height again. "Yeah. I guess I did."

I shrug, my tone turning as saccharine as my girlish grin. "Happens."

And without missing a beat, this man says, "I bet it happens to you a lot."

*Now, hold the fuck up.* "What's that supposed to—"

But he doesn't let me finish.

"Look, there's a lot going on here," he says, with enough sense to finally look mildly uncomfortable. "How 'bout I go inside and work on my social deconditioning and I'll let somebody else deal with all this." He says it while waving in the general direction of the car before pausing his hand directly in front of my face. Like *I'm* the asshole.

"Yeah, that's probably for the best," I say, dismissing him by turning my attention back to my phone.

In my peripheral view, I vaguely see his thick eyebrows rise as he mouths something that looks a lot like *Wow* as he retreats. I nearly bite my tongue off to keep from engaging further.

And did I already mention the universe hates me? Because not even two seconds later, a car door slams behind me and when I look to the side mirror, an actual real-life uniformed officer is approaching.

I roll my window down and smile up at him, in an attempt to juxtapose the smoke billowing from my ears.

"Ma'am," he begins. "You know you're parked in front of a yellow curb?"

I try to remember if it's illegal to scream in an officer's presence if you're not screaming *at* the officer. Just a scream. Just to get it out.

"Mm-hmm," I begin, through closed lips. I don't yet trust myself to open my mouth (for fear of the scream). "Got it," I say, once it feels safe to speak. "I'm moving."

I shovel the last of the donut into my mouth while crawling over the center console. *Fucking cops. Fucking men. Fucking Zola's weak-ass fucking bladder.*

Once I've settled into the driver's seat, I turn to wave at the officer walking back to his cruiser and lock eyes with *Mr. Save the Day Samaritan.*

"I bet you're loving this," I yell through the now open window.

"I don't even know what *this* is," he shouts back before disappearing inside, behind the obnoxiously sunshiny beach display I suddenly want to destroy.

When Zola opens the passenger door a few minutes later, I'm parked as far from the entrance and any yellow curbs as humanly possible, replaying the nightmare that just unfolded on a loop. Only in my version, there's violence.

She sees me fully reclined in the driver's seat with an arm slung over my eyes, but she can't possibly know the emotional minefield she's entering.

"Hey," she says casually, buckling her seat belt. "I couldn't find you. Why'd you move?"

*Don't hit a pregnant woman, don't hit a pregnant woman, don't hit a pregnant woman.*

"Is there wine at the house or should I stop on the way?"

# 3

ZOLA AND I ARE HUDDLED OVER THE COFFEE TABLE, UNpacking our snack haul, when Mom emerges from her *Why don't you love me?* cave of despondency. She's in the same tattered breakup uniform I've seen too many times: a raggedy sweatshirt she stole from an old college boyfriend and a satin bonnet that barely covers her two-week-old wash 'n' go.

The smile on her face when she sees us is more physiological mechanics than actual emotion, but I don't take it personally. *Real* smiles come at stage two (or even three: *back in the saddle*).

"I didn't realize you were back already," she says to us both, but her arms are outstretched to Zola. Misery does love company, after all. "I got your text. I'm so sorry, baby."

I leave space for Zola to talk about losing her job, but she forces a tight smile and reaches for a bag of chips to busy her hands instead. And when Mom says, "I can't believe Eliza did you like that, after all this time," Zola's eyes dart to mine over her can of sparkling water, silently screaming for help with sisterly telepathy, well-honed over a lifetime.

She doesn't want to talk about this. Not now. Maybe not at all, with Mom.

"We needed to stock up on rations," I interject.

Mom pulls me into a hug of my own and I bristle at the frailness of her body, the weakness of her embrace, and how she rests her weight on me when I hadn't offered to prop her up.

I know she wants me to ask about all the ways *whatshisname* wronged her over the many *weeks* of their deep (and not at all exaggerated) love affair, but it's all I can do not to peel the sweatshirt off Mom's limp frame and search for the once-vibrant woman who used to wear this skin.

Mom releases me before collapsing onto the couch beside Zola, reaching out for Zo's belly to greet the baby and offer what minimal support she can muster. Zola's rigid frame visibly untenses. She lifts the unclaimed half of her blanket in invitation. Mom accepts it gladly.

"We're about to watch something," I announce from my seat in the worn recliner that used to be Dad's go-to spot.

"That actually sounds perfect," Mom says, tucking Zo's blanket up to her chin.

Hoping to capitalize on the tenuous peace we've achieved, I turn the TV on, clearing my throat with the gusto of a smoker with a pack-a-day habit. A wordless proclamation that we have officially switched gears. For the runtime of whatever's about to be on the screen, nobody's allowed to bring up anything miserable. Those are the rules. I just decided.

"So, are we feeling a movie? Or should we go straight-up murder show marathon?" I'm obviously only asking to be polite. Blunt force trauma is always the clear winner.

"Ugh, no true crime," Zola whines. "Last time you were home, I had nightmares for a month. You're such a—"

"Choose your words wisely," I say, slicing the air with the remote. "I'm not above reporting our shared account to Netflix. Pretty sure the penalty for that now is jail."

Zola pretends to throw the tiniest handful of popcorn in

my direction before bringing it to her mouth. "Can we please just watch something that doesn't end in me sleeping with the lights on?"

This isn't my first time deflecting a suggested *Dateline* detox—or intensive psychoanalysis to identify why I seek out humanity's most gruesome acts as a form of entertainment. The truth is, I just take comfort in *knowing.* Knowing with absolute certainty which stories will *not* have a happy ending, and working backward to uncover all the reasons why.

"Boo," I chant through a mouthful of frozen cookie dough. "You're lame."

"Don't make me pull the baby card. Do you really want your nephew thinking the world is all lies, betrayal, and revenge before he's even born?"

"Better he knows now," I tell her.

But even as I say it, I navigate our search to the comedies. Zola's right, laughter's got to be better for the baby than, well—homicide.

"I'll see your comedy," Zola starts, "and raise you—"

"Rom-com?" Mom interjects, and though her delivery doesn't pack much of a punch, the suggestion is a fighting word and she knows it.

I pantomime a swoon. "The one where a quirky yet adorable caricature of a woman throws her life's work away at the first hint of validation from the shirtless D-lister promising forever?" Then I go stoic. "I've already seen it, and spoiler alert, the heroine ends up worse off than she started."

Zola's head's been lolling since the word *caricature.*

"Oh god, relax. We're picking a movie, not tearing down the patriarchy. I wish I'd had a chance to get you in front of Eliza before . . ." Zo trails off, before redirecting. "Maybe she would've known how to deal with all *this.*"

Zola waves in my general direction as she says it. Her hand

circling my face from afar. Flashes of the Whole Foods "parking attendant" making a similar gesture burn red-hot in my memory.

"I just wish they'd call the genre what it is," I snap. "Fantasy! But they play in our faces with these unrealistic men, when I'm not sure they've ever had an actual conversation with a real one. And it perpetuates this arcane metric of female success. Spoon-feeding us unattainable relationship standards, while men get to consume media that fails to mention they'll be held to any standards at all. I take offense at that. And after what Jason did to you, you should too."

The moment his name leaves my lips, I regret it. Zola's smile falls and her hands reach for her belly.

"Shit, Zo. Sorry. I just meant—"

But it's too late. And this time, I deserve it.

"You think if I spend a couple hours watching sappy montages of people falling in love, I'm gonna forget Jason's trash? If the promise of *happily ever after* buys me some modicum of temporary peace, I don't see what's wrong with that. Believe it or not we don't all need to watch people get stuffed into freezers to remember life isn't all rainbows."

I always forget how fast Zola can still *big sister* me into submission.

When she sees she's got the upper hand, she presses on. "*I'm* the one who got knocked up, dumped on my ass, *and* fired! Yet somehow you get to be bitter? Please make it make sense."

On cue, Mom's crossed leg bounces her foot up and down. Her foot in that nasty leopard slipper—the pièce de résistance of her breakup uniform. She's seated now, but the house is forever haunted by the sound of her shuffling around for dark chocolate and red wine. Too wrecked by *Tom, Dick,* or *Tyrone* to even lift her feet off the ground.

Zola's gaze follows mine. I don't have to say a word—she gets it. We've both been trapped in Mom's toxic cycle of *he loves me, he loves me not.* Only, Zola's response was to become immune to heartbreak where I became immune to love. She still believes in fairy tales. I don't know what I believe in.

"Fair enough," Zola says, sounding eerily calm.

She flicks popcorn kernels from her swollen abdomen with a smirk, repositioning herself to use Mom as a footrest. Since we were kids that's how we sit when we have something real to say. Whoever has their feet on Mom has the floor.

My eyes are on Zo, silently begging her not to call me out. I don't have the energy for a run-in with Mom right now. Zola's eyes are filled with amusement in return like, *Relax. I've got this.*

I'm most definitely not relaxed, but I am somewhat intrigued.

"Mom, you know I love you," she starts. "But I think the stench of our respective romantic failures is souring poor Kaia. So, I'm gonna need you to speed up your recovery."

Mom looks like she might burst into tears if given the chance, but before she can, Zola continues.

"Because I've got a project in mind that demands our full attention," Zo says, wagging her eyebrows. "All three of us."

Mom looks at me expectantly, like maybe I'll be leading the next part of this family meeting, but all I can do is shrug. I'm as lost as she is.

We turn our attention back to Zola as she pulls herself into a sitting position, eyes blazing. Now I'm *seriously* intrigued.

Zola sets her sights on me, and I recognize that same spark she'd tried to hide earlier. But it's back now, and this time, it's packing heat. "Did you mean what you said at the grocery store? About helping me start my own thing? Getting my name on the door?"

In all the years I've known Zola, the look she's giving me

now has never *not* led to trouble. I manage the weakest, barely perceptible, most noncommittal nod, but Zola's eyes ignite, like I've just taken a blood oath.

"It's come to my attention, dear sister," Zola begins, "that you've become too cynical for your own good. So, before this little baby shoots his giant head out of my once-bangin' body, it will be my mission—my *job*—to help you find love."

I sputter-choke on my water.

"Whoa, what? Me?" I say, wiping my chin with the back of my hand. "I thought we were gonna fix *Mom*."

"Hey!" Mom shouts, kicking a slipper at me. Thank god she misses, because—ew.

"Sorry." I laugh. "But let's be real, I'm the last person under this roof who needs a life coach."

"Hey!" Mom and Zola shout in unison this time.

"Sorry," I say again. "But . . . well—"

Luckily, before I can keep digging, Zola throws back the blanket and damn near sprints into the kitchen to retrieve her giant tote bag from the island.

Mom and I stare in silence as she fishes around in there before hoisting up an unmarked black binder like a torch. Ready to set my world on fire.

"I'd like to formally announce that I'll be opening my own matchmaking firm," Zola declares to the room—though she still hasn't taken her eyes off the binder.

But then she *does* take her eyes off it, and now, they're once again looking directly at me.

"And Kaia here has generously volunteered to be my very first client."

I whisper the next part, the way I would if approaching a rabid dog or wild animal. "Zo. Maybe I could help by like passing out business cards or watching the baby."

She doesn't respond. I'm not totally sure she can even hear me. Her singular focus remains on that binder, flipping through the pages with a look on her face that leaves me genuinely concerned she may be in the throes of a psychotic break.

I look to Mom for backup, but even as she cringes for my benefit, it doesn't hide the first genuine smile I've seen in her eyes since I got home. I'm relieved to see signs of life, but also—*traitor.*

I try again. "Zo."

"Here," Zola says, splaying the binder open on the coffee table so I'm staring into the article that will be my demise. "I prepped this presentation for Eliza before—"

"She fired you," I finish for her this time. If I'm going down, I'm taking everybody with me. "Anyone else need wine for this?" I ask, rising from my chair.

Zola's glare is ice, but Mom raises a hand and I high-five it on my way to the kitchen.

Before I can pull away, Mom wraps her fingers around mine and squeezes. Just for a moment—there and gone—but there's a silent promise in her grasp that says, *I'm trying.*

The whole first floor of the house is open, so there's nowhere to truly escape, but I still spend longer than necessary uncorking the rosé I picked up earlier. Moving my body a little offers an outlet for my mounting anxiety. And it can't hurt to put some distance between myself and Zola's *evil genius* energy.

"An-y-way." Zola says those three syllables more deliberately than anyone in the history of the world. A less than subtle indication that she's reclaiming her time. "I had a pitch ready for our next social media push. It's based on this: thirty-six questions psychologists say can lead any two people to fall in love."

I reenter the lion's den, snatching the printout from Zola's hands as I sip my afternoon wine like the lady of leisure I am now.

"Let's see," I say, flopping sideways into the recliner so my legs dangle over the armrest. A lady of leisure, sure, but never *a lady.* I could swear Mom actually giggles into her wineglass.

I rattle off a few of the less invasive bullet points from Zola's article.

"Who's your ideal dinner guest? Would you want to be famous? Wait," I say, getting tripped up on the third one. "Doesn't everyone rehearse phone calls before making them?"

Mom and Zo laugh like I've delivered a punch line. *Note to self: apparently no, everyone does not.*

"I think there's something here," Zola says, with renewed focus.

She sounds like she's seated at a conference table, while I'm still lying here in yoga pants, picking cookie dough chunks from my teeth.

"It's gimmicky enough to hit on socials, but there's real scientific backing for the client. For Kaia," Zola clarifies. *Threatens.*

A few sips of rosé with a splash of midday collusion, and Mom's almost giddy. "Yesss. Zo, you're a genius."

"Duh," Zola says, flipping her boho braids behind her shoulder.

"You're both hilarious," I say through a snarl. "Can we please get back to picking a movie?"

"No," Zola insists. "This is happening."

She looks so serious I'm legitimately worried that she *is* serious.

"You were right," she says, using my three favorite words against me. "I need to at least *try* to get my own thing going, and you need to get out of your own way too. You're an adult now. You can't hide behind pithy one-liners and casual sex forever."

"But if not for casual sex," I retort, "then *why are there men*?"

Zola throws her hands in the air. "I rest my case."

Usually, I don't mind having the spotlight on me. As the younger sibling, I sort of revel in it, but this is different. This is an ambush!

"I'm sorry, I didn't realize not falling for every guy who flexes in my direction is cause for an intervention."

"Well, maybe it is," Mom says, betraying me for the second time. "Nobody's trying to marry you off, but I figured at some point in the last four years, you would've brought somebody home. Or gone to theirs."

"Or gone to dinner," Zo jabs, under her breath.

I snap my fingers theatrically. "I knew I forgot something. I thought I was supposed to be building a life for myself. But I was there to find a *man*."

Zola scans the room like the mystery life I speak of must be hiding somewhere around the corner. "Oh, is *that* why you were able to pick up and leave with three days' notice? Because of this robust life you've established."

"Zo," Mom warns, but her effort to shut Zola up is half-assed, and we all know it.

"You got your degree, but you act funny when I ask about job prospects," Zola continues. "You say *love* like it's a dirty word. Even picking a movie just led to a dissertation about how the modern woman's better off alone. You're practically begging for an intervention."

"Well, this has been enlightening," I say, already moving toward the nearest exit. "So glad I came home to help out. Zola, good luck on your new venture. Mom, please enjoy my wine."

Zola lies back on the couch, effectively giving up on me, but Mom's not put off as easily.

"Honey, don't leave," she says with a sigh.

And I can't stand being the reason that flicker of light in Mom's eyes has gone out again, but if this confrontation is any indication of what's coming this summer, I'm going to need something stronger than rosé.

# 4

**W**HAT IS IT ABOUT FAMILY AND OLD STOMPING GROUNDS that brings out your angsty inner teen in sixty seconds or less? Back in city limits and immediately back in time. As evidenced by the surreal string of texts hitting my phone.

**5:16pm**

**Liv:** You should come! Everybody's here

Liv Foster's been my best friend since forever. Which is why when she says "everybody," I die a little, picturing the impromptu high school reunion of my literal nightmares. It's also the reason I can't figure out why this invite sounds like an afterthought.

**Me:** You're already there? Why didn't you hit me earlier? And since when does Speckled Pig do private events?

**Liv:** These are all questions you can ask when you get here. COME!

I hear it in her usual singsong tone but still take notice that this must've been why Liv couldn't pick me up earlier. I hadn't expected her to drop everything for my last-minute return, but I also kind of had.

**Me:** Today's already been a week.

**Liv:** My train's in a couple hours. You have a hard out!

**Me:** should we just meet up in the city next week then?

Liv's been in Manhattan since her parents divorced the summer before she started NYU. Pitting Mommy and Daddy against each other kept Liv well fed and well housed all four years, despite the city's soaring real estate costs. Oh, to have estranged parents desperate to buy your love. I can't even get a three-dollar birthday card out of dear old dad. Of course, that would require that he remember a birthday.

**Liv:** JUST COME!

I'm tapping out a firmer no, when Liv says a few of my favorite *shut-me-up* words:

**Liv:** I'll buy all your drinks.

Talk about burying the lead.

**Me:** On my way.

It might've been my responsibility to notice the charge on Mom's car was in the red before ducking onto these backstreets to avoid rush-hour traffic, but I didn't. And what good is that kind of thinking anyway, now that I've already lurched to a dead stop on the road's nonexistent shoulder.

I allow myself exactly five seconds to curse everyone and everything before flipping on my hazards and assessing my surroundings.

Minutes ago, I would've described the lush Connecticut greenery overtaking this two-lane road against a backdrop of a true-blue evening sky as picturesque. But in this current predicament, my brain is doing its fun little party trick—mentally cataloging all the cold cases I've seen that begin under circumstances similar to my own. Overgrown woods aren't quite as *picturesque* if your lifeless body is being hurled into them.

Cell service out here has always been spotty at best, but even the universe must realize that particular joke is played out. On my third attempt, the search results for local tow companies magically load.

Before my finger can tap *call* on the first link, something big pulls up behind me. Parked, bumper to bumper—so close I can't make out what it is. Probably one of those white conversion vans with "candy" and "puppies" inside.

Mom better be kind when choosing the photo to run with the story of my disappearance. And Zola already knows to wipe my search histories clean.

A knock at the window interrupts my panic. The glass is almost completely filled by the nondescript gray fabric covering this guy's broad abdomen—easily the width of two of mine. So much for overpowering him.

I take my eyes off the window just long enough to unlock my phone and debate whether I should use this last opportunity to call the police or Zola. Something tells me the latter might actually be the smarter choice. I've seen *Taken,* and Liam Neeson's got nothing on Zo.

The guy raps on my window again, his face replacing his body in my view. The sight of it shakes me to my very core.

*Fuck, fuck, fuck, fuck, fuck.*

Of course, when *Mr. Save the Day (Again) Samaritan* isn't enforcing parking ordinances at local grocery stores, he's some sort of F-150-driving forest ranger. And *of course* he is here with me now.

"Hey," he yells. Even the glass muffling his voice doesn't hide his amusement. "Need some help?"

Where's the guy in the ski mask when you want him?

"No thanks," I say, trying to remember what are words. "I'm good."

I give a lame little wave when I say the last part, to really sell it.

He's not convinced. "Cars fly down this road. Let me at least get you off the bend."

I hold up my phone and say, "My boyfriend's actually on his way now." Impressed by how effortlessly I deliver the lie.

"Oh, cool," he says. "I'll wait in my truck till he gets here. Make sure you're good."

I don't take my eyes off his truck in the rearview as I call for a tow. I only pray they won't hang up on me when I ask if, in addition to the auto service, they're also willing to fake date me for a few minutes.

They answer on the first ring. "Pops Towing."

"Hey, my car just died. Is there somebody who can meet me out in Westport?"

"Yeah. I'm actually out that way now," he says, like the absolute hero he is. "What are your cross streets?"

"I'm at Greens Farm and . . ." I scan the street, embarrassed that I have absolutely no clue.

"Maple?" he suggests. "Westbound?"

"Maybe . . . yeah?" I offer, weakly.

"White Audi?"

"Yeah, how'd you—"

Before I can finish my question, there's another knock on my window. Whole Foods guy is back, holding his phone up so I can see the active call. When he puts it back to his ear, I hear him through the window, but also through my phone.

"You're gonna have to come out now, so I can hook you up to my truck."

And then I burst into flames.

When my foot hits the pavement, his tow truck comes into full view and my face burns red-hot. The side door is tagged with POPS' AUTO SHOP and what must be their logo: a cartoon drawing of a Black man in a rocking chair wearing a Kool-Aid grin. Not exactly the slaughter mobile I'd imagined.

He walks me to the passenger side to get the door. I'm tempted to point out that I can open my own door *thankyouverymuch,* but I can't form the words around my own foot, still lodged firmly in my mouth. I squeak out a pathetic "Thanks" instead. Because though technically I still didn't order his saving, in this moment, I am, in fact, in need of it.

His legs make quick work of the jog back to the driver's side. Even in this behemoth of a vehicle, this guy dwarfs the cabin with his presence. Well, him and the elephant-size discomfort shoehorned between us.

I don't know how long I've had this death grip on my phone, but when my fingers start to cramp, I loosen it—though I refuse to release it entirely. What else am I going to do with my hands?

"I'm just gonna pull in front," he says, maneuvering the truck into position and jumping out to get to work.

I'm alone in the pristine cab, hammering out a message to Zola with entirely too much backstory, when the door opens again. Sooner than I'd expected. The truck shifts under his weight, and I freeze. Like if I'm still enough, he might not notice me. Sitting here. In his truck.

The heat of his body beside me is suffocating enough, but when he reaches into the center console for a business card, his knuckles skim my elbow, and I jump out of my skin.

"Sorry," he says, trying to cover his laugh.

I attempt to play off my obvious overreaction. Adjusting my body again and again, with equally jerky movements as if perhaps that's just how bodies move. It is not.

I know I should leave it alone now, but I simply cannot.

"Oh, it's me!" I screech, before trying again. "I mean mine. My fault." And then, because my brain has short-circuited, I keep saying all the words. "I was in the way. That was my bad. With your fingers."

"You're good," he says, lip still quirking as he jots notes on his clipboard.

I've only been in this guy's presence for a matter of minutes, but already I recognize that thing his mouth is doing as he bites back his smile.

After my reaction to the accidental elbow graze, I don't blame him for announcing his plans to reach over into the glove box to retrieve a stapler. His movements are focused and direct—he hardly enters my bubble—but it doesn't stop anxiety from prickling the tips of my fingers now that we're only inches apart.

I direct all my focus to the first thing I see to ground myself, fixating on the subtleties of every tattoo painting his arms as they flex and relax with each stroke of his pen.

I craft a detailed backstory for every intricate symbol and decide on hyperspecific names for the colored ink bringing them to life. But when the malachite stem of a carmine dahlia leads directly into a vein that snakes up his forearm, my eyes stray from the flower, following the lines of his biceps instead.

It'd be easier to pretend he hadn't caught my gaze trailing across his skin if he wasn't sinking his teeth into his bottom lip like that.

Mischief dances in his eyes as he clears his throat. "What's your name?"

"Kaia?" I say, like I'm guessing. "Harper."

He mouths it silently as he makes that final note on his paperwork. I'd never really considered the exact shapes my name might make crossing a person's lips, but now that I've seen it form on his mouth, I won't forget.

He releases his paper from the clamp and holds it out to me, careful not to let so much as a stray fingernail cross onto my side of the console.

"That's everything you'll need."

"Thanks," I say, pretending to survey it before shoving it into my purse.

"Should we wait for your boyfriend here? Or I can take you to the shop or a charge station and he can meet us there."

"Oh! My *boyfriend*." I enunciate it, as if it's my first time hearing the word in my life.

6:12 P.M. Shit. If I don't get to Liv soon, I'll miss her completely.

"Actually, is there any way you could take me to the Speckled Pig and I'll grab the car tomorrow? We're so close, and that's where I'm supposed to meet . . . him . . . my boyfriend."

"Yeah," he says, eyeing me. "Sure."

"He's already there," I continue. "So . . ."

"Got it," he says, pulling onto the road with Mom's car trailing pathetically behind. "Speckled Pig it is."

The silence between us stretches so thick, I'd swear I could reach out and touch it. When the *ping* of my phone echoes off the hard lines of the cab, it might as well be on surround sound. His eyes follow the noise down to the phone in my lap. I flip it over, as if he might be able to read Zola's message through the lock screen. X-ray vision doesn't feel like an entirely implausible feature of eyes as dark as his.

When another message pings, he says, "Feel free to do what you need to do. Make a call or whatever."

Since I can't call my nonexistent boyfriend to let him know I'm running late, I opt for the next best plan: sitting in total silence until, with any luck, I cease to exist.

But another shrill *ping* from my phone sends me over the edge. A little yelp slipping through my lips. Now I have no choice but to make literally any other sound to cover up whatever that was.

Unfortunately, the first sound that comes to mind is words. And not just any words.

"No wonder you know so much about parking lots."

I would've fared better with the axe murderer.

"I actually consider myself a sort of plainclothes parking attendant," he says, mocking my words from earlier.

When he turns to smile at me, I'm hit by the direct force of it for the first time, and goddamn. A little warning would've been nice.

He's got one of those smiles you don't just *see,* you *feel.* Deep and dimpled, with so much genuine emotion behind it that it's impossible not to smile back. This is also the first time I'm actually seeing his face without my vision being clouded by rage and shame. It's a good face, if you're into that *yacht on the South of France* cologne ad sort of thing.

"So, what's at Speckled Pig?" he asks, letting me off the hook from further talk of our earlier run-in. "Besides your boyfriend."

I try to avoid his accompanying smile and the clear confirmation he knows I'm full of shit, but my very specific brand of awkwardness won't allow it.

"Okay, maybe *boyfriend* wasn't the right word. They're a friend. Well, *she. She's* a friend."

He nods in assumed understanding, and for some reason unbeknownst to me, I'm suddenly desperate to clarify the exceedingly *hetero* nature of my sexuality to this complete stranger.

"No! Not like that," I yell, with more urgency than necessary. "Not that there's anything wrong with that." *Nice.* "But she's really a friend. My best friend. And she's heading out soon, which is why I need to get there. I was just trying to throw you off earlier with the boyfriend thing in case you were planning to . . ."

He raises an eyebrow for me to continue.

". . . kill me?" That horrified look on his face might actually be even better than his smile. "It's been suggested that I watch too much true crime."

His laugh comes on slow and easy. "Man, what is it with women and those shows? My ex used to watch all that stuff on repeat. She'd be all excited like '*Ohhh, I bet he cheats,*' as if that's a good enough reason to put rat poison in the guy's burger and bury him under a rosebush. I never knew if she had me watch it as entertainment or a warning."

"Maybe a little bit of both," I say with a shrug.

"Damn. That's exactly what she used to say."

"Well, she sounds lovely. You were a fool to let her go."

There's another lull in the conversation, but this time, silence doesn't accompany it. I hadn't even noticed he'd turned the radio on in the background until he starts humming along. Effortlessly alternating between the harmony and melody of the music floating through the speakers.

"You sing?" I ask, before I can stop myself.

His eyes go wide, like a deer in the headlights of a freight train. It's a welcome change to see *him* squirm for once.

"Only in the truck," he admits, finally.

I want to tell him he's actually pretty good, but the flimsy subject change he rushes for is for his own benefit this time.

"I think I went to a watch party at this place when I was like eighteen."

A strategically placed sports reference to combat his falsetto, no doubt. Still, I let him have it.

"Yay, sports," I say, with an accompanying *rah-rah* fist pump.

He laughs again, but now that I'm better prepared, I manage to keep my own face flat, even as his sparkles.

"Back then, it was more like, *yay bartenders who don't check IDs,*" he says, turning onto the main drag. "I've never been that into sports."

My frantic texts to Liv are stuck on read, and I swear, if she leaves for her train before I even get there, I'm never leaving the house again. The house, where Zola and Mom are waiting for me. Ready to continue judging *my* life and *my* failings, while also expecting me to help them sort out theirs.

I mutter an absent-minded response to him about how *everyone has their thing* but I'm too distracted by the traffic to say anything more. Maybe I should've had him drop me at a charge station after all. At least then, if I miss Liv, I could've just gone home.

"What's your thing?" he asks. "Are you in school?"

"Just graduated," is all I offer, as another minute slips away.

His smile deepens. "Oh, that's dope. What's your degree in?"

I shift in my seat at the turn the conversation's taking and say only: "Education."

I'm so not in the mood for *get to know you*s.

"That's what's up. Out there shaping the future."

His genuine excitement about a career I have no interest in pursuing brings on a familiar stomach drop. Like being on a roller coaster, bottoming out. Because, no, I'm not going to be shaping "the future." I don't even know how I'm going to shape my own.

I know this is where I should be all, *where'd you go to school, what'd you study, did you like it?* But I can't force any of it out past the tightness forming in my chest. I sink my teeth into my dread and my cheek. Wishing both the traffic and the conversation away.

When his words break though my thoughts once more, I very seriously consider how badly hurt I'd be if I tucked and rolled my way out of this.

"I did a few years at UConn, before . . ."

And I'm still biting my cheek to keep quiet, but I must not be biting down hard enough.

"Mm-hmm." The sound comes out more deliberate and harsher than I'd meant for it to. Stalling the conversation cold.

"Sorry," I say, hating myself a little more with each passing moment I'm in this truck. "My head's just somewhere else."

This time, there's no question he gets the message, because all he says as he flips on his blinker to turn into the Speckled Pig lot is: "Understood."

He doesn't put the truck in park when he pulls up to the restaurant, but at this point, I'm just grateful he comes to a complete stop.

"Well, thanks for the ride," I say, because I'm not a complete asshole. "And the tow."

"No problem, Kaia. Have a good night."

Those parting words play on repeat as I watch him drive out of sight. My name, a challenge he doesn't explain.

*No problem, Kaia.*

But then I understand, and once I do, no walk has ever felt more shameful than the one I make to the bar's entrance. Because, it never even occurred to me to ask his name.

Turns out, I *am* a complete asshole after all.

# 5

THE BELL ABOVE THE DOOR IS STILL ANNOUNCING MY arrival when Liv's welcome scream rings out through the packed bar area. She bounces over and her infectious energy draws a little shoulder shimmy from me. The whole display is very on-brand for us, and I immediately feel like an idiot for thinking she was blowing me off.

"Oh my god, Kai!" she squeals into our hug.

Liv's basically a *bubble* in human form—that airy, flighty, *POP! POP!* And though on the surface she looks just as delicate, fragile even, that's never stopped her from finding the light in any room and bending it to her will. But right now, instead of her usual rainbow refraction, she's a bubble going *POP!* in black leather and lace.

"Oh my god, hi!" I mirror, glancing around the bar to make sure I didn't miss the costume memo. "What are you wearing?"

I barely get the words out before Liv grabs my hand to drag me through the crowd of mostly familiar faces. Though I'm pretty sure I spot a nose job or two. She leads me down the oh-so-elegantly wood-paneled hallway to the bathroom at the bar's end.

If it means avoiding small talk with guys who peaked in high school and the women who love them, I'll gladly stay in this dingy stall watching Liv pee for the foreseeable future. And we might need that long for me to wrap my head around the story she's telling.

A few weeks ago, when Liv texted about her drunken graduation night hookup, she'd sounded embarrassed to have chosen the least *Liv* guy in that particular Lower East Side bar, but like any good confessional, the sanctity of the women's restroom has revealed a new truth.

Today, to my abject horror, Liv is in love.

"Are we talking about Leather Vest?" I ask, praying it's anyone but Leather Vest. "Is that why you're in cosplay tonight?"

Liv follows me out to the sinks. Her blond ponytail bounces innocently in the mirror ahead, but her grip is surprisingly strong when she yanks me back to face her pout.

"Okay. We cannot call him that anymore." Her green eyes are alight with excitement or hope or one of the other painfully naïve emotions she embodies so easily at the start of every new something with every new somebody.

This is usually the point where I'd warn her that she's doing it again and remind her that if history has taught us anything, it's that this feeling, like this relationship, is temporary. But right now, she's looking at me like a little kid who still believes in Santa Claus.

So, for now, I choose the path of least resistance.

"What's his name again?" I ask, pulling my phone out to stalk him a little. It's more than I usually offer at this stage, and my reward for my generosity is watching Liv vibrate out of her skin.

"Travis!" she screams at a decibel that should be criminal.

"Does he have a last name?" I ask at a more reasonable volume. "Or should I just type in *Travis* to see if Instagram guesses the right one?"

Liv steals my phone to pull up the guitarist formerly known as Leather Vest. I yank my pineapple to the side, clearing the curls from my eyes to stare at the screen. I'm going to need all my senses for this one.

"Liv," I warn, scrolling through the Marilyn Manson parody before me. *Can you even be a parody of a parody?*

"Don't!" she whines. "You have to get to know him."

"I *have* to?" I ask, already brainstorming excuses to *not.*

Her expressive-ass ponytail bobs with her nodding head.

*Fine,* I mime, with a dramatic shrug that looks more tortured than I feel. Because, even clad in black leather, Liv makes me feel light. Well, light-*er.* So it's no wonder she's always been able to bend me to her will too.

I missed that. I missed us.

When we open the bathroom door to make our exit down the hall, I'm smacked in the face by the deafening wave of our hometown friends' hometown conversations, floating around this hometown bar.

A not-so-small part of me wishes I could click my heels three times to be back in that tow truck rerouting us anywhere but here. But after my earlier performance, I might not be welcome. The thought upsets me more than it should. The thought of him, and the way he looked saying my name that last time. I can't believe I never even asked his name.

I only notice Liv's come to a stop ahead of me when I slam into her.

"Why do you look like that?" she asks, blocking my path. "What just happened?"

"Nothing," I say, because it *is* nothing. "It's a long story."

Liv's silence urges me to tell it anyway, so of course I do.

"I had to get a tow earlier and ended up sort of fighting with the driver."

Saying it out loud sounds ridiculous, but as always, Liv's quick to offer me a pass.

"Did he deserve it?"

"He really, *really* didn't," I admit.

"Meh," she decides. "Don't be so hard on yourself. Look at me—"

"Oh, I am," I joke, assessing her ensemble again.

"In what world am *I* dating a rocker?"

"You're right. Yours is worse."

She rightfully ignores me.

"And *you're* yelling at strangers," she continues. "We're like animals being released from captivity into the real world. None of us know how to act. But tonight, we don't have to. You're home and we're together. And there's alcohol," she says, grabbing both of my shoulders and shaking. "So maybe for the next couple hours we let ourselves act like kids again and pretend life isn't about to drop-kick us into the deep end."

Liv links her arm through mine, moving us down the hallway once more, and I'm happy to follow. Because she really does know how to find the light.

At the end of the hallway, we spill out into the bar again, and the scene playing out leaves me mentally cataloging and reassessing every life choice that's led me here tonight. You know that saying "You can't go home again"? Turns out you can, it's just depressing as fuck.

"I see the football team is still *pro-warm-booze-before-sundown,*" I say, scanning and judging. Judging and scanning.

I haven't had a chance to properly fix my face, when our forever cheer captain spots us in the crowd. Michelle Meyer has been on the top of every physical and social pyramid since she moved to Connecticut's Gold Coast in middle school. She's the kind of person for whom the world will always make way. And now she's making way right at us—or Liv rather.

"Ahh!" Michelle and Liv both scream in wordless greeting.

Michelle doesn't waste any energy acknowledging my existence, as the giddy pair start volleying NYU-alum-specific inside jokes back and forth. I don't appreciate anyone talking to my best friend like she's their best friend, but I set my face on *bored* rather than brooding. I know better than to have a lovers' quarrel in front of the other woman.

When Michelle finally trains her glassy vodka soda eyes on me, a lazy smile of recognition forms on her perfectly pink lips. She's finally placed me. I wasn't sure she'd get there. It's not that I was unpopular in high school, but I was only cool by proxy. To Liv.

Michelle raises her drink, a finger lifted from her sweaty glass to point at me. "You're Zola's sister, right?"

Correction: cool by proxy to Liv *and Zola*. It's not news. My high school made space for exactly one transcendent Black girl at a time. Zola got there first.

"Weren't you in Kentucky?" she continues, a gentle sway to both her stance and her words.

"Kansas," I yell, over the music.

"Yeah, Kansas," she says, nose scrunched by the apparent adorableness of the locale. "Same thing though, yeah?"

Liv enters the conversation before I can respond to the assertion that any place outside the Tri-State is all the *same thing*.

"Kai's gonna be a teacher," she says, beaming. "I would've killed to have a teacher like her."

My face heats under their spotlight as they watch me expectantly. The only thing I want to do less than teach for pay that borders on offensive is admit that truth out loud, in front of

Michelle's Botox frozen Spock brow. There's only one way out of this. *Deflect, deflect, deflect.* If there was money in *that,* maybe I'd have a career path I could get behind.

Luckily, I've always got a tight five ready.

"And if that doesn't work out, I saw they're hiring at the Starbucks downtown." I raise crossed fingers into the air and pause for the silent snare drum. "Taking down union busters with a discounted macchiato in hand sounds like a lovely little Tuesday."

Liv's face screws up in concern at my performance, but before she can respond, a cheer erupts from the crowd. A resurrected call-and-response time warp from the longest four years of my life. And just like that, I'm back at the big Friday night game watching Asher Hall on the field, while *he* watches these same *will hurkey for booze* girlies. Though that particular star quarterback is noticeably and unfortunately absent from tonight's reunion.

The cheer teases out another darker flashback, but I don't let that one play out. One mental breakdown at a time, please.

Michelle's eyes are still vodka-vacant and her smile is rabid as she yells, "That's my cue!" And as quickly as she surfaced, she's lost to the swarm of ex-cheerleaders getting into formation.

My disapproval is palpable as I take in the insurance liability before me.

Liv's disapproval is palpable, too, but her stare is trained on me. "Be nice."

Turning away from everyone and everything else, I meet the warning in Liv's eyes and enunciate my words above the fray: "I'm too sober for this."

By our third drink, Liv and I have retreated into our own world the way we have since we were young. Huddled together, co-dependently swearing to never love another the way we love each other—and incessantly checking train times. Liv's already missed the first three she'd meant to take.

Three drinks, it would seem, is also the exact amount of alcohol required for me to start confessing the deep dark stuff.

I expect Liv to die laughing when I tell her about Zola's matchmaking ambush, but she's uncharacteristically quiet.

"Why aren't you saying anything?" I ask, when I can't take the silence any longer.

A lazy smile spreads across her lips as she chases her straw down with her tongue. She finally catches it and takes a long sip before speaking.

"You're considering it, aren't you?"

I can't swallow my own sip fast enough. "Hellllll no."

Liv shakes her head, braving my glare to *boop* my nose.

"I know you," she says. And even though her words are slower and drenched in tequila now, they still sound like *POP! POP!* "You can't say no to them. They've got that Harper hold on you."

*That Harper hold.* I don't have to ask what she means by it.

Liv was there in the weeks after my dad left, when there was no order in our world anymore—no constants, no control. She saw how it changed me to realize how vulnerable we'd been. How fragile our world was that it could be destroyed by one man's *goodbye.*

All my dad had to do was flick a finger to turn over the ignition, and everything came crashing down. Our old lives, and old selves, shattered.

One moment we were the people we'd always been, and the next, we became something different. I just made sure my "different" was stronger, so I couldn't be torn down like that again. So even if everyone around me fell, I'd still be standing. Ready to help them get back up. I never paused to consider if the thing holding *me* up was muscle or scar tissue.

"You should have seen them," I say, surprised by how quickly I sober at the thought of Mom and Zola. "And Zo," I whine. "I want this for her. I want her to have something nobody can take from her. But there's gotta be another way."

"Zo would be doing you a favor by keeping you off the apps. I've been swiping up here for years. That shit is horrendous." Liv braces for impact as she continues. "And I love you, but you, my friend, have looked fucking miserable all night. A little dumb fun isn't the worst thing that could happen to you. Or a crush. I haven't heard you talk about a guy since—"

"That guy with the hands?" I ask, cupping the air above my lap.

"Ew, god, no."

"Okay, but I do kinda miss him."

"That's 'cause you're disgusting," she says, a little too quickly. "No, it was the one who'd come see you at the bar every night. We tailgated with him when I was in town."

"Oh! Adam."

"Wait, I thought Adam was gay."

"He is."

"Then why would I be talking about Adam, Kai?"

I shrug as Liv's phone vibrates in her hand.

"Well," she says, face going momentarily blank to unlock her phone, "if we just scanned the last four years of your dating history and all we came up with was a creep and a gay guy, my vote on this thing with Zo is a hard yes."

Liv reads her new text and cartoon heart eyes bug out of her face. Girls' night is officially over.

I signal the bartender to run our tab. "Thank Daddy Foster for the drinks."

"Please stop calling him that," Liv says, rolling her eyes at my long-running joke. "I can stay a little longer. Travis can wait."

She places her phone face down on the bar as she says it. I know she means it—she'd stay if I asked. But I also know she wants to go. I can already see the Liv-shaped hole she's about to leave, running out the front door. Besides, now *I* get to go home and eat snacks. Tonight, I'm winning.

I wave her off and order my Uber to make our exit official. "I should get back anyway. Broken hearts to heal, babies to deliver."

"Isn't Zola like seven months along?"

"You know she's always been an overachiever," I say, pulling Liv in for one last hug. "Now, let's get you to your train."

The déjà vu of sneaking back into Mom's with a buzz is as disorienting as the strobing lights of the muted TV Mom's currently staring through. But the stakes of getting caught now aren't a lecture or grounding, the way they were for teenage me. Now, even so much as a tipsy stutter step will be confirmation of Zola's assessment that I'm the less adult-y adult. Worse yet, it'd be all the proof she needs that her earlier words struck the exact soft spot she'd been aiming for.

Luckily though, when I poke my head into the living room, Mom raises a finger to her weak *welcome home* smile, before pointing toward a sleeping Zola—hands wrapped gently around her midsection. I still have to remind myself that it's not just a *belly.* There's an actual baby in there.

It's been the *Harper girls* for so long now, I can't imagine it any other way. But everything is about to change. In so many ways, it already has.

As I scale the stairs, I steal one final glance at Zola and Mom the way I have countless times before, and I wish life would slow down a little. My eyes linger on the familiar scene below, until I'm distracted by a glint on the coffee table. The flashing TV reflects off the silver rings of Zola's work binder, still splayed open the way it'd been before I left—back when Zola looked like a mogul in the making and Mom looked like her old self. It catches the light like a tiny flare declaring a state of emergency.

When my head hits my pillow, it's spinning from more than just the margaritas. This is the longest I've been still enough to take everything in. The two people I love most in this world are out there. Knocked down and hurting. Mom needs this distraction. Zola needs a foothold. They need my help to get back up.

They need me to do this, and if one last Harper girls hurrah is the bridge between the way things are and whatever's coming next for us all, that's as good a reason as any. And it's not the worst thing if that comes with a few free dinners and an LLC.

Before I can talk myself out of it, I send a text to the group chat that will either be exactly what we all need *or* the thing that sets in motion a series of catastrophic events that will leave us all forever scarred.

Only one way to find out.

**9:24pm**

**Me:** Fine. I'll do it.

Before my phone even registers that the message has been *Delivered,* I hear the shrill excitement of my very *not-asleep* sister's voice screeching:

"Oh my god! She said yes!"

The happy shrieks and squeals coming from the living room make two things perfectly clear:

1. I'm doing this.
2. I was never not going to.

# 6

AS A KID, I HAD NIGHT TERRORS. AFTER A FEW QUIET HOURS each evening, I'd shoot up in bed, certain the *terrible thing* had finally found me. My family would wake to the horror of screams that tore at my throat and my parents' hearts until they were raw. It was the *not knowing* that left me inconsolable—not knowing what was coming for me. Not knowing when or why.

By the time I'd come back to consciousness and the saner side of my meltdown, I'd demand definitive answers to all life's unimaginables. I needed to talk through every possible worst-case scenario. A doomsday prepper with pigtail puffs.

Exhausted by my morbid line of incessant questioning, my mom eventually decided it was safer to keep me awake than risk me falling back into another nightmare and beginning the whole mess again. She'd sit me in front of cartoon marathons and pray the vibrant lights and colors would chase away the bad guys in my mind.

It never worked. I didn't want a distraction, I wanted to be prepared for the things nobody else wanted to talk about. It wasn't until I graduated from Disney to *Dateline* that I actually found a little peace. Say what you will about being a true crime addict, but for a kid who grew up afraid of the boogeyman, it was basically survival research.

Now, my antennae remain firmly up at all times, which is why as soon as I step into the hallway on Saturday morning, I already sense trouble.

"Uh, morning?" I say, when Zola and Mom fail to notice my arrival in the dining room.

Mom turns to greet me, the angle of her body bringing the scene behind her into full view. Apparently where I used to start the day early to avoid nightmares, today I've left the safety of my bed and stumbled straight into the waking kind.

"What the . . . ?" I say, horrified. "Zo. No."

"It's too late," Zola says without looking up from her seat at the head of the table. She pauses shuffling crisp pink papers just long enough to turn a small stack toward me. "You can't back out now. I already mocked up the logo."

*XO by Zo.* Okay, that's kind of adorable.

"But did you also rob a Staples" I ask. And then, ignoring the alarm bells telling me to run, I hear myself say, "What is all this?"

That's all the invitation Zola needs. She nods once, and Mom reaches for my shoulders. Ushering me toward my seat, like a lamb to the slaughter.

"Welcome," Zola says dramatically, "to the first day of the rest of your life."

She opens her arms to frame the table as I take it in. I never knew a few manila folders could be so ominous.

Mom retrieves a plate of assorted baked goods and a take-out carafe of black coffee from the kitchen island at my back. I haven't had a chance to properly discern the hierarchy of Zola's makeshift enterprise, but Mom's vibe is giving *entry-level.* The anti–Tina Knowles.

I break off a chunk of a blueberry muffin, before abandoning it on the center tray in favor of a pain au chocolat. How they managed to pull all this together after I passed out last night is beyond me, but clearly, they've been busy. If this was happening to anyone else, I'd almost be impressed. *Almost.*

"Kaia," Zola starts, with a shit-eating grin plastered on her pretty little face. "You are about to embark on a transformative journey that will change the very course of your life. When this is all said and done, I'm confident you'll be a new woman. Perhaps even a woman in love."

Zola's doing entirely too much, but I thaw a bit when Mom lets out a little squeak and squeezes my hand.

Zo continues her pitch, which I imagine is similar to what it'd be like to be sold a dilapidated time-share in nowhere Idaho or a wood-paneled station wagon without an engine.

"With our limited time frame," she says, pointing down at her belly, "I've designed an expedited membership package. A two-month commitment, with targeted coaching and three perfect matches I'll be personally selecting to . . . break through all that," she says, pointing this time to my face, frozen mid-snarl.

When Zola wraps up her introduction, Mom walks me through a more detailed timeline. It all starts with that thirty-six-step questionnaire Zola showed us the other night. Based on my answers to those prompts, she'll take two weeks to find suitable contenders.

"Before you meet the guys," Mom explains, taking the reins, "you'll get to look at their completed questionnaires, and they get to read yours too. You'll meet one of our bachelors each week, on a date that we'll plan especially for you. Isn't this great?"

Mom hasn't used this tone on me since she tried to convince me to give a speech at her second wedding to a near stranger. She's handling me, but she's also smiling. *Really* smiling.

Still, I've got to ask: "And if I hate them?"

"Typical," Zola says, making a note in what must be *my file.*

I sit a little taller in my chair to get a peek inside, but I catch myself before Zola and Mom notice. That slipup would've indicated interest—a weakness I can't afford against this united front.

I abandon my curiosity, narrowing my eyes instead. "It's a valid question."

Mom steps in to diffuse the tension. "Let's just cross that bridge when we come to it."

Zola reclaims the stage. "I need a shiny, happy success story to hard launch this thing. And what's shinier and happier than this face?" she says, squeezing my puff pastry–stuffed cheeks.

"Zo." I don't waste time pretending not to beg. "I'll find you better faces. There are a lot of thirsty girls home for the summer."

She waves the suggestion away with a literal flick of her hand. "This isn't like your apps. Do you know how long it takes to vet quality clients? Background checks, online sweeps—I don't have time for all that. Ideally the first pairing will be locked in before the launch party."

"The launch party?" I say, but Zola's words are coming too fast and furious for her to register the question.

Mom places a calendar of events on top of the mess of papers I'm shuffling through, as Zola continues.

"And the first couple has to be *good.* They have to look aspirational. This has to look like the answer."

"To who?" I yell, scanning the room for the live audience I must've missed upon entry.

Zola rubs her temples as if *I'm* the one stressing *her* out. "Kai, it's not like you'll be mic'd, but if we don't get some content, we might as well not even do it."

"Great," I say, refilling my coffee mug. "Let's not do it!"

But as Zola starts naming off various strategies to go viral, it's clear I'm shouting into the wind.

There was a time Zola would've been able to run on this high all day, so when she relocates to the couch for a nap instead of basking in the glow of my defeat, I silently thank my future nephew for taking her out.

Without the adrenaline of this morning's festivities, Mom also comes back down to Earth, curling into that old recliner the way she always does between failed relationships. It might not be as murder-y as my comfort watches, but true crime is still less gruesome than siphoning comfort from a memory-foam-filled relic of a past life. Mom sinks into its familiar depressions the way she used to sink into Dad's arms.

I've given up on trying to get her to toss the chair, but that doesn't mean I have to watch her get her fix.

"Anybody need anything from the world?" I ask, whispering like it's the volume of the question that disturbs people trying to sleep, not the question itself. "I'm gonna run out."

Zola's eyes pop open. "Can you grab me a burger on your way back? With bacon. Oh! And a milkshake—but only if they have strawberry." She pulls herself into a sitting position. "Actually, I'll just come. But you're driving."

Zola not trusting me to order her lunch is offensive, but at the mention of driving, I know better than to defend my many competencies. Because Mom's car, which I'd been planning to take, is still locked up behind the metal gates of an impound two towns over.

# 7

I SHOULD'VE KNOWN ZOLA COMING WOULD MEAN MORE THAN a quick detour at the Duchess drive-through. Twenty-five uninterrupted minutes dragging me for a dumb mistake is worth more to her than gold. This passenger princess is having the time of her life.

"You're just lucky the tow guy got you off the road before someone smashed into you. This could have been so much worse."

She pauses to lick BBQ sauce from a strip of bacon with so much enthusiasm, it's near pornographic. I avert my eyes to give the pair a moment of privacy, but unfortunately, I can't avert my ears as she continues.

"You could've charged at home for like ten minutes and avoided all this."

I consider reminding Zo that if we're going to *coulda, woulda, shoulda* my unfavorable charging consequences, we should keep the tow and wish away late-night dating app hookups. But she's already continuing her lecture without me.

"And why not have him tow you to a charge station? Why choose the most expensive and inconvenient option possible?"

*Hormones, just hormones,* I tell myself, though this particular *Zolaism* isn't the baby's fault. Unsolicited opinions are the only kind Zo's got.

Luckily, her judgments and her burger provide Zola all the company she needs. She hardly seems to notice how quickly I leave her behind once we're parked outside the shop. But I hadn't realized what I'd be walking into, and as I step through the lobby doors, I almost wish I wasn't experiencing it alone.

The energy is different in here—pulsing cool and low with the bass line. Street art renderings of Black icons line the walls from the cash register all the way to the vending machines in back. Familiar figures taking on new life under soft studio lights. Immortalized, reverently, by the detailed stroke of a brush.

I scan the portraits that seem to leap off the walls, but even the walls themselves tug at my gaze. Striking city scenes and intricate landscapes shouting the words to their own stories. Just as rich and alive as each subject within the frames and treated with as much care.

It's like stepping inside the pages of a love letter to the culture.

I'm still studying the floor-to-ceiling murals, reveling in all the hidden treasures the artist left to be discovered, when a voice rumbles behind me.

"So how was it? Those bartenders still corrupting our youth?"

His words pull me from my trance. Deading my perusal so abruptly that I physically trip over myself as I spin toward him.

There's not even time for me to put my own hands out to catch my fall, before his are on me—steadying me, with a firm but gentle certainty.

Once I'm no longer a fall risk, he releases me. "Shit, sorry. I didn't mean to scare you."

"No!" I say, too forcefully. "I mean, no—you didn't. I just wasn't paying attention. Or I was paying too *much* attention. To all this." I raise my hands to our surroundings. As if perhaps he's unaware that he's in the presence of magic. "I wasn't expecting this place to be so . . ."

But finding the words to convey stepping through that vortex of a front door is futile.

He brings both of his delicately veined hands up to adjust his Kith hat, and I blame my earlier perusal of the murals for the way I also study him now. My brain, immersed in this world where everything is art. Including each graceful movement his fingers make before he tucks them into his crossed arms.

"I wanted it to be a place you could lose a little time," he tells me. "But most people who come through hardly notice. Probably woulda been better off putting those hours toward a commissioned piece, but once I see it—" He brings a graceful finger to his temple, with a shrug. "It's over."

My eyes bug out of my head. "*You* did this?"

"I did," he says, assessing the walls with me, like he's seeing them for the first time again.

"It's—" I start, but words fail me again. "I feel like I should've paid an entry fee to get in."

I hadn't committed his laughter to memory, but the husky sound brings a familiar warmth to my belly. And *that,* I do remember. Luckily, staring at his work affords me a necessary distraction from whatever's happening to my insides.

He stands beside me, turned toward a muraled wall in quiet contemplation. My eyes dart between the art and the artist in front of it.

His profile is all hard lines and chiseled edges—torched steel, right at home in this auto shop—but there's a softness to his nose that I hadn't noticed yesterday. Rounded curves that offset the otherwise statuesque features I'd initially found intimidating. Though his demeanor is proving to be anything but.

When his dimple pops in quiet pride, I'm incapable of keeping my own face passive. He's the one controlling my smile now—like some sort of master puppeteer.

I'd planned to put the "*one green eye, one blue eye,*" thing I saw in a movie on Zola's questionnaire to piss her off, but now when she asks my ideal physical type, I fear I must paste a picture of this man.

His expression shifts to thinly veiled amusement when he notices me watching him. Again. "Don't let this fool you," he says, keeping the air between us light. "Pops wouldn't let me touch his garage. It's still foul as ever back there."

"Well, I appreciate the warning," I tell him. "I'll try not to be too disappointed."

He holds a hand out to direct me toward the register, and we make our way across the lobby. "So, how'd your night turn out? Worth the trouble?"

The look on my face gives me away.

He smiles. "That bad?"

But before either of us can say more, Zola bursts through the front door waving my forgotten tow paperwork in the air like she's trying to land a 747. I rush to intercept her, but her sight line is already locked on something more interesting behind me. Or *someone.*

"Hey," she says, marching past me with a fake-ass smile plastered on her face. "I'm Kaia's sister, Zola."

"Nice to meet you," he says, glancing toward me in a way that says, *Watch how easy this is.* And enunciates, "I'm Ro," like *R* and *O* are the Sesame Street letters of the day.

"No way." Zola giggles. Yes, *giggles.* "Everyone calls me *Zo.* How funny: Zo and Ro."

I know my pregnant sister is not flirting with this man in broad daylight.

"The only people who call you *Zo* are me and Mom," I say, openly hating.

She's undeterred. "I just wanted to pop in to give this to my forgetful baby sis. But it looks like you two are doing just fine without me."

She finally directs her attention back to me, with her eyebrows raised and nostrils flared in that way that silently screams: *Girl!*

"Okay, Zo*la*," I say, hitting the last syllable of her name extra-hard. "You've been a huge help. I'll see you back at home."

"So, you work here, Ro?" Zola asks, as if I haven't spoken a word.

"Right now, yeah," he tells her. "It's my dad's shop. I've been in town a couple months helping out."

Zola pretends to survey the space before setting her sights right back on Ro. "It's so nice. Does your girlfriend help out too?"

*I'm dead.*

Ro bites his lip to keep from laughing and shakes his head. "Nah. Ya know, it's funny, I've never dated a girl who was real into cars."

Having completed the transition from twenty-six-year-old woman to meddling auntie, Zola sucks her teeth. "Imagine that."

I'm firing off all types of sisterly telepathy and universal girl-code death stares, but Zola's on a mission.

"So, if your girlfriend isn't into cars, how does she spend her time?"

*Goodbye forever.*

Ro's eyes volley between us like he's sorting out a riddle. "I don't have one," he says, giving Zola exactly what she wants. "I'm single."

"You don't say," Zola says, elbowing me.

Welp. I tried to get the car back, but it lives here now. Ro can keep it. He can sell it. He can set it on fire for all I care. I'm leaving and so is Zola.

"Zola, don't you have somewhere to be?" I say, trying (and failing) to sound intimidating. Unfortunately, as far as Zola's concerned, I no longer exist.

"So, do you work every weekend, Ro?"

"Not every weekend," he says, playing along. "If I'm not picking girls up on the side of the road and delivering them to neighborhood sports bars, I'm usually off Fridays."

"Wait!" Zola yells. "*You're* the guy who saved Kaia yesterday?"

I sneer. "Okay, I wouldn't exactly say *saved*."

Ro laughs. "Nah. Kaia doesn't strike me as someone who needs saving. Just a ride every now and then. And a charge wouldn't hurt. But yeah, that was me."

Zola's wild eyes land on me, and I'm terrified.

"Oh my god, Kai, I just had the best idea! Maybe Ro's available for our little project."

"Zola," I say, desperate to stop her. Just once I'd like to leave this guy's presence with my dignity somewhat intact.

"He could be my first pick for—"

"Stop," I yell. "He doesn't need to hear all this, he's just the tow truck guy."

The carelessness of my words stuns us all into a silence that goes on a beat too long. As if not speaking might give someone a chance to re-pin the live grenade I've just hurled.

"Okay," Zo says too calmly. Blinking away her dreams of future family dinners with the guy beside me. The one who currently looks like he's been punched in the gut while his guard was down.

"I'll go, and just see you back at home," she continues. "Ro, it was really nice to meet you. And your place is great, by the way. I need to get the name of the artist you used."

Ro nods once, crossing his arms tightly over his chest when he says, "That would be me."

It's such a departure from how he'd looked and sounded talking about his work before. And it's my fault.

Zola's eyebrows lift at the news, but she leaves it alone. "Well, thanks again for all your help."

"It's all good," he tells her, without a hint of his earlier levity. "That's my job." And when he continues, he's still speaking to Zola, but his gaze and his words are directed at me—daggers hurling toward their target. "I'm just the tow truck guy."

*Shit.*

It wasn't that bad. My comment was a fact, not a judgment. He probably didn't even think anything of it. Ro's just silently running my card like he does for every customer. Because that's what I am to him—a customer. An elitist prick of a customer, but a customer just the same. I came to pick up my car, and that's what I'm doing. In twenty minutes, he'll forget I even exist.

*Don't make it a thing. Just because you overthink everything doesn't mean he does—he's a guy.*

But even as I think it, I know I'm full of shit.

Ro looks hurt. I hurt him.

I have to say something. I have to explain—

"Car'll be out front," he says, handing me the receipt that concludes our transaction. "Have a great day."

I pause for a beat. Silent and still. I'm waiting for him to say my name, I realize. *Have a great day, Kaia.*

I want to see the shape of it on his lips. To hear the challenge in it before I go. For some reason it's important to me that he says it.

But when the customer behind me moves to the counter to take my spot, Ro's smile sparkles for them, and I know I've been dismissed. He's not going to say it.

"Thanks, Ro," I whisper.

And as I turn toward the exit, I tell myself the heat at my back is embarrassment—not Ro's eyes burning holes right through me.

It's entirely possible that the air freshener dangling from the rear-view mirror is a standard thing Pops' includes for all its customers, but there's also a chance Ro put it in here for me. Before I showed up to prove that I really am the absolute worst. Either way, I've been watching it oscillate so intensely that by the time I get home, I'm practically hypnotized.

Mom's back in her recliner. Her eyes are glued to her phone, and what sounds like another social media self-help reel. But she watches self-appointed Insta gurus the same way I consume fitspo. Chronically, while living in direct contradiction of the thirty-second clickbait loop.

Only, where I question the effectiveness of standing core work while approving offensively high service fees on Thai delivery, Mom inhales virtual therapy sound bites while going the opposite of *no contact.* I guarantee that in between sage-advice snippets, she's switching over to her burner account. Secretly stalking the mistresses and ghosts of relationships past.

I can't care about any of that right now though. I've got to gauge how much she already knows.

"Hey," I say, feigning calm. It's so put on that I might as well be whistling with my hands buried in my pockets. "Zo beat me back?"

"She's running a few more errands," Mom says, not giving anything away. "More stuff for the baby."

That buys me at least a couple hours before I have to answer for—

"Zola said she met the man who helped you out yesterday."

*Welp.*

Mom doesn't offer anything more. She's making me work for it.

She swivels to face me so I sit, building a protective buffer of decorative couch pillows between us. "What else did she say?"

"She said if she wasn't already knocked up . . ." Mom trails off but lets her eyebrows rise and fall to finish her thought.

"Mom, with the eyebrows. Please."

She's still laughing when she says, "So, what do you say? Should I tell the boss to add the tow truck guy to our lineup?"

Hearing *those* words echoed back makes me want to suffocate myself in these cushions. But, because I'm me, I don't hide from my shame—I turn it inside out till it's something I can get my hands around. Anger.

"Is it even possible to have a conversation in this house that doesn't center around men? What is it with you guys? It's fucking sad."

"Okay, first of all, I don't care how grown you think you are. Watch your mouth." Mom holds her finger out so straight and sharp it cuts me down to size. "I'll give you a pass this time, because you've obviously lost your mind, and right now that seems like the more pressing issue. But Kaia Rose, I am not the one. This is *my* house."

"Yes, ma'am," I say, feeling like a child, but also loving this glimpse of who Mom used to be in the *before* times.

And she's right—no matter how grown I am out in the world, in this house, I'm her child. Which is why I transition so seamlessly from full-blown tantrum to being laid out on the couch with my feet in Mom's lap, listing out my failings from the past twelve hours. In chronological order.

"Kai, it sounds like what you said to this guy is really bothering you. Or *all* the things you said to him."

"Mom," I whine, but that lone word is the entirety of my argument.

So she continues. "Go back and apologize."

"Okay, I think that's a little aggressive."

"Fine, don't *go,*" she says, standing to grab my phone from the coffee table. "But if you treated him badly and shouldn't have, you're gonna replay what happened and a *would-be apology* in your mind all day. Or knowing you, quite possibly for years to come. Might as well just call him and get it over with."

I make no move toward the phone, but she's right. I've only been trapped in this shame montage for the past twenty-four hours, and already I want out.

Sensing my internal debate, Mom goes in for the kill. "You have a big heart, sweetie. But don't worry, I won't tell." Then she lowers her voice to a whisper and places the phone on my stomach. "Promise."

Afrobeats is playing in the background when Ro answers. Even through the phone, that place is a vibe.

"Pops'."

I recognize his voice and this thing my stomach does in response to it, but still I ask: "Hey. Is Ro available?" to buy myself another second.

"It's Ro."

I scale the stairs three at a time in search of a door to close. Mom's way too quiet to *not* be listening in.

"Hey, it's Kaia. Harper. From earlier?" I stammer, hoping not to sound too breathless as I pace the length of the bedroom.

It's the same room I grew up sleeping in, but I'd never call it *mine.* Mom trades out decor the way she does men—or rather she redesigns her surroundings to *match* her men, so now it's basically a yoga studio with a daybed in the bay window.

"Yeah, hey. What's up?" he says, snapping me back to the present. "Everything good with the car?"

"Yeah, the car's great, you guys did a great job."

*Charging the battery?*

"Anyway," I start, but I can't risk any more small talk. "I felt weird after I left. That comment I made . . . It sounded bad, but I didn't mean anything by it."

"Okay."

"I don't want you to think I was judging you for being a tow truck driver. That's so not who I am."

And then, because apparently, I have to hit some sort of quota—I say more words.

"I mean nobody's just any one thing, right? Like you're an artist, you're . . . somebody's ex-boyfriend," I say, recounting the nonexistent details I know about Ro's life. "And you're *also*—"

"The tow truck guy?" he asks, dryly, but I swear I hear his teeth scrape that lip.

"Well, yeah," I say seriously. "For now."

"So let me get this straight," he starts. "You called to apologize for calling me 'just the tow truck guy,' by calling me, 'the tow truck guy . . . *for now.*'"

"I mean—yes?" I say, as I debate which of us hates me more right now.

"Okay," I start again. "Full disclosure, I was worried my sister was gonna out me. I'm doing an excruciatingly embarrassing favor for her, and I didn't want her to put my business out there."

Ro's quiet and I can't tell if he's listening politely or doling out additional rope for me to keep hanging myself with.

"It's this matchmaking thing. That's what she does."

"Like for fun?" he says. His first sign of life in a minute.

"Like for work."

"Ya know," he says, and he's definitely smiling now. "I can see that. She'd probably be pretty good at it too. Maybe I should use her."

"I am. Sort of," I admit for the first time. "That's the favor. And I panicked when I realized she was gonna tell you about it. But now *I'm* telling you about it, so basically, I was an asshole for nothing."

At this point I have no pride left to tarnish, so I come clean about all of it.

Ro's so quiet after I finish that I have to check to make sure the call didn't drop.

Finally, he lets out a laugh so big and sudden that I'm as shocked to hear it as I am relieved. And now I'm smiling too.

"Okay," he says. "I've gotta know how this one ends."

# 8

BEFORE THIS MORNING, I'D NEVER CONCEPTUALIZED HOW big a number thirty-six is. Making a thirty-six-minute drive, paying a thirty-six-dollar tab, eating thirty-six sour gummies till your tongue goes raw—none of it's storyworthy.

However, answering thirty-six questions, like what I'd regret most should I suddenly drop dead tomorrow, is enough to put me off the grand slam breakfast I'd demanded from Zola in exchange for completing her questionnaire. And from the smirk on her face, she knew I was getting the shit end of this deal.

I push the barstool back from the kitchen island, staring into the pendants overhead like the cheat codes to this thing might be inscribed on their domed metal canopies.

"So, what do you think?" Zola asks from the far side of the counter. "Good, right?"

But not even the smell of bacon wafting from Zo's skillet can improve my mood.

I pluck a pancake from the cooling rack, folding it like a taco, before ripping into it with bared teeth. "I'm in hell."

Zola's hand finds her hip and her robe falls open slightly, exposing the tiniest sliver of a growing belly peeking out from the T-shirt that fit differently just a few weeks ago. She's become a human mile marker for a future I'm not exactly racing toward.

"It's not that bad," she says, reaching out for the papers I'd sooner chew up and swallow than have her read.

"Well, it's not great either," I say, without loosening my death grip on the questionnaire. My eyes dart toward the living room as I map out an escape route.

Zola follows my gaze, before narrowing her eyes at me. "You know I have to read it."

"Well, yeah," I say. "But, like, . . . right in front of me?"

I thought contemplating a footrace through Mom's house was childish enough, but Zola does me one better. Launching a silver dollar pancake at me like we're in a high school cafeteria, mid food fight.

My hands instinctively rise to shield my face, which means, of course, that I'm no longer gripping the papers. Two sets of frantic eyes land on the questionnaire, now abandoned on the counter, but only one of us was prepared for this.

Zola snatches the pages away a half second before my own hands pathetically slam down on the empty counter.

"Nice," I say, like she should be ashamed of her guerrilla tactics. Like I didn't just put everything I had into trying to beat her at the same game.

Zola settles onto the neighboring barstool and I drown my nerves in bacon grease and maple syrup. I wouldn't admit to stress eating, but the speed at which I've just mauled my short stack suggests I'm not *not* stress eating.

Zola's quiet as she reviews my work. It's like being called out in a lecture hall by that professor who holds an inexplicable vendetta against you. The one who's refused to properly pronounce your name all semester, no matter how many times you correct them. The one for whom you seriously consider changing it to "Kay-uh."

I'm refilling my coffee mug again, watching Zola over the bitter dregs of grounds sloshing out of the French press, when she finally speaks.

"Hmm."

*That's it?!*

"What?" I ask, as she studies me—mouth: pursed; face: stank.

She fans the pages out before me, like the issue is glaring enough to catch at a glance.

"I mean, you definitely completed *someone's* questionnaire."

She stands, dumping my coffee-colored sludge into the sink before filling the kettle with fresh water and scooping grounds into the press. I scan the pages, attempting to see it through Zola's eyes, but I don't get it.

She swipes the papers from my hands, and this time, to my horror, she clears her throat to read it aloud.

"*I wish I had someone with whom I could share . . .*" she begins. "And you—my sister, Kaia Harper—wrote: *my hopes and dreams for the future.*"

"And . . . ?"

"And, no the fuck you don't. Who is this person?" she asks, turning the pages over in her hands.

"What did you want me to put? *Someone with whom I could share my dry humor, dark love of crime TV, and an extra-large pizza so I don't have to cook*?"

She shrugs. "I mean . . ."

The fact that I actually tried and still managed to fail is more proof I didn't need that this plan has been trash from go.

"I thought you'd be happy. I gave you what you wanted."

"What *I* wanted?" Zola asks.

"Your exact words were: *shiny, happy success story.*" My tone is more bitter than coffee ground sludge.

The kettle's whistle cuts through our debate like a referee calling halftime. But when Zola joins me again at the island, I know there will be no breaks given.

"So, in order to find you a match, you assumed I'd want you to pretend to be a different person?"

It feels like a trick question.

"Kai," she starts again. "When did you get like this?"

The thing about the telepathic bond of sisters is that you don't get to decide how or when they use it. Zola's face tells me she can more than *sense* my internal debate—she can actually hear it.

"Say it," she tells me.

But I'm so used to choking the words down that it's nearly impossible to let them past the vise I secured years ago.

"What's going on?" Zola asks, her prodding gentle. The light touch is my undoing.

"I don't know how to do this," I admit.

"Answer questions honestly?" she asks, holding up the questionnaire. "Yeah, that's pretty obvious."

"If someone could leave *you,*" I say, meaning every word of this, "what hope is there for the rest of us?

"And then there's Mom," I continue, but Zola stops me. Physically raising her hand before I can say more.

"Will you quit with this? This isn't about me and Mom. It's about you. You're young and hot and so smart it's fucking annoying. But for some reason you've preemptively become this embittered old lady who avoids anything meaningful or real. I don't want that for you. You deserve to be screwed over by guys in your own unique way. To learn to hate them slowly. Over many, many years. Like the rest of us."

"Is that the new company motto?" I ask. "Because if so, it's fire."

Zola slaps my arm on her way back to the stove. "This isn't about turning you into someone you think *they* want—fuck that. These guys are gonna be lucky to get to know you. But it's gotta be *you*. And this," she says, chucking my questionnaire into the recycling bin, "ain't it."

What I'm *not* going to do is fill out a whole new questionnaire with Zola watching over my shoulder. Which is why I'm now driving around aimlessly with a fresh set of the same thirty-six questions screaming for attention from their spot in the center console.

At least, I'd thought I'd been driving aimlessly. It's not until I'm parked outside the tow yard, wondering if Ro works on Thursdays, that I realize my subconscious had very specific plans of its own.

Talking to him the other day had been easier than I'd expected it to be. Even for just those few minutes, it was such a relief to find a person out here who didn't feel like part of my past. Who wasn't trying to remind me of who I'd been at eighteen.

But now that I'm here, I'm not convinced that's a good enough reason to show up at a stranger's job unannounced. Sure, Ro had begged to see the questionnaire, but I highly doubt he expected me to hand deliver it. I wouldn't be surprised if he'd forgotten about it completely.

Before anyone can prove I've temporarily lost my mind, I scan the lot and slide my sunglasses up my nose. *Because apparently that makes me invisible.* I turn the steering wheel toward the exit, fully aware that my behavior is bordering on creepy now. And by "bordering" I mean that if the roles were reversed, I'd already have Ro's name and detailed description on an offender registry or two.

I can almost taste my freedom, but there goes the universe again. Thinking she's so damn funny.

Ro steps out of the open garage doors, yanking a towel from his back pocket. He balls it up to fire off at someone or something inside, and his head tilts up toward the sky. Mouth breaking wide into a laugh. Even at this distance, I can feel the honeyed warmth of it.

He smiles, like nothing in the world matters more than this moment, and I forget I'm supposed to be escaping. Besides, on the mortification spectrum, being caught mid-getaway has to be worse than an awkward hello, right? *RIGHT?*

I don't have time to reach a verdict before our eyes lock across the parking lot. Ro's thick eyebrows crinkle in confusion as I step out of the car—and very briefly consider slashing my own tire to have a legitimate excuse for being here.

But as quickly as his confusion comes, it's replaced by another one of his smiles. This one reaches both corners of his eyes and I can't help but smile back.

Ro's long legs and heavy boots close the distance between us. "Aye! What up, E?"

"E?"

"Yeah. Like your battery."

"Very funny," I say, rolling my eyes in mock annoyance. "I hope it's not weird I just showed up like this, I know you're busy—"

"Nah, it's dead today. Pops is in there with way too much time on his hands. Tryin' to school me on his old man jams, but he can't tell me nothing I don't already know." Ro raises his voice to a yell at the end, though I doubt his dad can hear the challenge from this distance. "I could actually use some backup," he says, holding an arm out for me to lead the way back to the garage. "Maybe he'll stop cheating if we've got a witness."

I don't know what kind of reception I'd been expecting, but it wasn't this.

I'm still trying to conjure up a lie for when his dad inevitably asks why I'm here, when a Ro look-alike emerges from behind the hood of a black BMW. I freeze at the threshold like a vampire awaiting a formal invitation.

"Yo, Pops," Ro says, walking past me. "This is Kaia. Her car was here over the weekend."

"It's nice to meet you, Kaia," his dad says, assessing me. "Car still giving you trouble? Son, go ahead and pull her paperwork for me."

"Nah, it was just a quick job," Ro says, conveniently leaving out that the "job" was a thirty-minute charge I should've done myself.

"Yeah. No, everything's good Mr. . . . ?"

"Jackson," he says. "Or you can call me Pops. Everyone else does." He laughs as he holds his hands out to his namesake garage. "Still blame Ro for that one. Had all his little friends calling me that so long, it stuck."

"Don't act like you don't love it, PJ," Ro says, catching the towel his dad throws in his direction this time.

My head volleys between their broad smiles, equally bright against their smooth skin. Each of their brown eyes so dark they'd be black if not for the tiniest hint of gold at their edges. Crinkling into crescent moons when they laugh their same easy laugh. His dad really said *copy & paste.* The only notable difference is Mr. Jackson's dimple is on his right cheek, where Ro's digs into the left—two sides of the same face.

"Mr. Jackson," I decide. "I just came by to drop something off. For Ro."

Ro raises an eyebrow in my direction again, surprised by the news.

But Mr. Jackson's attention is elsewhere. "Boy, you got about thirty seconds left on this song before you gotta write my name on that winner's board again. I know you don't think distracting me with this young lady's gonna save you."

"I already got this one and you know it."

"There you go, tryin' to change the rules on me," Mr. Jackson says, laughing. "Kaia, I'm sorry you have to see this. I promise you never met a man worse at losing than my boy."

And there it is, like clockwork. Any time I see dads with their kids, dads who stayed, there's always *a moment.* A moment I get a glimpse of what life could be like. A moment I have to force a smile as I swallow heavy past a familiar pang in my chest.

Ro's laugh puts a welcome end to that moment. "Man, don't do me like that, Pops!"

"Okay," I say, raising my hand. "I think I'm a little lost."

Mr. Jackson walks out from behind the car and turns up the music. "It's how we pass the time out here. Gotta name every artist and song before it ends. Till *one of us* don't know," he says through a smirk that reminds me so much of his son.

". . . And this man *knows* I know this song," Ro finishes.

"I don't need your outta tune self serenading me like you're finna ask me to go steady. I need a *name,*" Mr. Jackson says, clapping his hands together to drive it home. "You ain't got that, take your L like a man and stop embarrassing yourself in front of Kaia here."

That shuts Ro up quick. His arms cross above his head and his eyes dart back and forth as he racks his brain. The notes are fading out. There are only a few seconds left, and at this point we all know Ro's not getting it. Mr. Jackson's already doing a celebratory dance that ages him by about a decade, while Ro looks like he could flip the Beamer with his bare hands.

"Have You Seen Her," I must say out loud, because both their heads whip around to me. Since they're still waiting, I follow it up with the winning answer. "The Chi-Lites."

"The Chi-Lites!" Ro echoes, walking over to high-five me. He's still clasping my hand in the air when he turns toward Mr. Jackson. "We're taking that point. Kaia's on my team now."

"Oh, it's like that," his dad says, laughing.

"It's just like that."

"Okay, I see you," Mr. Jackson says. "I'm gonna give y'all that one, but next time I'm bringing your mother. Then you know it's over."

Ro flinches. "Damn. If you thought my dad was bad . . ."

"Chi-Lites," Mr. Jackson says as he adds my *K* to Ro's *R* on the leader board, like it's nothing. "Your parents did all right with you."

"My mom," I say, correcting him. "Breakup songs are our unofficial family anthem."

"I hear that," he says, even though he can't possibly know the half of it. "Now if you two will excuse me, somebody's gotta do some work around here. Y'all can go do your victory lap inside."

"Your dad's great," I say as soon as the lobby door closes behind us.

Ro smiles. "He's a piece of work." But behind the jab, all I hear is love. "So, what's up? You said you have something for me?"

"Yeah, I was out and remembered I had this on me." I reach into my pocket for the questionnaire. "I think you mentioned wanting to see it, so I figured . . ."

Ro's eyes light up like a kid on Christmas, but as he reads it, the humor on his face morphs into something else.

"Shit, this is intense. I thought it'd ask favorite movies or something. Not '*Describe your childhood trauma and how it fucked you up.*'"

"It does not say that," I say, laughing. "But it *is* a lot. Zola's a lot. She swears if two people compare their answers to these questions they'll—"

"Lose their will to live?" Ro says, looking either terrified or impressed. It's too soon to say which.

My laughs comes out like a bark, but Ro's reaction to the sound looks like pride.

"I think in therapy that's called a breakthrough," I say, still smiling.

Ro moves behind the register. "I didn't realize therapy and matchmaking had so much in common," he says, fishing a pen from between the rows of the keyboard. "But I'm down."

He's folded over the counter as he scribbles words onto the questionnaire that was meant to be mine. I don't stop him. For some reason nothing feels as important as reading Ro's answers to these questions I've been mocking all day.

"How many guys are filling this out for you?" he asks, without looking up from his work.

"Three. But they're not doing it *for me.* They don't even know me."

His head snaps up, eyes locking with mine. "Then why are they doing it?"

He asks it so earnestly, like it's the most obvious question in the world, but I don't have an answer. Unless you count figuring out ways to blow them off, I haven't spent much time thinking about these guys at all. Let alone trying to determine their motivations for agreeing to this. So I say something I do know to be true.

"My sister can be pretty convincing."

The rolling timbre of Ro's laugh is like a lazy Sunday morning. "Say no more. She damn near had me introducing her to every skeleton in my closet too."

"She's got a gift," I tell him, attempting a not-so-subtle peek at his paper. "And embarrassing me is her lifeblood. So whyever the guys do it, I promise that's a major part of *her* motivation."

"I don't think it's embarrassing," he says easily. Like maybe he means it. "I think it's dope. Not too many people would do something like this. I'm impressed, E."

"Can we negotiate my nickname before you commit to calling me *Empty*?"

"Only if you show me yours. The questionnaire you filled out."

It doesn't matter that I haven't yet filled mine out. My answer will always be the same: "Absolutely not."

"Aw, come on. I thought we were a team!"

"For musical trivia? Sure. For baring the inner workings of my cold black heart? No."

"Fair enough," he says, laughing. "But you don't get to see mine either."

I'm watching him tuck it under the cash drawer so intently that I jump a little when he slams the register shut. "Not until you're ready to swap."

"Well, your secrets are safe then," I say. "Because I'm not swapping."

That's what my mouth says, but my eyes are still zeroed in on Ro's hiding spot. When I look back to him, Ro's eyes are even brighter than usual, and when the corners of his lips quirk, I know it's not just 'cause he's caught me—he's fucking with me.

# 9

**7:26pm**

**Ro:** You're really not gonna give me anything?

IT'S BEEN A LITTLE OVER TWO WEEKS SINCE I LEFT RO WITH his questionnaire at the shop. Two weeks since Zola gave her lukewarm approval of my second attempt at my own questionnaire and scheduled dates with three potential matches. And two weeks since Ro has let me know a moment of peace.

**Ro:** Tell me something small. Ideal physical type.

**Ro:** I could probably guess that if I tried.

And now that I'm officially getting ready for date number one, Ro's all but foaming at the mouth for intel.

**Me:** I'd be so mad if he showed somebody my answers.

**Ro:** But you know he already has, right?

Oh great. A new fear to fixate on.

**Ro:** Come on, do it for the tow truck guy 😉

**Me:** You already forgave me for that. You can no longer use it against me.

But I'm smiling as I return my diffuser to its drawer. I'm obviously going to tell him.

I comb my memory for some personal favorites.

**Me:** Fine *clears throat*

**Me:** When asked about his ideal physical type, our first bachelor says it's "A girl who looks like my future wife."

**Ro:** YOOOO!

**Ro:** That's deep af

**Me:** That's a line.

**Ro:** well that line is deep af

Ro may actually be worse than Zola. He sounds like he's over there wrist-deep in a bowl of popcorn, giddy at the thought of my impending torture. But turning this whole thing into one long-running joke with Ro is also the only reason I've forgotten I'm supposed to be dreading it.

**Me:** Lol I can't with you.

**Me:** Ok, I gotta finish getting ready.

**Me:** Wish me luck. And keep an eye out for familiar sounding Amber Alerts.

**Ro:** I think those are for kids.

**Me:** Oh.

**Ro:** Idk what they call it when someone takes an adult woman hostage.

**Me:** Pretty sure it's called a relationship.

I flip my head from side to side, fluffing and teasing until my curls achieve their optimal poof. It's only when my phone is quiet and I'm alone deciding on a matte or glossy lip that the first spike of panic finally hits.

This setup has gone from a threat to a deal to a punch line. And now it's a reality.

Somewhere across town, there's a man who's conjured up an image of a woman in his mind that I'll now be judged against. So when the real me shows up instead of the questionnaire version he's already decided best suits him, I get to watch as he tries to fit me back into the box he's built me into. And he gets to spend the evening gauging just how easily me and my box fit into *his* world.

The knock at my bedroom door interrupts my thoughts, but the dread remains.

"You ready?" Zola's never been much for small talk.

Mom's standing beside her in the doorway, but her contributions begin and end at telling me how pretty I look. Over the past couple weeks, Mom's role in Zola's enterprise has become increasingly less pronounced.

Actually, her presence has been lacking overall. I've even been the one playing stand-in baby daddy at Zola's doctor's appointments and birthing classes. And while *sister wives-ing* this pregnancy *is* one of the reasons I'm home, I could've gone a lifetime without learning how to use the word *perineum* in a sentence, or knowing that Zola's should be oiled in preparation for the big day.

More than that, though, historically speaking, Mom going ghost has only ever meant one thing—but I can't think about her love life right now. Not when she and Zola have already zeroed in on me and mine.

"I was just about to head out," I say, as Zola follows me into the suddenly too-small and too-warm bathroom. Nerves heat my face as she watches me silently in the mirror.

"No," Zola says, finally turning to face me in the flesh. "Are you *ready*?"

The folder she holds in the air is marked with my first and last name, as if she'd otherwise confuse mine with one of her other nonexistent clients. The manila offering is an invitation behind the wizard's curtain.

"If I'm late because of this cloak-and-dagger reveal," I say, like I'm not dying for a peek, "I don't want to hear a word."

I can actually *hear* Mom holding her breath across the room now. Or shit, maybe that's me. I hope everyone will join me in pretending not to notice I'm now in a full sweat.

Zola opens the folder, and . . .

*Okkkkay, bachelor number one! Okkkkay, Zola!*

I'd seen his questionnaire that's now clipped behind the Polaroid, but the picture is new, and dare I say, Hemsworth adjacent in the best way. This may not be a complete waste of time after—

"Excuse me, what was that?" Zola's accusatory tone halts my movements. "Did you just try to *swipe* right?" She continues before I can deny the fact that I absolutely just attempted to swipe this very nondigital photo of this very nondigital man. "Mom, you saw that right?"

"There was something on the picture," I decide. But the lie's so flimsy, I can hardly keep a straight face as I deliver it.

"Did I call it or did I call it?" Zola says smugly, before joining Mom on the bed.

I do my best not to sound petulant when I bite back. "What's that supposed to mean?"

The question was directed at Zola, but Mom steps in, likely to take some sting out of the answer. "I'd wanted you to get the pictures when you got the questionnaires. To get you excited—"

"And *I*," Zola starts in, "knew your brain had become so

hardwired for the casual online thing that we'd have to force substance on you first, and make the physical piece an afterthought. We have to break these patterns, Kai. They're not serving you."

I pause to make sure we're still talking about me and not the woman currently seated to Zola's left. I want to again scream that I'm not the one with the problem, but I also want to get to the restaurant so I can see what this guy's working with below his headshot, so I snap a quick pic of my date for Liv and close the file. She hasn't been as involved in the lead-up as I'd expected her to be, but she's going to want to see *this.*

"Either way," I say, puckering into the mirror before turning to smack my lips at Zola for dramatic effect. "I would very much like to thank you for your service. Five stars."

No part of me expects to fall in love with this guy, but if the night ends with me falling into his bed, XO by Zo may have its first very satisfied customer.

Zola elbows Mom like she anticipated this moment. "Careful where you're pointing those things, little sister." Synchronized smirks hit their lips like they've rehearsed this part. "Universal matchmaking code dictates no sex till monogamy."

My shoulders sag in disbelief. "You one thousand percent just made that up."

Zola's eyes dance, as if my forced celibacy is her true victory. "Check the contract," she says, referring to the single piece of paper, smeared with remnants of chocolate croissants. A paper that would never hold up in a courtroom. *I don't think.*

I yank my purse onto my shoulder and spit parting words at Zola. "You are—and I can't stress this enough—fucking killing me."

"Language," Mom says, the same way she's been reflexively parroting since we were kids.

"I gave you access to my social schedule," I continue. "I don't remember giving you rights to my—"

"Flower?" Mom suggests.

"Ew," Zola says. And this time she has the decency to look just as disgusted as I am. "Mom."

Mom throws her hands up in surrender. "Kidding."

"Well, either way," I say, on my way out the door. "My peony. My choice."

The host stand is abandoned when I walk into Antonio's at 8:03. I expect the incoming texts from Zola to be a request for confirmation that I haven't stood her guy up, but as usual, Zo's full of surprises.

**8:03pm**

**Zola:** you and Ro are good now right?

**Zola:** can you send me his number?

**Me:** um. why?

She's still typing a response when the host finally emerges to ask how he can help. His words are all business, but his wandering eyes are drifting down to my peekaboo cleavage—currently more *peek* than *a-boo.*

Tonight's the first time I had an excuse to dig my outside clothes out of my suitcase, and it feels good to look good. Being back home has transformed me from a fully functioning human person back into somebody's daughter and little sister. I needed to be reminded who the fuck I am. *That's* why I got dressed tonight—not, I assure you, for this greasy teenager's approval.

I clear my throat and his eyes dart up almost impatiently. Like he's annoyed to find there's a human head resting atop the boobs he'd been ogling.

"I'm meeting someone," I say, and he looks even more disappointed to realize the boobs also speak. "The reservation should be under Harper or Zola."

The reservation is actually under XO by Zo (brand recognition and all that), but I'd rather call for Bloody Mary three times in the bathroom mirror than utter those six letters in public.

He scans the reservations list until his bushy brows furrow. *Yes, that one,* I silently confirm by raising my own. He registers the challenge on my face, and for the first time since I walked through the door, the smile on his lips is replaced by something that actually borders on professionalism.

"For two?" he confirms, grabbing an assortment of menus from the host stand. "You can follow me."

I'm relieved to find the small candlelit table empty as we approach—I need a minute to collect myself. I'm *less* relieved when the Peeping Tom host lingers beside me as I settle into my seat.

"Surprise," he says, and a pang of terror fires from my erratically beating heart to my fingertips. If Zo pops out from behind a planter and confesses to catfishing me with a seventeen-year-old on his last dose of Accutane, I swear to god.

I'm typing out a text to Liv that simply reads Chris Hansen—our long-shared predator alert—when Peeping Tom speaks again.

"This is my section. I'm gonna be taking care of you tonight."

"Oh," I say, my panic only somewhat assuaged. "Lucky me."

One of the many unpleasant consequences of being eye-fucked by someone who still counts half birthdays is that what once felt like a sexy amount of cleavage now feels obscene.

I'm discreetly tucking my breasts deeper into my bra, while

damning the broken system that demands I adjust *my* body for a little boy who never learned the word *no,* when bachelor number one's approach stalls my adjustments cold. Unfortunately, this temporary paralysis leaves me palming my own breast. Worse yet, before my brain can scream for me to *STOP TOUCHING YOUR NIPPLE, YOU PERVERT,* the nipple in question goes rogue—budding at the sight of him.

There's no truly inconspicuous way to stop feeling yourself up in public once you've been caught, but unlike my waiter du jour, the man standing before me is respectful enough to avert his gaze. I use the moment of privacy to right my shirt and appreciate my dinner companion.

After four years with salt of the earth guys in the Midwest, my expectations for men's dress options exist on a sliding scale that ranges from denim to *good* denim. So you'll forgive me the boardroom fantasy I indulge in as he shrugs out of his bespoke jacket, revealing a crisp white button-up that stretches in protest against his flexing pecs.

His blue eyes stare, unwavering, as he folds the discarded jacket over the back of his empty chair, before rounding the table to get to me. The smile he wears is both teasing and disarming. He's stalking me, and I, the feeblest of prey, reach out willingly for him to pull me up from my seat.

I'd never admit aloud what it does to me when he holds my hand in both of his, taking control of the movement, but *Toto, I have a feeling we're not in Kansas anymore.*

The slightest tug at my hand invites me into his quick introductory hug. Against the contrast of his firm body and slightly stubbled cheek pressing into mine, my own body goes soft. I momentarily sink deeper into the embrace and the scent of his soap and something faintly spicy as it ensnares my senses. But he doesn't linger. Nothing about the gesture is overly intimate and I appreciate that.

So far, he's doing everything right. But then, because they simply cannot help themselves, he does the thing they've all insisted on doing since ancient man choked out his inaugural grunt—he speaks.

"Ryan Burgess," he proclaims, taking his seat before I've found mine again. "I hope you weren't waiting long. It hadn't occurred to me that you'd beat me here."

Then *he chuckles.*

"Fifteen minutes late seems to be the new normal for you girls. I've taken to building that buffer in for myself now too. Seems only fair."

If he wasn't so tickled by the many micro-misogynies he's doling out, he'd see the physical effect his "joke" has on me—a verbal cold shower, immediately cooling any dull embers of attraction that had briefly sparked.

"The partner track doesn't come with a work-life balance as it is, I'm afraid. I can't afford to be kept waiting. You'd be amazed by how much I can accomplish in fifteen minutes."

I ignore his smirk at the most unsexy sex reference ever uttered in favor of recalling the details of Ryan's questionnaire. Now that there's exactly zero sexual tension clouding my brain, I recall Zola's brief rundown. Ryan Burgess is a *box checker,* as she put it. Great schooling (Yale, as I'm sure he'll be announcing loudly and often), great prospects (on track to be his firm's youngest partner), great future (in a Greenwich, Connecticut, zip code, no doubt). Unfortunately, as far as I can tell, he's not a particularly *great* person.

"You're . . ." Ryan begins again, searching his Ivy League brain. "A teacher, right? So, you don't have to worry about the whole work-life thing."

This time my fiery glare finds its target.

"Hey, I envy it," he says, backpedaling only somewhat. "That's the way to go. My parents were already six figures in debt to Yale Law when I realized I'd all but signed my life away. Far too late to pivot to a job with summers off."

Only used car salesmen and this fucking guy laugh at their own jokes this much. I'm sure of it.

"I've been out with quite a few teachers. I get the appeal. Not a field where you fall down the corporate ladder if you need off for weddings and babies and all that. It makes sense."

"Actually," I interject, and it's only when the word hangs between us that I realize it's the first I've uttered since Ryan stormed in—a sexy, egotistical tornado, sucking up all the air in the room. "It's the *men* in my family who sparked my interest in education."

*Shit,* I think to myself. I'm surprised to have made a careless admission on which I have no intention of elaborating.

But I should've known better than to worry about Ryan latching onto a thought that doesn't center on him entirely. Instead, he cranes his neck to see over my hair, head pivoting as he surveys the restaurant.

"Where is she?" he says, mostly to himself.

I turn to follow his view. "Who?"

"The waitress." He makes a show of checking his watch, as if he's being kept from more important matters. "Now I have to apologize doubly. This time for *her* tardiness." He says this as if his entitlement is somehow for my benefit. "Whenever she does finally grace us with her presence, please feel free to order anything you like. Zola mentioned you're currently living at home? Tonight's my treat. And thanks for waiting to order. You wouldn't believe how rare that home training is these days."

I check the restaurant's perimeter greenery once more. I'm disappointed not to find Zo beneath the faux olive trees, filming what I've now come to hope is a prank. But my mood improves somewhat when I see our *waitress* returning. Penis and all.

"Sorry for the wait," he says, as he presents my cocktail. "Bartenders made me dig the grapefruits outta the walk-in for your twist."

I raise my poetically timed drink delivery toward my date. "It seems, I, too, was raised by wolves." And I turn back toward Peeping Tom, who's suddenly become the lesser of two evils, to say, "Cheers, Tom."

His eyes dart nervously across the table and back again. "Uh. My name is Jared."

I drain the glass as Ryan and Jared (*apparently*) look on in disgust and awe, respectively. In my best mock-Stepford, I dab the corners of my mouth with my cloth napkin.

"My mistake," I say, before tapping the rim. "Jared, I'm gonna do one more of these."

And then, because how much or little I enjoy my evening will correlate directly with how miserable I can make Ryan, I turn to him in invitation. "And for tonight's sponsor? Anything you like."

I expect his cool blue eyes to blaze, but Ryan's face flashes from shock to intrigue.

He nods toward the glass I'm currently rubbing sweat from. "Bourbon?"

"Mezcal," I correct.

His eyebrow quirks like he's impressed, and I cannot express how little I care to impress this man.

With renewed intensity to his eye contact, Ryan speaks again, but this time he's finally addressing our waiter when he says, "Make it two."

The rest of the evening follows the same tiresome cycle—trading insults masquerading as flirty first date banter. Me, trying like hell to bury this fucking guy beneath the spike of my stiletto, and him, in return, laughing his grating old boys' club chortle like we're in on the joke together.

By the time the dessert cart rolls around, I'm:

1. fairly certain Zola has no future in matchmaking,
2. ready to light this guy up in tomorrow's postmortem, and
3. shmammered.

"So, Zola—*my sister*—set this up."

It's a clarification that would've made more sense earlier in the night, but I thought I'd have figured it out by now. After two hours, I still don't get it.

"You're paying her for this service. And this," I say, gesturing between us, "is the match she chose."

Ryan's nod is coupled with a sigh as he leans into the table, his angular chin propped up on steepled fingertips. "Look, I'm an old-school guy—"

"Ya don't say."

"I was on the apps for a while after Eliza declined my last contract renewal."

*There it is. One matchmaker's trash, I guess.*

"But the females on there . . ." he continues. And not for the first time tonight, I wonder why Zola hates me. "They're a different breed. I don't have a clue what they want, but it's not the kind of relationship I'm looking for."

As I remove my bag from the chairback, I'm still mentally stuck back at "females," but Ryan doesn't pause long enough for me to catch up.

"Zola called at the right time," he continues. "Said she wanted to keep working with me. Convinced me to try it her way this time. Some shit about slaying your dating demons, I don't know.

The deck she sent had a picture of you, and she cut Eliza's prices in half. I liked everything I saw."

Ryan seems to be attempting some version of bro vulnerability—I wonder if that was also in Zola's dating guide. The one she'd conveniently forgotten to give me.

His misguided words don't move me, but they do cut through my mental fog enough for me to refocus on retrieving the phone from my purse. But the missed message notifications on the lock screen briefly distract me from ordering a car.

**8:07pm**

**Zola:** I need Ro's help with something.

I'd already wanted to get home to see the look on Zo's face when I tear our contract to shreds in front of her, but reading the Nm. Got it text that follows makes getting home even more urgent. I need to know what she wants with Ro.

But both of those plans are quickly forgotten when I read the other awaiting texts.

**8:52pm**

**Ro:** I expect updates!

**9:47pm**

**Ro:** You forget about me?

I'd promised to send Ro the play-by-play as the night progressed, but he's lucky to have avoided my real-time updates. And I can sum up the experience for him easily:

**10:12pm**

**Me:** OMG. SENDD HELP P

**Ro:** Ha that bad? What happened?

"Can I offer you a ride?" Ryan interrupts without looking up from signing the check he'd insisted on paying. Not that I put up much of a fight. I'll file tonight away as charity work of sorts—attempted rehab of a broken man.

His shirtsleeves are rolled up to his elbows now, tie hanging open around his neck. There's no denying that Ryan Burgess is the stuff late-night fantasies are made of. But even this current state of buzzy undress on a man who's been turning heads all night isn't enough to warm the shivers trailing down my spine at the prospect of spending another moment in his company.

"I have a Lyft coming," I lie.

My phone pings in my hand. I check it immediately, sparing no thought to first date etiquette.

**Ro:** You ok? Where are you?

**Me:** Antonios. getting a car. gotta get outta here

**Ro:** That's right by me. I can be there in 5. Can Uber beat that?

I check. No, Uber cannot beat that. Nor can Lyft.

**Me:** You sure?

**Ro:** Yes. Already walking out.

The sound of Ryan clearing his throat provides a necessary reminder that he's still here. The expression he wears could be mistaken for boredom, if not for the indignant posture of his left eyebrow and the slight flare of his nose. Like he said at the top of the evening, Ryan is not a man who likes to be kept waiting. It's also painfully clear that he's not a man who should've been seated across from me tonight.

"Look," I begin, focused intently on unsloshing the words in my brain before they leave my lips. "I appreciate you coming, but I think I'm gonna head out."

The only confirmation I have that Ryan even heard me is the subtle shake of his head that acts as a dismissal, before he reclines slightly in his chair and takes out his phone. Without my permission, and most certainly as a result of that fourth cocktail, my eyes roam over his broad chest and the pull of those buttons. Snapping a mental image before I go. I continue down his arms to his hands, mostly hidden behind the table—and I know this man is not doing what I think he's doing.

"Was that a swipe?" I ask, appalled. "Are you on an app right now?"

Ryan's scoff is incredulous—*I hope he chokes on it.* "You really think I took a peak train back from the city to *not* get laid tonight?"

Then he keeps right on swiping. Above the table, now. For all of Antonio's to see.

I'll never know if Ryan hears it as a reaction to the alcohol or his limitless audacity, but when my stomach gurgles a warning, I stand abruptly. "I think I'm gonna be sick."

And when my phone pings in my hand, Ro's here text is the most beautiful prose I've ever read.

I launch myself into Ro's truck.

"I thought you needed a ride, not a getaway," Ro says, laughing. "If we're about to end up on the news, maybe an Uber's the right way to go. You're cute and all, but—"

"Just drive!" I yell, laughing as I recline the seat completely, committing to the scene Ro's set.

He shakes his head as he shifts into gear. "Well, hi to you too."

My stomach is still less than thrilled with me as we make our way through town. I open the window, breathing deeply so the fresh air can replace the toxins currently off-gassing in my liver.

"I don't normally drink like this on first dates," I say, unsure what compelled me to explain myself.

"I'm not judging you," he says. He's driving with purpose, though I haven't actually told him where to take me. "You gonna tell me what happened back there?"

My head falls to the crook of my elbow, resting on the window. "You wouldn't believe it if I did."

At the next red light, Ro turns to me, his face relaxed and open as he waits. I meet his eyes, and I'm relieved by the warm depths of his dark gaze, when moments before, I'd seen Ryan's sharp blue frost. And there's no challenge or baiting in his tone when he speaks next. There's only an invitation, when he smiles and says, "Try me."

# 10

YOU CAN TELL A LOT ABOUT A PERSON BY THEIR PIZZA topping of choice. Pepperoni is for risk-takers—the ones who don't bother asking what is it *really* and where exactly does it come from? Pineapple, obviously, is for sociopaths. Or people from L.A., but what's the difference? Anything other than a plain slice is an admission.

But I didn't agree to stop at Ro's go-to spot for a psychoanalysis of his late-night order. I'm just here to soak up my blood alcohol content and the night's ick with a greasy slice or four.

"Thanks for joining me for second dinner," I say, shifting to make space for a guy struggling with an unwieldy take-out pie.

When he walks between me and Ro to cover his pizza in assorted spices, Ro steps around him to join me again. The movement leaves me pinned between Ro's chest and the wall. His shoulders tense, almost imperceptibly, as his body registers the feel of mine, but he doesn't back away.

Each exhale of Ro's minty breath is only inches from me now as he speaks. "Everyone knows a slice doesn't count. Couldn't let you leave a date hungry."

I'm doing my best to focus on his words, but my brain is

singularly focused on the feel of his cool, steady breath on me, and trying to guess if he stopped to brush his teeth on his way out the door.

My unfocused eyes meet his expectant ones. Apparently, it's my turn to talk.

"It wasn't even your date," I say, only about 60 percent sure I've chosen an appropriate response.

The corner of his top lip jumps a little before he hits me with a smile that makes me feel way too childish and way too grown, all at once. "Doesn't matter. House rules growing up were you don't leave till you're full. I woulda been dodging my mom's slippers if she ever found out I sent you home hungry."

When the guy at the oven yells out our order, we make our way through the crowd. Ro towers over everyone at the counter as he grabs our tray.

"What is it with Black moms and slippers?" I ask.

"Plausible deniability," he shouts over the crowd. "We stay scared, but ain't nobody ever called CPS over a house shoe."

Ro nods toward the front door and I follow him outside with a handful of napkins and the waters we already paid for.

The street is mostly empty and completely quiet. A stark difference from the chaos we left behind inside.

"This place is going off," I say, choosing a bench for us. "Is it always like this?"

He nods, divvying up our food. "Worth it though. Best slice between here and the city."

I make a face like *we'll see about that,* but as soon as I bite into mine, my eyes close and an *mmmm* escapes from someplace deep.

Ro pumps the air, victorious. "What'd I say?"

I elbow him. "Or maybe I'm just drunk and hungry." It's not easy to play coy about a meal you're actively inhaling, but I manage.

Ro shakes his head. "I'm still mad you went to an Italian joint and got salad. Would've had you pegged for the chicken parm."

"My salad was delicious, thank you very much," I say, yanking the cheese from my teeth to cut it. "But I do get down with some chicken parm. I just ordered whatever sounded quick."

"Damn," he says, "you knew the night was over before you even ordered?"

"Well, I'm pretty sure *his* night kept going," I admit. "Just not with me."

Ro chokes on a mushroom. And I am vindicated.

"No fucking way," he says, in equal parts shock, horror, and excitement. An entirely appropriate response from start to finish.

I nod, sipping my water through a satisfied smile. "I can now officially check *watching my date set up another date* off my bingo card. I shouldn't even be surprised. Guys are always finding new and inventive ways to fail."

"That's what you think?"

"It's what I *know*. A fact, proven time after time, by every guy in the history of the world."

"Not *every* guy?"

"Every single one."

Ro leans back on the bench before abandoning his slice in the empty space beside him. He crosses his arms in front of his chest but continues speaking before I can ask about his plans for that half-eaten slice. "There had to be one who didn't fuck up like that. Somebody who at least made it through dinner."

My eyebrow raises suggestively. "I mean, I did my thing a little at school."

Ro untucks his hand from his bicep, holding it up to stop me. "Nah, nah, nah, nah. I don't need to hear about all that."

"Well, if none of those guys count . . ." I'm not dying to confess my more casual exploits to Ro, but I don't hate making him squirm. And squirm he does.

When I've had my fun, I start again. "There was one guy. I thought I was gonna marry him." Ro looks intrigued, until I continue. "But I don't know if that counts since half the student section thought Asher Hall was their boyfriend."

"Asher," Ro repeats. "Well, if that's not a white guy . . ."

My barking laugh comes out in a rush. "Actually, he was mixed. And fine as hell. He was the captain of our high school football team, so my friend Liv and I used to go watch him play every Friday night. Never missed a game." I smile at the memory. It feels, somehow, like a lifetime ago and just yesterday, all at once. "We were down so bad. Thought he was scoring touchdowns just for us. Out there every week, waiting for him to scale the bleachers to profess his love. In hindsight I realize I probably should've started our great love affair by introducing myself."

Ro cringes and I close my eyes, nodding at the ancient missed connection. But my smile fades in anticipation of the part that comes next.

"I never worked up the nerve. And this was all right around the time my dad left—on a Thursday. Which I only know because I remember I'd been crying for a full twenty-four hours by the time Liv came over. I think she figured going to the game would help. That had always been the highlight of our weeks. But have you ever tried to paint a *#28* over teenage girl tears?"

At some point during my story, Ro righted his body. He's leaning forward now, elbows digging into each parted thigh, at full attention. Like he doesn't want to miss a word.

"She managed to get me to the game though. And she was right—everything was exactly the same as always. Asher was still playing his ass off and the girls in the stands were still losing their minds. It should've been comforting. Seeing that not everything had changed. But it felt like another betrayal."

The familiar hollowing of my stomach transports me back to that night in the bleachers. Emptiness returning with the memory, even after all this time.

"I was pissed nobody else's world had been destroyed. So even though it *looked* the same, it *felt* completely different. Standing there, like I was in a performance of a moment instead of actually living it. Everything was in 2D: the set, the characters. There was the hometown hero, who was always gonna go home with whichever cheerleader forgot her bloomers that week. The girls in the stands, playing their supporting role of the adoring fans. And I knew that was supposed to be my role too. It always had been, but I didn't want to play it anymore. I didn't want to be a part of this thing that suddenly felt like a lie, like everything else in my life—my dad, my family, my whole world. It had all been a lie. I couldn't be part of another one. So I walked home alone and that was that. The fairy tale was over."

Ro's face reflects the weight of all the words I hadn't meant to say, and I'm desperate to unsay them. To move past them, at least.

"Let's just say that was the last time I ever pretended to enjoy football. And I never painted another guy's number on a tear-stained cheek. But I think we can all agree I'm probably better for it."

Ro's head tilts back and forth like he's weighing it all out. "You and your dad all right now?"

"Uh, no."

Over the years I've found that if you just leave it there, people rarely ask for more. They're probably relieved not to have to listen to another story about another girl with daddy issues.

But Ro doesn't rush to fill the silence or change the subject the way so many do. He's not suddenly avoiding eye contact or looking at me like I'm broken. There's no race to find that toxic silver lining to make it all better. He's just waiting. Listening.

Which is probably the reason I keep going.

"The only way my mom could handle my dad leaving was to decide he'd made the decision under some sort of duress. A temporary break from reality. She was so sure he'd come to his senses and come home. But I knew he wasn't coming back for us. He'd woken up one day and wanted an entirely different life. One that didn't include me and Zola. And that hasn't changed."

I hear truths tumbling from my mezcal-loosened lips, like this is normal dinner conversation. Like I'm not sharing my world and my wounds with him, when I hadn't even planned to share this bench.

"Call it whatever you want—a midlife crisis, a psychotic break. Leaving was the first honest thing he did. Maybe ever. Who would choose to go back to living the lie?" My laugh is darker than I mean for it to be, but I guess it's what's real. "The first guy to ever ghost me."

"And now you think that's all guys."

I fold what's left of my slice into the grease-stained paper plate. Grateful to give my hands something to do other than sweat.

"But am I wrong?" I ask. "Take tonight. I tried it Zola's way and still ended up on a dirty bench with a slice." When I realize what I've said, I try to save it. "No offense," I say, leaning into him in apology.

"Oh, I'm offended," he says, shouldering me, so I know we're okay. "But not by that comment."

"I'm not even hating. I just think everyone's so desperate to find their *person* that they don't bother finding out who *they* are first. I'm not gonna waste my time trying to become the thing somebody else wants, just for him to look at me one day and decide he doesn't want it anymore."

Ro watches me thoughtfully, considering my words. Likely trying to find the safest point of entry. "Isn't that the whole point though? To find somebody you don't have to change for?"

I shrug, and I'd usually leave it there, but there's something about the space Ro leaves open that makes me want to fill it.

"It's a nice thought," I admit. "But even basic attraction is all presentation. An act. That's why I prefer the apps. At least people on there are more obvious about it. I respect that more than a guy undressing me with his eyes while telling me that it was my sparkling personality he noticed from across the room. Lying to get into bed, lying to get into a relationship, and then we both have to keep lying to make it work." I continue, because I can't not. "As soon as one person stops lying, everything falls apart. Because none of it was ever real to begin with."

I should quit, but then another wave of mezcal-flavored truth serum bubbles out of me.

"And no, this isn't me thinking every guy's my dad, it's me knowing what happens when a woman accidentally lets herself be honest or human. Or worst of all, inconvenient."

"Ah," he says. "We're not talking about what *people* do in relationships. It's men."

"Come on. Guys'll throw a whole life away when it stops being easy. Stops being fun."

Ro nods, but I wouldn't call it agreement. "Maybe some guys. But no shot that's what everybody's doing. Or no relationship would last."

"They don't! That's the point."

Ro collects my discarded plate with his and reaches a long arm out to deposit them in the trash can at the far side of our bench. He doesn't say a word, but I can see in his eyes that he has Thoughts™.

"Don't worry," he says finally. "I'm not gonna try to change your mind tonight."

"You couldn't if you wanted to."

"Yeah, I'm kinda gettin' that," he says with a look I can't quite name. He lets out a heavy exhale and with it, he releases the heaviness of our conversation. "How we feeling over there, E? That pizza help?"

"If I close one eye, there's only two of you now," I say, only half joking. "I think I'll do one more for the road."

Ducking inside for a last slice gives Ro a chance to grab the truck, and me an opportunity to find the off switch for whatever valve has malfunctioned in my brain. Talking to Ro is way too easy—it's a liability—and as much as I'd love to blame the alcohol, the truth is, it's him. It's every time I see him.

Just this once, I'd love to leave him without having to dissect my every social failing.

Ro's got the truck iced out by the time I meet him out front. On another warm summer night, I'd welcome the AC, but when I get drunk, I get tired, and when I get tired, I get cold.

I hardly register the shiver ripple up my spine. "Thanks for waiting. Pizza was the thing I missed most when I was in Kansas. Don't tell Zola I said that."

Ro laughs and wordlessly reaches into the back seat to retrieve an enormous black hoodie. He's already turned the air off, but I don't argue when he holds it out to me. I slip into the plushness, burying my nose in the cowl neck once it's over my head. Because I'm cold. Obviously. Not because it smells clean and earthy, a little minty, with the tiniest hint of musk. Just like him.

"What were you doing in Kansas?"

I turn toward his voice and the outline of his strong profile.

The visual serves as a reminder that if I can see him, he can see me too. So I should probably stop sniffing his clothes.

"Oh," I say, almost forgetting I'd mentioned it. "That's where I went to school. The University of Kansas."

"Well, damn, E. That's your problem. What's an East Coast girl gonna do with the guys in Kansas?"

"Oh, you East Coasters had my heart plenty black and dead by the time I left," I say, laughing. "But shocking as it may be, I went for the school. Not the men. And Kansas has a great early education program."

"Oh, are we talking about that now? The other day, it was off-limits."

"Please don't. I still feel terrible about that," I admit freely. "I don't know if it makes it better or worse, but it really had nothing to do with you. Everything's just been so off since I got back—Zola had been in my ear that whole day, I thought my best friend was blowing me off, and you caught me mid-realization that what had felt like four years of forward progress might've been a giant fucking circle that dropped me off right back where I started. You were just at the wrong place at the wrong time."

No more than a single breath passes after I finish, a single beat, but it's enough time for me to want to take it all back. "Sorry. That probably doesn't make sense out of context. Ignore me. I'm drunk."

Ro smiles, and it's even more brilliant in the moonlight somehow. "I don't think you're that drunk anymore."

He pulls away from the stop sign, leaving the moment and my confessions behind.

We're a few miles down the road when Ro breaks our comfortable silence. "I still don't get what kind of *break the internet, straight to jail without passing go* dirt Zola has on you to get you to agree to these dates. The more I get to know you, the less sense it makes."

"I'm gonna take that as a compliment," I say, laughing.

"You should! You don't seem like you get caught up doing things you don't want to."

"You've met my sister," I joke, hoping maybe this time he'll let me off the hook.

The hum of Ro's tires on the highway fills the silence until he offers me an out I should take. "It doesn't matter if it makes sense to me. You know what you're doing."

"I thought I did."

Even to me, the words sound cryptic. But I've been trying to answer this question myself for weeks. I didn't expect to do it tonight with an audience.

"This one doesn't have a quick answer," I say, offering him one last chance to stop the clock on this impromptu therapy session.

But he doesn't take it. "I've got time."

I try to remember how I got here, but it goes so much further back than coming home.

"My dad was hilarious," I say, before I can stop myself. "Sometimes it's the only good thing I remember about him. If he was around, somebody was laughing. I used to love that—how laughter followed him. And my mom was all heart. Zola's always been exactly *Zola*—this genius firecracker of a person. Everybody in my family had their thing. But I could never figure mine out. It was like everything good had already been spoken for before I came along. So I just tried to fly under the radar. I used to prefer it that way."

At the stop sign Ro looks at me. His eye contact is so focused and intense that I know his silence is not for lack of interest.

"But then my dad left, and nothing fit together the way it

had before. He took the laughter with him. And my mom's giant heart that had always been her superpower became an overnight liability. She'd go from being a puddle on the kitchen floor to some random guy's fiancée and back again."

We still haven't moved from the stop sign. Ro still hasn't stopped watching me. And despite my better judgment, I still haven't stopped talking.

"Zola stepped up to keep things on track. She shouldered a lot of it, and I think it burned her out. And it sounds pathetic now, but when everything fell apart like that, I finally saw an opening. My mom and Zo needed me. I became the bridge between the bleeding heart and the brain. And I did it well. The three of us made sense together. It feels like that again now."

"And that's why you're doing this? To hold them together. To help them make sense."

"It's not like I have anything better going on," I try, but by the look on Ro's face, he's unamused.

"Every day before I came home, the same questions ran through my mind on a loop: *Who am I? What do I want? Where do I go from here?* They're the same questions I've been asking myself forever. And I'd always assumed the answers were gonna be *out there,* but clearly that was wrong, because I've been out there now, and I'm just as lost as I ever was."

Ro pulls to a stop outside my front door as I finish.

"Maybe to get better answers, I need to start asking better questions. Might as well try thirty-six of Zola's."

I start to shrug out of Ro's hoodie, but he stops me. In the dim of night, I can't make out every detail of Ro's features, but I've already mentally mapped and memorized his face, his smile. I know the exact shape of his dimple, and I know that right now it's there. On full display.

"Keep it. You've still got another twenty feet or so to go. Besides, it'll give me an excuse to see you again. To find out how it ends."

"Don't worry," I tell him as I hop down from his truck. "I'd never fade to black on you. Not after you saved me. Twice."

# 11

**7:46am**

**Ro:** Morning. How you feeling?

**Me:** Like I want to crawl into a dark hole where only me and that pizza exist.

**Me:** And then die there

**Me:** I'm so sorry about last night.

**Ro:** Why?

**Me:** I think the clinical term is Emotionally Slutty™

**Me:** I normally wait until I'm alone to hit rock bottom.

**Ro:** Nah, you were fine.

**Ro:** Idk if this will help your hangover, but did your sister tell you she hit me up?

**Ro:** I had an interesting voicemail waiting for me this morning.

**Me:** Oh fuck. No.

**Ro:** Ha. I'll wait to hit her back then.

**Me:** I apologize in advance for whatever she wants.

**Ro:** It's work actually. For her company.

**Me:** The gift that keeps on giving.

**Me:** I can't believe I have to do this two more times.

**Ro:** Your next date is when? Next Saturday?

**Me:** yes. Don't remind me

**Ro:** looking for an out?

**Me:** What'd you have in mind?

**Ro:** I'm going to a street art exhibition in the city.

**Me:** OMG Yes.

**Me:** Wait, that was an invitation right?

**Ro:** Ha. Yes.

**Me:** then YES!

**Me:** Now I just have to survive this hangover. Thoughts and prayers, appreciated.

**Ro:** I'm sure you'll pull through.

I'M WATCHING THE TRAILER FOR A NEW CRIME SHOW AND TRYing to decide which breakfast item pairs best with Pedialyte, when my bedroom door creaks open. A rogue braid and Zo's belly cross the threshold first, quickly followed by the rest of her.

Her exaggerated footsteps are meant to mime stealth, but she's about a trimester too late for that. I watch her unnatural movements toward the bed in silent amusement until we lock eyes. And it's Zola who has the audacity to look annoyed.

"You could have said something."

"You could've knocked," I say through a stretch.

"I wanted to get the highlights from last night before you were awake enough to filter out all the good stuff."

Zola scoots in beside me and I'm lucky she leaves me any space at all.

"What good stuff? There was no good stuff. That guy had zero redeeming qualities other than—"

"His face, his body, his salary, his pedigree, his drive, his—"

"Elitism, his flagrant chauvinism, his trigger-happy Bumble finger."

"His what?"

"And why wasn't I offered a peek at your groundbreaking matchmaking deck?" I ask, cutting to the chase.

Her face goes cherub, but her words are an admission when she says, "He told you?"

"*You* should've told me."

"That I'd special ordered you a date with your worst nightmare? Would you still have gone?"

*No.*

"Yes," is what I actually say.

But as I stand to make space for my lie, Zola's already shaking her head. "We had to get that guy out of the way. The big bad thing you stay ready for. You had to get the fight out of your system so we could move on. Think of it like aversion therapy."

My jaw is on the floor, stuck somewhere between being wildly offended at how she played me and being wildly impressed *at how she played me.*

"Well, I guess that answers the question of whether or not matchmakers answer to an ethics board."

I wait for Zola to defend herself, but she's already lost to me. Engrossed in whatever or whoever is on her phone.

"Jason?" I ask.

Zola lets out a heavy sigh and finds her belly with her free hand. That's all the answer I need.

Then she reaches out a hand for me to help her out of bed too. "For someone who doesn't want this baby, he sure has a lot of questions," she says with a sad smile.

"You think he's trying to come back?"

Zola doesn't answer. She's still protecting him with whatever she's not saying. I've always known there had to be more to their story, but I don't push for it. At a certain point, do the details even matter?

"Fucking guys," is all I say, wrapping Zola into a hug.

She laughs into my hair. "The whole point of this is to get you to stop saying stuff like that. But I'll give you a pass this time since your date sucked. And since you're making waffles."

"Oh, am I?"

"Mm-hmm. With whipped cream. Fresh. Not that crap from the can."

"Fine," I concede. "But you're on coffee duty. And while you make it, you can explain why you're hitting Ro up behind my back."

"In my defense, I did ask you for his number first."

It's a weak argument and we both know it. "Most people would've waited for a response."

"You were busy," she says, holding a cup of coffee out to me, as either an olive branch or a bribe. "And I have a company to run. I really don't see what the big deal is. You guys are friends now, right?"

"And what exactly does *my* friend have to do with *your* company?"

Zola's posture visibly relaxes at my subtle interest. She finally hands over the mug as she speaks, certain she's been forgiven.

"I need his help. I can do most of this alone if I have to, but this"—she scrolls through her photos until she finds her logo mock-up—"isn't gonna work. This company can't look like something I started out of my childhood bedroom."

"Even though you did."

"Correct, Kaia. Thank you for connecting those dots."

"So, you want to ask Ro to help with your logo."

When Zola warms up my coffee without my asking, I know her plans for Ro are bigger than that.

"Actually, I want him to help me with all my visuals," she

says, and I can practically hear the gears in her head turning. "Cohesive color palettes and designs for brand recognition, graphic design help for the site; I even thought it could be cool to commission him for some bare-bones portraits that we could use in place of client photos. A *not completely blind* date, with a twist to set us apart. We could target creatives and entrepreneurs. They'd eat that shit up."

I don't bother telling her that I actually love the idea. She's patting herself on the back enough for us both.

"What makes you think Ro would even know how to do this?" I ask, inviting Zola to join me back down here on Earth. "Yes, the art at the shop is incredible, but what you're describing is something totally different. You need a brand strategist or something."

She's pulling something up on her phone before I've even finished. When she slides the second barstool up beside me to share her screen, I see just how far behind I am.

"What is this?" I ask, though the website address bar makes it obvious. It's Ro. RoJackson.com. And it's everything Zola just described, and so much more. A Tribeca design firm with his name. "How did you find this?"

"I googled him before I even left the parking lot that day. I can't believe you didn't. Look at this!"

And I am. But I'm struggling to make this new information fit into who I'd already decided Ro was. A box I hadn't realized I'd been building him into in that familiar way I never want done to me.

I'm scrolling intently through Ro's expertly crafted site, but I stop myself from clicking the *About Me* page. Whatever it says about Ro, I'd rather hear directly from him.

"Why is he working at that tow place?" I whisper, mostly to myself.

*He's just the tow truck guy.*

"So, can I set up a call with him?" I hardly register the question, until Zo repeats it. "He wants you to sign off first. Can I tell him you're good with it?"

"I'll tell him," I say too quickly.

Zola must hear the ownership in those words, but she doesn't ask. She does, however, smile at me in a way that makes me wish I'd stayed in bed.

I'm deeply regretting adding whipped cream and maple syrup to my hangover, when Mom walks in from the garage.

"She lives," Mom says, shopping bags dangling from her wrists. At least one of us woke up ready to carpe diem this fine Sunday. "Does sleeping till noon mean you actually had fun last night?"

"You guys are the ones who wanted me to be more social," I say, pushing my plate away in surrender. "I'm just following orders."

"And exactly which part of our *orders* were you following when you slipped into this," Mom says, holding Ro's hoodie in the air like a smoking gun.

Zola's eyes go wide. "And you made *me* seem like the one keeping secrets! I thought you said the date was a bust."

"Relax," I say, yanking the sweatshirt from Zola, mid-sniff. "It's Ro's. He picked me up after your guy showed his ass."

"Hellooo, plot twist," Zola sings, salivating. "No wonder you didn't want me calling him."

Mom, on the other hand, looks like she's mentally solving for pi. "Wait, this is the tow truck driver, right?"

"Yes!" Zola answers for me. "Kaia's knight in overpriced streetwear."

"He picks up cars off the side of the road for a living." After seeing Ro's site, I'm not sure this is technically true, but I've gone too far to double back. So I double down instead. "Knightly rescues don't usually come with an invoice."

"Well, was he working last night when he saved you from the big bad wolf?" Zola says with that same damn smirk.

"We're friends."

"So that's a no," Zola says, taking the final word.

She can have it.

My stomach is protesting, my head is pounding, and frankly I don't have the energy to go another round with these two.

By the time Mom calls out, "Don't leave! We're just having fun," I'm already gone.

# 12

I EXPECTED TO HAVE TO FIGHT HARDER TO PUSH THE NEXT date back a week, but when I tell Zola about Ro's show, she can't really argue. Ro's not only helping with her site, he's cutting his design rates by more than half so Zo can afford him. Sparing me for a night is the actual least she could do for him in return.

"I can't believe you're going out of town with a guy you hardly even know," Liv says that Saturday from my bed.

"We're driving an hour away," I remind her. Still disappointed that her being *here* means she won't be *there*. "It's not like we're flying to Bali."

I'd been so ready for a night with Liv in the city—my excitement had almost been enough for me to forgive her for ignoring my Chris Hansen SOS. But when I told her that Ro and I would be by her place later, she informed me that *she* was already on her way out. Because of course she was. We've been out of sync all summer.

"Still," she says, texting more than talking. I don't ask who with. Or who she came to Connecticut for today. If her Instagram stories are any indication, Liv's entire summer has been spent following Travis from gig to gig. "Quite a leap to go from complaining about driving twenty minutes to meet a guy for dinner."

"In my defense, I tried to cancel this, too, when I realized you were heading home. I didn't know I needed to book time with you weeks in advance."

"Nuh-uh," she says, holding a finger up to stop me. "Don't put this on me. You made this plan all by yourself. You want to go. And you're allowed to wanna go!"

"Well, I can't say I'm mad he got me out of going on another date. He could've sent an itinerary for a night in Poughkeepsie, and I would've been immediately down."

"I bet you would've." Her singsong tone is heavy on an implication that I willfully ignore. "But for the record," Liv says, rolling over on the mattress to make eye contact. "I wouldn't be so sure you're not going on a date. When a guy invites you to—"

"Guys can't have friends?"

"Don't be that girl. Of course, guys can have friends," she says, turning her phone to reveal the archives of Ro's Instagram grid. If she accidentally likes something, I'm fleeing to Canada. "But guys that look like *this* don't have friends that look like you."

"Ro's the only person I talk to out here who doesn't remember what I looked like in braces. And with you otherwise occupied in the city, I'm in no position to pass up new friends."

"With benefits," Liv suggests, matter-of-factly. Like it's a given.

"Right," I say, sarcastically. "Because that always ends well."

•

I'd planned for my exit to coincide with Mom and Zola's gym run, but as I jam the contents of our kitchen pantry into my crossbody, Mom joins us downstairs wearing a full face of makeup and her favorite jeans. I don't know what (or who) was worth canceling on Zo for, but I make a mental note to text my sister later to find out if we're mad about it.

Liv rushes Mom, shouting her standard "*Miss Harper!*" into their hug, and I'm glad her genuine excitement at seeing my mom overshadows my unease. Liv pulls back. "Wait. Miss? Ms.? You kept Harper last time, right?"

Mom laughs. "Girl, some days, I don't even know. But you're grown now. Just call me Angela."

I cross my arms over my chest. "Can you imagine guys having this conversation? Their names and identities legally bound to their relationship status."

Liv's and Mom's matching eye rolls might as well be choreographed.

"She's like one of those dolls," Liv says, switching to her infomercial voice when she continues. "Just pull the string in back and she'll spit out one of ten preprogrammed phrases damning the patriarchy."

Mom slaps Liv's arm and they have a quick laugh at my expense, until they feel the heat of my stare.

"You're no fun." Mom's words are as juvenile as her eye roll.

But I'm unbothered—singing, "I never claimed to be," while shoving a protein bar into my purse for the ride. It's an easy drive, but Ro's already seen me drunk. He doesn't need to see me hangry.

I'm attempting to coax Liv toward the door, when Mom asks, "So what are you up to this summer, Livvie?"

Liv sidesteps me to take a seat at the kitchen island, raising a hand to her chest in feigned disbelief. "Does this mean Kaia hasn't been complaining about me touring divey concert halls with my *boyfriend*? I'm shocked!"

She wants me to bite, but I can let one go by. I'm nobody's windup doll.

Liv's eyebrows lift gently in approval of my restraint before she turns back to my mom. "Unfortunately, that part of the summer is almost over. My dad lined up a bunch of interviews for me starting Monday. Deutsche Bank, J.P. Morgan, Morgan Stanley. So now I have to at least pretend to be serious." She says it nonchalantly, as if she didn't just name-drop Manhattan's titans of wealth management. "And I'm still waiting to see if I made it to the next round at Goldman Sachs."

At the same time Mom shrieks something like, "Okkkay, little Livvie," I yell, "What the fuck?!" But when I see their faces, I wish I would've erred more on the side of *little Livvie.*

"Sorry," I say, indiscriminately. "But—what? I had no idea."

It's not the first time since I got home that I've felt this distance between me and Liv. It's not even the first time I've felt it today.

"Of course, you didn't," she says, and though she's still smiling, Liv's tone is more growl than *POP!* Apparently, it's not her first time feeling the distance either.

It's only the three of us here, but with the way they're judging me, I might as well be naked onstage at Madison Square Garden, asking them to use *onomatopoeia* in a sentence.

"Okay," I say, physically pulling Liv out of her chair now. "As soon as I get back, I promise we'll do a lightning round Q&A on our five-year plans and set aside a night to sell band merch at whatever venue Travis has lined up next. But right now, I really do have someplace I need to be."

"Go on then," Mom says, standing to see us off at the door.

"But Liv's right. It's time to get serious. Summer won't last forever."

"Promise?" I yell back, as if I'll have somewhere better to be by fall.

But luckily, the closing garage door drowns out whatever Mom's saying about me under her breath.

# 13

THE SUN GLINTS OFF THE GLASS LOBBY DOOR AS I PULL into Ro's lot, but its shine is nothing compared to his smile. He's beaming.

It takes more effort than it should to walk to the entrance like a human and not like a human who knows she's being watched. I try to focus on *not* wondering how long Ro's been at the door waiting for me like this. Until now, I'd never seen a man go *golden retriever* in real life, but the mental image it conjures—phantom tail wagging and all—lightens the weight of the anvil Liv's words left lodged in my stomach.

*Guys that look like* this *don't have friends that look like you.*

"I still need a few more minutes," he says, holding the door wide for me.

With each step I take toward Ro, my nerves dissolve a little more. Like just sharing his air makes it easier to breathe. But I meant what I told Liv earlier—a casual hookup with an actual friend is just not a thing. Not a thing *I'm* signing up for, anyway.

So when Ro squeezes the back of my neck as I slide through the space he's left for me between his chest and the doorframe, I ignore my body's response to his touch. I ignore the goosebumps that prickle across my exposed flesh—my skin reaching out to get even a fraction of an inch closer.

"You cool to hang for a few?" he asks, pulling his hand away before I can embarrass myself by leaning into it.

"This is your day," I say, regaining some physical distance and my composure. "I'm only here for a change of scenery."

Ro disappears up the stairs, seemingly oblivious to the way my body briefly betrayed me back there. I unlock my phone for company as I wait. Scanning the weekly ads emailed from my pharmacy and scrolling through other assorted nothingness to look busy.

Ro's dad's voice booms through the lobby as the garage doors shut behind him. "He gotcha on payroll now?"

I return his easy smile, because it's good to see him—but also because, considering my professional prospects, that's actually not a terrible option.

"Ro just ran up," I explain, as Mr. Jackson takes me into one of those dad half hugs and leads me toward the register.

"You two headin' out soon?"

I nod, leaning my hip into the counter. "Yeah, in a couple minutes. He's just wrapping up."

"Sounds about right," Mr. Jackson says with a laugh. "That boy's always needed 'one more minute.' Used to drive his mother nuts. The mind of an artist, I suppose."

"I wouldn't know. Only thing I paint are my nails, and even those look like I do 'em blindfolded."

"Yeah?" he says, grabbing a towel to wipe the grime from his hands. "I just assumed. Ro doesn't usually take us laymen to these shows. He'll share his finished stuff sometimes, but otherwise keeps all that to himself. Been that way since ol' *whatshername.* Glad to see he's breaking his own rules today."

"Oh. I didn't realize—" *And what is her name?* I can't ask aloud.

"You ready?" Ro says, walking up with a black leather bag slung over his shoulder.

Mr. Jackson winks at me before shaking Ro's hand, like they're finalizing a business deal.

"Take care of yourself while I'm gone."

I expect those words to come from Mr. Jackson, but it's Ro saying them. "Mom's on her way," he continues. "Try to go easy on her."

Mr. Jackson must be confused by the exchange, too, because when I turn to say a last goodbye, his eyes are clouding over. Searching for understanding, and a million miles away.

Between Liv's certainty that I'm on an accidental date, that thing my body did at the shop, and the bomb Ro's dad casually dropped before we left, my mind's working overtime as Ro and I start our drive.

It might be time to unpause those apps again. Breaking Zo's *no sex* rule with a guy lying about his name, age, height, income, relationship, and felony status might actually *help* clarify things in my life for once.

"You good?" Ro asks, finally. He's been watching me since we passed the Connecticut–New York state line. "You still want to do this?"

"Of course! Sorry, I'm just stuck in my head."

"Should I be worried?"

I wince at the memory I know we're both revisiting now. The last time being "stuck in my head" and stuck in this truck resulted in me not so politely asking Ro to *shutthefuckup.* "I think you're in the clear."

His elbow nudges mine on the console, and I appreciate the gentle ways he checks in. Though his next inquiry isn't nearly as subtle.

"Anything specific going on up there?"

"Kinda," I start, attempting to meet his directness. "I'm trying to figure out why I'm here. Why you wanted me to come. Your dad said something about you only doing art stuff with art people."

"Those technical terms? *Art stuff* and *art people.*" Ro's words are as relaxed as his posture. "Don't listen to Pops. I just don't bring *him*. Last time he was at a show, he was all loud, talking 'bout Banksy like he'd discovered an unknown artist on the come up."

His sarcasm is laced with an obvious affection for his father.

"So, I *shouldn't* lead with the Van Gogh trivia I memorized last night?"

Ro laughs. "Naw, but if you got anything on that new Mona Lisa joint . . ."

And I hate how acutely aware I am that our arms are still almost touching on the console.

"I asked you to come because I like hanging out with you," he says easily. "And because even if you don't know all the *art words,* you get it. More than most people. I watched you in the shop that day," he admits, without looking embarrassed. "The way you studied murals most people don't even look up from their phones long enough to notice. It's wallpaper to them. But you really saw 'em. Felt like you saw me too." His eyes dart toward me and back to the road so fast, I might've imagined it. "I just wanted you to see a little more."

I'm quiet again, searching for the right response, but what do you say when someone hands you something sacred?

Ro and I hardly notice the traffic that turns what should've been a one-hour drive into two. We're too deep in the throes of the musical trivia game I walked in on him and his dad playing at the shop.

My abs physically ache from laughing at how bad Ro is at losing. After a particularly poor showing on a Kendrick Lamar round I'd expected to be a *gimme* for him, Ro eyed a passing service station with a little too much interest. Very likely considering the most efficient means of unloading his problem passenger. But as we cross the bridge into Manhattan, I'm still here. And impressively, so is Ro. We both know he's going down, but he's going down swinging.

"Try again," Ro offers, leaving the artist for me this time.

"Pfft. Please," I say, offended he thought he'd get me with this. "If you're coming for me with some Aaliyah, you're the one who needs to *try again*."

Ro kisses his fingertips and raises his pointer and middle finger to the sky. "Rest in peace, Babygirl."

We let the song play, and when the chorus drops, Ro hits me with a falsetto I could never have seen coming. But then again, I'd also never expected spending two hours on the torn pleather seats of an off-duty tow truck to be the most fun I've had all summer.

In what feels like a blink, we're driving along the Hudson River toward Manhattan's named streets downtown. I don't hesitate when Ro asks if I'm hungry. The answer is: always.

"You have a place in mind or should I look something up?"

"I know a spot," he says, baiting me with a look. "If you're feeling adventurous."

I don't hesitate this time either. "Immediately yes."

We pass a stretch of vacant curb that would be a snug fit to park a Hot Wheels, but before Ro's rear bumper passes it completely, he hits the brakes.

"Think I can make it?"

I don't bother looking again or mincing my words. I've seen all I need to see.

"Sure don't."

"Care to place a wager on that?"

"I mean *I'm* good to let this one go, but if *you* feel like leaving your insurance information on dashboards around town, I'm not gonna get in your way."

"What happened to your sense of adventure?"

"I wasn't aware it would involve public vandalism."

Ro's laugh fills the cabin as he leaves the too-small-spot behind. "You've got no faith in me, E. I'm hurt."

I suck my teeth. "Damn, I kinda thought you'd at least try to prove me wrong."

The afternoon sun has been cooking the cab all day, and the lack of shade on this stretch of Seventh Avenue offers no relief. I forgo the buttons of my cropped knit sweater in favor of convenience, peeling it over my head all at once. But when I emerge from the discarded fabric, Ro's eyes are on me, dusky and alert, following the thin straps of my tank top toward the scoop at my neck. Lingering there just long enough that my skin flushes for an entirely different reason than the sun.

His observation of me is penetrating, but I wouldn't call the sensation that accompanies it *uncomfortable.* My body, flaming and thrumming to attention as I shift in my seat to relieve the tightness coiling between my thighs. Ro follows my movements like his gaze is bound to my body by string.

He shakes his head, flicking his eyes back to the road to sever our connection.

"Nah," he says, in response to my forgotten challenge. "You got in my head. Made me all nervous."

•

A delivery truck abandoning its parking spot saves us from an overpriced garage, but it doesn't save me from Ro's continued insistence that he could've fit back in that first spot.

Today's my first time back in the city since coming home though, and we couldn't have chosen a better or more cloudless day for it. Not even Ro's overly descriptive parking simulations can ruin it for me.

Ro hasn't told me where we're eating yet but when he joins me on the sidewalk, he extends an arm to show me the way. "You think you'd ever move out here?"

"If I could figure out how to do it without seven roommates and a Top Ramen food allowance," I decide. "You remember me talking about my friend Liv? She's in Tribeca. We used to always talk about me taking her roommate's spot after graduation, but I get the feeling she might be doing her own thing now. And I don't know if I wanna be this far from Zola and the baby anyway."

"You'd be an hour away," he says, but he corrects himself when I raise my brows. "Fine, but two max. And it's New York. You gotta try it once. What's that thing they say about living here? Come before you get too soft, leave before you get too hard."

He nudges my hip with his own as he says it. It's gentle, playful, but at the vaguely sexual nature of his words, I go a little wobbly, like it's my first time on legs.

I steal a glance at Ro as I regain my balance, and though his eyes are straight ahead, they're sparkling again. Mischievous, like he knows exactly what he's doing. Like he's doing it on purpose.

Ro slows at a building with a highly Instagrammable floral facade. "This is it," he says, as the cute hostess emerges.

The eagerness of her friendly greeting shifts the air between

Ro and me, and whatever challenge had been in his eyes a moment ago is gone with the breeze.

We're led to what's arguably the best table in the patio's corner, and my touristy *I♥NY* glow returns. I could melt into the warmth of this afternoon in this city. But when my rose-colored gaze finally lands on the menu before me, I pale a little.

"The Raw Bar," I read in horror. "Okay, there's a chance I overstated just how adventurous I am with my food."

"Aw, come on. My boy Paul says this place is the new Catch. I bet they'll even throw something on the grill for ya. If you ask nice."

Ro wastes no time selecting a tray of assorted local oysters and has the audacity to *boo* when I order a fully cooked shrimp linguine.

"What about you?" I ask, once we're alone with our cocktails and each other. "What's stopping you from moving out here?"

He brings his margarita to his lips, licking the salt from its rim. "I actually have a spot uptown," he says way too casually. "I'm subletting it right now."

"How did I not know that?"

He winks and manages, somehow, to not look like a pervert. "I'm full of surprises, E."

"Is this when we finally talk about you having a secret company?"

I hadn't meant for it to come out like an accusation, but here we are.

He narrows his eyes at me. "A secret company?"

"Okay, not secret. But the one you failed to mention."

Ro's face is unreadable as he studies mine. I'd wanted to bring this up a million times but hoped it would happen naturally. Casually. But there's nothing casual about my tone. Ro's not alone in trying to figure out why that is.

"It just hadn't come up yet. I didn't realize you'd look me up so quick."

"Technically Zola looked you up."

Ro's eyebrow quirks at something he hears in my tone. "You said you were cool with me helping her out. Is it weird that I'm working with your sister?"

*Yes,* I think. But admitting that out loud would make me the worst sister ever—and helping Zola set up her future should be my focus. Not staking a claim on a guy I have no rights to. A guy I have no intention of fucking things up with by . . . well, fucking him.

"Of course not," I promise instead. "I was just surprised. We'd talked about your art—"

Ro shakes his head. "This isn't art. It's business. And it's not even one I spend much of my time on lately."

My silence invites him to say more, the way his so often has for me.

"My dad had some health stuff come up outta nowhere a while back."

My cocktail goes bitter on my tongue. Sharp and biting with worry. "Is he okay?"

Ro smiles, but the warmth of it doesn't reach me the way it usually does.

"Yeah, he's doing all right. But some of the words doctors threw around back then—"

Ro's eyelids close so briefly that if I hadn't learned their cadence, I might've mistaken it for a blink, but it's something else involuntary. It's his body remembering. Reliving it, and grieving, even now.

"Everything they were saying felt like a death sentence. And ultimately, I guess it is, just not in the way I'd thought. Pops is doing good right now, he is. And I'm grateful for it. But finding out he was sick, realizing that any of us can get sick, at any time, made me grow up real quick. Before that, my life had always been good, but only 'cause I'd been lucky. And luck ain't a guarantee."

Ro's lean fingers circle the rim of his glass as he speaks. The movement as hypnotic as his voice, his words, his story.

"Art had been my life forever, but it wasn't safe. And back then that's what I needed. For everything and everyone to be safe. Since I couldn't control *that,* the best I could get was security. Stability. So that's what I started chasing."

I want to ask Ro to hurry toward the part where he promises his dad's going to be okay. That *he's* okay too. I want to pull his fingers from the cool sweat of his glass and warm them in mine, until the heat of our touch warms his smile again.

But I don't do any of that. And as Ro continues, his honeyed tone, thick with emotion, slows my thoughts and movements until everything goes still. I'm transfixed again, and I tell myself it's for the best.

"That's why I started the design firm. I had the degree, so it felt like a natural step. I'd never wanted to run a company, but all of a sudden just getting it off the ground became the only thing that mattered to me. I let myself be consumed by the idea of it. And it took off a little, but I couldn't crave it the way I craved the canvas. I never loved it like that. Then my dad's stuff leveled out for a while, and I just got tired of running from shit. Which is all the company had ever been—a place to hide. I'm not meant to be the suit-and-tie guy setting meetings. So, in the end, the firm turned out to be the hobby I needed to put away so I could focus on my art. Not the other way around."

Ro ducks his head like his brief and completely understandable confusion had been something silly. I'm relieved to find humor in his eyes again, but I refuse to let him feel like a punch line.

"I get it," I say, plainly. "Even separate from everything your dad was going through, it makes sense. Sometimes people have to leave the thing they love for a minute, so when they come back to it, they know they're actually choosing it."

Ro's mouth curls in anticipation. "If only my ex had been as understanding," he says, sipping his now watered-down margarita to his lips. "My focus shifted to my dad and the company. Hers shifted to my roommate's bed."

"NO!"

I'm practically doubled over the table in horror, but Ro doesn't look bothered in the least. In fact, he looks more pleased by his story's shocking finale than he has since we started talking.

He shoos away the memory of her along with my outrage. "It's all good. She fit me about as well as that suit and tie."

"Fuck" is all I get out before the waitress returns with our food, but Ro nods like I've said everything.

When our waitress turns her back to go, I scrunch my nose at Ro's plate like the child that I am. "I hope you're not expecting me to help with those."

"You're not gonna try one?" he says, holding an oyster out to me in equal parts offering and challenge.

"Fine," I say, rolling my eyes. "*One.* You're on your own for the rest."

"You're no fun."

"Why do people keep telling me that? I never claimed to be."

Ro squeezes a little lemon and hot sauce on his, so I follow his lead, resisting the urge to plug my nose.

"Bottoms up," he says, jiggling his half shell in the air. But the moment that oyster slides onto his tongue, Ro's smug grin disappears.

"What the fuck was that?" he says, coughing. "Is that what it's supposed to taste like? Why the fuck do people eat these things?"

Nobody in life has ever chugged a glass of water quicker. And I cannot stop laughing.

"It's not funny!" he shouts.

"It is though." I swipe at my tears. "Oh my god, you should see your face."

"You're cold, E," Ro says, still looking like he might be sick.

"And you're dramatic. It wasn't that bad. I actually kind of liked it."

Of course, I'm lying. If I wanted a mouth full of dirty seawater, I'd jump in the East River.

His dimple digs into his cheek even before his smile appears, and he gestures toward the tray. "Have at it then."

"Hell no. But I will share some of my pasta with you. That's just the kind of girl I am."

"Gee, thanks," Ro says unamused.

But he pushes the extra plate over to my side of the table just the same.

"So, if things are going better, why haven't you moved back here yet?" I ask, after a surprisingly comfortable silence. "Did you start getting too hard?"

It was meant to be a casual continuation of Ro's earlier idiom, but I'm not surprised it leaves him choking on a crustacean. It's a saying that requires a little context. And ample warning.

He switches to water once he's recovered. "We still need help at the shop till we can set up something long term," he says as if every son would uproot their life like he has. "I grew up at that garage, so it's easier for me to slide back in than train somebody new right now. I can paint from anywhere. And take dope design gigs that pop up unexpectedly."

"Zo's plans are dope enough to get you out of retirement?"

"She has some cool ideas. And I never officially retired, I just recommitted elsewhere."

"I like that framing," I admit.

"That's all life is."

And I wonder if those four simple words might just be the key to it all. If anyone can teach me something about the art of reframing, it's this artist quietly watching me from behind his glass.

"What?" I ask, touching my mouth to feel for any errant Tajín.

His eyes heat slightly as he follows the movement. I pretend not to notice.

"You," he says, lifting his hand toward the city at my back. "Here. It makes sense. I'm trying to imagine you in Kansas. I can't see it."

"It's just a place," I tell him, but since it's Ro, I already know I'll say the thing I usually don't. "My dad's from out there. Kansas. It's where he went to school—also for education, actually."

"Ah," he says, decided. "So you were following your dad."

My lips purse at the oversimplification, but I can't fault him for it. I lived it and still don't really understand.

"No?" I say, like it's a guess. Because it kind of is. "I didn't even tell him when I applied. I didn't tell anyone. I knew it didn't make sense so I didn't wanna have to defend it. I mean, I hated this man, and here I was walking in his footsteps."

No wonder I'm so fucking lost. I followed a ghost expecting to end up found.

"I grew up watching basketball with him," I say, smiling at a memory of Dad for the first time in a long time. "He'd buy me these *Chalk 'Em* Kansas shirts, and I'd wear them around all proud, knowing nobody out here knew what it meant. It was like a language only the two of us could speak. Our little secret." I sigh at how silly it sounds now that I'm supposedly all grown up. "Things were hard here by the time I applied to schools. Zola was already living with her ex, and my mom was in a deeply toxic cycle with husband number two. I needed to not be here, but I didn't know where to go. When it was finally time to decide, the only other place that came to mind was Kansas. So—"

"So you left."

I nod my confirmation.

"I knew it was a mistake almost immediately," I say aloud for the first time. "But I was too proud to admit I had no clue what I was doing. I kinda hoped even the wrong decision would buy me enough time to figure it out, but admittedly there were some holes in the plan."

I hope my laugh doesn't sound as forced as it feels.

"Because now I'm back here with a degree that feels like a lie and connections that don't matter."

"Did you at least hit your dad up while you were out there?"

I'm shaking my head before he's even finished asking the question.

"Being there didn't change anything for me," I say, realizing how true the words are as I say them. "I didn't want to talk to him. Let alone see him."

"But there had to be a part of you that wanted something from him."

"I think there's always gonna be a part of me that wants something from him. But I've gotta be okay even if I never get it."

I smile too brightly and raise my glass in a weak attempt to end on a lighter note. "A toast to daddy issues?"

Ro's drink remains planted on the table. "I'm not toasting that."

"Fiiine." I roll my eyes, but there's no heat in the expression. "You pick something."

Ro swirls his glass, eyes trained on his clinking ice cubes.

The patio around us is alive with the sounds of forks scraping flatware, laughter mounting with each next sip of a summer cocktail, and speakers blasting a soundtrack better suited for a

Meatpacking nightclub. But when Ro's eyes meet mine again, everything quiets, like the world is holding its breath.

*Or maybe that's just me.*

"To reframing," he says, finally. "To being back in the right place, at the right time."

My face falls before I can catch it, but I don't know why. It's a perfectly fitting and fine toast. Even if, maybe, I'd been hoping for more.

I shift my glass toward his, but Ro's not finished. And the familiar glint in his eyes is replaced by something I can't quite place as he finishes.

"And to doing it with the right person."

When our drinks connect, the world exhales and the noise returns. It's not a moment too soon, either, because even the city at full volume is only just enough to drown out the pounding in my chest.

# 14

ZOLA HAD BEEN QUICK TO EMBARRASS HERSELF IN FRONT of Ro when she met him. Mom saw his socials and made it perfectly clear she thinks "*that boy is foooine.*" And when I told Liv about him, she applauded as she dove down her own Ro Jackson Instagram rabbit hole. Still, watching complete strangers respond to Ro out in the world is a whole new study in human behavior.

The cute hostess lingered, the waitress batted her eyelashes so hard she almost took flight. Random doormen don't let Ro pass without engaging him in conversation. You'd even think the guy with the chinchilla on his shoulder at the Fourteenth Street station was an old friend by the way he chatted Ro up.

Seeing Ro through everyone else's eyes is like seeing him for the first time all over again. It makes me wonder about the guy under all that shiny packaging. He seems so *good.* And there's nothing scarier to me than a guy everybody thinks is *good.*

We're at a hole-in-the-wall consignment shop in the Village when Ro brings up my next date.

"Can we not?" I ask, thumbing through vintage jackets that cost more than I've got in my bank account. "Tell me something else about you. Save me the Google search."

"You already know all the big stuff," he says, passing behind me so close that the heathered cotton of his shirt brushes against my bare arm.

"It's just you and your parents, right? No brothers or sisters?"

"Nah, but my parents both came from big families so I've got way too many damn cousins," he says, laughing. "We were that house on the block where somebody was always coming or going. And Pops has been playing surrogate dad to all the kids in the neighborhood as long as I can remember, so even as an only child, I've never been alone a day in my life."

Ro slips into a worn leather jacket from the rack, and my stomach drops a little at how good he looks. It's been happening all day—he smiles and my cheeks flush, he guides the small of my back and my whole body tenses. But that's not why we're here. Today's supposed to be my safe space away from all that. Ro's supposed to be my safe space away from all that.

*Say something,* I tell myself. Something *friendly.*

"Can your dad take me in too?" I don't wait for my awkward joke to fall flat before I rush to explain. "It just sounds like a nice way to grow up."

Ro shrugs off the jacket. "What about you? You and Zola seem close."

"We are, yeah," I say, turning back to the rack. "But when your family's as small as ours, you kind of have to be."

"It's wild how different the two of you seem."

"Yup." It's not the first time someone's pointed this out to me. "She's the firecracker. I'm the fizzle."

His face screws up tighter than when he ate the oyster. "Whoa. That's not what I meant at all."

I trace the stitching on an old denim jacket. "Sorry. Childish insecurities die hard, I guess."

"Maybe I should dig up my old sketchbooks to even the scales. My teenage insecurities had their own fan art." Ro never breaks eye contact, but he's still trying on old hats as he speaks. I'm grateful not to feel like I'm onstage. "But don't apologize, I like when you let the real stuff slip. Helps me figure you out."

My brows knit together pleadingly. "Please don't try. It's so much more fun to diagnose everyone else."

"You sure?"

His full attention is on me now, and I'm pinned under the weight of it.

"I can be gentle."

A tentative nod is all the agreement I can give.

"You're a maze," he says, before I can change my mind. "You let me make a little progress in one direction, but throw up a wall before I get too far. So I gotta back up or find a different path, before you cut me off again. It's why that night at the pizza place was so different. Why I couldn't stop watching you with the mural that day at the garage. There are these moments you forget to be on guard. You forget to put up the walls. I guess I hoped today could be that too. Not even for me, for real. For you. So, at least for a little while, you could just *be*."

I'm quiet when he finishes, but once again, our shared silence isn't uncomfortable.

"How do you do that?" I ask, finally.

"Do what?"

"Say a thing so real and honest like it's the most natural thing in the world."

"Isn't it?"

"No," I say, certain. "It isn't."

"Does it bother you?"

I don't even have to think about it.

"No," I say, just as sure. "It doesn't."

# 15

THE REST OF THE AFTERNOON FLIES BY, AND BEFORE I know it, we're running late for the show. I spend the whole ride to Harlem watching my phone, willing the traffic to ease up so we can make up some time. And apparently, I'm not subtle about it.

"Is it working?" Ro says, his eyes still straight ahead.

"Is what working?"

"That death stare you're giving the clock. You figure out how to freeze time yet?"

"I can't stand you," I say, smiling big so he knows I'm joking. "I feel bad. I don't want you to be late because you were trying to entertain me. And yes, for your information, it *is* working. Pretty sure I shaved thirty seconds off the clock. So, you are welcome."

Ro laughs. "Well, I appreciate you looking out, but don't worry about me. It's an art show. The walls aren't going anywhere. We could be an hour late and still be right on time."

Luckily, we're not an hour late, but we're pushing it. You'd never know it though by watching Ro amble across 125th Street, looking around at everything and nothing at all, like it's the most fascinating thing he's seen all day.

"Don't we need to get in there?" I ask, trying, unsuccessfully, to hurry him along. "What are you doing?"

Ro grabs my hand. He does it to slow me down, but even after we fall into step, he doesn't immediately release me. My breath slows to match his lazy rhythm. Coming and going as evenly as Ro's steps.

He continues scanning the street as we walk. No longer holding hands, but still together.

"What?" I ask, unable to deny my curiosity any longer.

"Nothing. Everything. There's so much going on out here. So much inspiration if you pay attention. I'm just paying attention."

"Should I expect your next piece to be an ode to that street vendor?"

Ro laughs, and I claim the breathy sound as a victory.

"It's not that literal. It's more about the energy of a place. The texture of it. How it feels to be here, now. All of it sits up here," he says, tapping his head. "Becoming whatever it's gonna be."

Ro leans into me, and past the heat of his bare arm on mine, I try to focus on his words. He points as he speaks so I can see what he does.

"Those lines of that old building. That shadow, there, under the busted streetlamp. The curve of that door. All these paper-thin blades of grass shooting up around this hydrant. Because life's always gonna force its way through."

He pauses, and without permission, my heels rise from the cement. My toes working to get a little closer to whatever his next words will be.

Ro reaches a hand out toward my face, and I don't know if my feet will ever land on solid ground again.

"The way this curl moves with every step you take when you

think we're late." His fingers never meet my skin before he lowers his hand, letting it drop back down to his side. "I wanna remember it all. And one day, I'll paint it. In ways I can't even recognize. But it starts here," he says, gesturing to the city around us. "If you pay attention."

"You're so lucky you get to see the world like that." I wish I could crawl inside Ro to *feel* the way he does. "I don't think my brain works that way."

"It's mostly conditioning," he tells me. "Practice."

I nod in near understanding, but I want to hear it in his words, so I can hear it exactly.

"I remember being a kid—my teachers used to tell me to stay focused. Stay on task. Finish fast, finish first. They'd praise me when I got from point A to point B with as little interruption as possible. But I don't think it's about how much you can get done in the shortest amount of time, all at the same time. The beauty's in the detours. Life's in the detours. Those moments in between the things we're told to care about. But it's hard to train your brain to go against what you've been taught. It's hard to slow down. It not a talent you just *have.* It's a discipline. A resistance."

That familiar calm washes over me as I watch Ro's hand dangle at his side. I don't think I would've noticed it just moments ago, when I was racing down the block like the world was on fire. Running scared so I didn't become somebody else's inconvenience.

I would've missed it.

Missed seeing his long, delicate fingers curled around the thick summer air, heavy with promise. His hand, palming vacant space, waiting to be filled.

*Seeing,* though, is only half of it. Because I still don't let myself reach out to fill the space between his fingers with my own. I hesitate just a second too long, until a couple spills out of the studio, and the moment passes us by.

Ro catches the door to hold it open for me, and I clasp my own hands together to fill the sudden loss of our connection. Shrugging off my disappointment as I pass him to enter.

"Maybe the world would be better if it were run by artists," I say as I step inside.

And the bass of his voice rattles the air at my back when he whispers, "Maybe one day we'll get to find out."

I didn't know I had an image of what we'd be walking into tonight, but I must've, because as soon as we're inside, I realize just how wrong I'd been.

This studio isn't the sterile white art cliché of my imagination. There are no suited-up cater waiters passing tiny glasses of boiled shrimp and cocktail sauce. Instead, it's a neon-lit halal street truck that had to have been deconstructed and rebuilt inside to fit through the doors. There's no delicate champagne flutes clinking along to classical music. The liquor is brown and the bass line is turned up. This place is real and alive, and it makes me feel alive too.

Heavy wood beams run overhead. Floor-to-ceiling windows perfectly framing the city like a postcard. The whole place and everyone in it is a work of art. But surrounded by elegantly wrapped turbans and slinky dresses, I suddenly feel very *Connecticut*.

Ro's hand finds the small of my back as he directs me farther into the space. Without pausing to think better of it, I settle into his touch. Throughout the day, I've become more used to his hands on me—always innocent, but growing more familiar.

I've also come to expect heads turning to seek Ro out as he

passes. It's been like that all day, but it's different here. People don't just turn to observe him, they smile and nod in recognition.

A particularly enthusiastic voice shouting "*Ayyye!*" rises above the indiscriminate murmurs of the crowd.

Ro's face lights up as a man with a well-oiled salt-and-pepper beard and black linen pants reaches past me to dap him up. "Wasn't sure you'd make it out."

"Ah, you know I wouldn't miss it," Ro says, stepping back to bring me into the conversation. "Kaia, this is Paul. He puts this exhibit on every year."

"Hey," I say, ignoring Paul's obvious and prolonged appraisal of me. "It's nice to meet you. This place is incredible."

"Dope, right? Unfortunately, it's only ours for the night."

Paul must see the confusion on my face.

"We're at a different venue every time," he explains. "It's how we get new artists to come through. Helps us keep it fresh. That way we're more accessible to young up-and-comers in different communities. We're out in Greenpoint in a few weeks."

"Oh, I love that," I say, beginning to understand Paul's appeal.

"It's real cool," he continues. "Been a lotta fun to watch this thing grow. And your boy here's been with us since the beginning." Paul clasps a hand onto Ro's shoulder. "Since he was just a scrawny kid finger painting comic books with Mommy's watercolors."

"That's not how I remember it," Ro says, laughing. "But yeah, Paul's the one who got me to take all this seriously. Brought me out for his shows, lined up some gallery consultancies so I could pay for a place I had no business renting. That part's true. Everything else . . ."

"You come ready to work?" Paul asks, switching focus. "You know half these artists came out to see you."

"Nah, man," Ro says, inviting me back in with his eye contact. "We're just here checking out what everyone else has goin' on tonight."

"Come on," Paul says, pressing him. "Give 'em something easy." Before Ro can turn him down again, Paul goes in for the kill. "I know you got your bag around here somewhere."

Ro reaches for the back of his neck sheepishly. A little boy caught with his hand in the cookie jar.

He nods toward the entrance. "Coat check."

When Ro looks at me, the dimple popping on his cheek gives him away—he wants to do it.

"You cool if I throw a little paint at the wall? Just to get this guy off my back."

"Of course," I say, surprised by the change in our itinerary, but without a moment's pause. "Do your thing."

"I'll keep her company while you're gone," Paul promises. "We won't even miss you."

Before he runs off, Ro pulls me into him and whispers, "I'd tell you to watch out for this guy, but if anything goes down, smart money's on you."

Without Ro between us, Paul and I struggle through a few attempts at surface conversation that all end with him telling me, "That's what's up." I'm relieved when he steals two unnamed cocktails from a passing tray.

"Thanks for comin' out," he says, handing me a glass. "It's good for Ro to have somebody with him at these things again. This industry's wild, man. Watching him do it alone for so long was rough."

I'm not usually much of a bourbon fan, but I'm grateful that sipping the drink offers an excuse for my silence. I'm here with Ro, but I'm not here *with* Ro.

Before Paul excuses himself to help set up Ro's workstation, he hands me his jack-of-all-trades business card should I ever "need anything." Though I'm not sure what I could really need from a Gallery Consultant/Community Outreach Specialist/Financial Adviser. Not that I'm in any position to judge. If I printed off business cards of my own, my hyphenate would be something like *Professional Deflector/Recent Day Drinker/Future Pyramid Scheme Bottom.*

I start an aimless lap around the main room, for fear that if someone takes pity on the lonely girl biting her nails in the middle of the gallery, they'll know I'm an outsider as soon as the conversation turns to *mediums* and I tell them I'm usually a small. But when I'm only a few portraits into my perusal a funny thing happens: Pretending to focus on the art *actually* shifts my focus to the art. I forget to feel like I don't belong.

There's a natural flow to the room that I'm swept into. Momentum carries me past some, while I stop at others that refuse to be overlooked.

A still of an old Black woman alone at a bus stop leaves me rooted to the floor for what could be minutes or hours. Had I not been paying attention, I might have considered her expression passive, blank even. A simple image of a simple moment in time. But thanks to Ro's lesson outside, I *am* paying attention, so I see her, fully. I see a longing in her eyes and sadness folded into every crease above her barely perceptible smile. It's a window into the life of a stranger, but it also feels like a mirror I can't look away from.

Commotion on the far side of the gallery pulls me from my trance. I move toward the crowd forming at an installation on the opposite side of the room and freeze in my tracks when I'm close enough to find the source of the excitement.

Ro.

He's facing the wall—the shirt he'd been wearing earlier left crumpled in the corner near his black leather tote. His strong back and broad shoulders heave as he catches his breath in what used to be a white undershirt, now recklessly splattered with the spray from his brush. There's a layer of fresh sweat on his skin that leaves him glowing under the studio lights. He's art in his own right—a molten sculpture of liquefied bronze, taking its final shape.

It's only when I finally force my eyes away from Ro that the canvas behind him comes into focus. The instant it does, I forget everything and everyone else. Just like he said, it's impossible to pinpoint any discrete shapes or discernible figures, but I *know* I'm looking at our moment from the street outside. I feel it. The energy and the texture of it. And now I can see it too. Ro's showing us the world through his eyes. He's showing me. And the beauty in his generosity and in the work itself steals the breath from my lungs, screwing a tightness in my chest.

It's stunning, this thing he just created out of thin air. A painting that didn't exist an hour ago, a painting I'll know forever. Raw inspiration splayed against the wall with as much honesty as there is grace. A piece so perfectly Ro, on full display.

When the crowd offers its boisterous approval, Ro spins to face us, as if our presence surprises him. Like he'd forgotten he'd been working with an audience all along. For the briefest moment, I worry we're intruding on something private, meant only to be shared between the art and the artist.

But then Ro finds me in the crowd, and the joy on his face does me in. His joy at sharing his world with me. His joy at my receiving it.

I join the rest of Ro's admirers in their applause. Ro's eyes, equal parts sure and shy, stay trained on me. And even in this crowded gallery, among a mass of bodies and noise under endless spotlights, I could swear it's only him and me.

I want to go to Ro—to congratulate him and study his piece for any messages he might've left for me. I want to be beside him, to share in the fervent energy pulsing from his skin, but bodies close in around him too quickly. An influx of people desperate for a piece of him move into his orbit, and I'm left just outside of it, standing still.

At the far end of the room, Paul nods with obvious pride and respect for his friend. When he sees me watching, he raises his drink in my direction, and though I return the gesture, the cool liquid on my tongue burns hot as I remember my place in all this. This is not *our* moment. It's Ro's.

I've only taken a few steps toward the quieter side of the gallery when my phone pings.

**10:17pm**

**Ro:** I don't see you.

**Me:** checking out some other work while you do your thing.

**Me:** That was incredible by the way! 😊

**Ro:** Thank you. But come back.

**Ro:** Or I'll come to you.

**Me:** No. You're busy! I'll find you when the crowd thins out.

**Ro:** You sure? I just need to talk to one BK curator. then we'll go.

**Ro:** Hungry? Dinner?

**Me:** Yeah, but take your time. Seriously. I'm good.

And I *am* good. It's the truth. But it's not the *whole* truth.

Walking away from him just now had been the first lie I'd told Ro since I met him.

It's more than a realization, it's a warning. Because even more than I'd wanted to go to him, I'd wanted to be easy. And I know exactly when and why people start lying to be easier for each other.

It wasn't supposed to be like that with Ro.

# 16

PAUL CATCHES UP TO US ON OUR WAY TO THE DINER AND casually invites himself to be our third. Ro apologizes for the intrusion more profusely than he should. I'm actually relieved by Paul's presence and the distraction he provides.

With Ro locked into a strategy session for their Greenpoint show, he doesn't notice that my attention's trained on his long fingers, absentmindedly painting his glass with beads of its own wetness. Doesn't see me memorizing the paint colors still flecked beneath each of his nails. He doesn't seem to feel the heat building between us in this red leather booth, leaving the backs of my thighs slick with sweat. Or how my body matches his, breath for breath, in a way it never did before today.

I'm grateful not to be alone with Ro. Not yet, anyway.

But soon we're back in his truck, heading home, and the easy silence we shared driving into the city is changed. Charged now, like the faintest spark of a single carelessly chosen word could ignite us into who knows what. And by the way his eyes stray from the road to seek me out in the darkness, I can't help but wonder if he feels it too.

He clears his throat, and I'm braced in anticipation.

"You got quiet after the show."

"Did I?" *Yes.* "Probably just tired." *Lie.* "Tonight really was incredible," I say, honestly. "You're amazing—your *work* is amazing. I could've watched you paint all night."

*You're amazing? Really?*

So much for a *single* careless word. I just sputtered out like ten. But as always, Ro doesn't push me where he knows I don't want to go.

"Sounds like the Brooklyn gallery wants to make an offer on the piece before I even set a price."

His news outranks my uncertainty. I whip around in my seat to face him, grabbing at his forearm with both of my hands without a second thought.

"They wanna buy it?!"

And the pride behind his smile lifts any remaining awkwardness that had settled between us.

"Dang, I kinda wanted that one," I joke. "Seriously though, I'm not surprised. You better do something special to celebrate this."

My hand hasn't left his arm, but I only realize it when his eyes fall to where we're still connected.

He smiles once more, but this time he bites it back a little when he says, "I already am."

I'm sure the pregnant lady, currently asleep in my bed, had planned to wait up and grill me about my day with Ro, but it's after 2:00 A.M. by the time I change into my pajamas.

I forgo my ten-step skin care ritual—the sign of a truly successful night out—and crawl into bed with Zola, her breath coming steady beside me. And as my evening with Ro replays behind my closed eyelids, I try not to let myself wonder what it might've been like to crawl into a different bed with a different someone's breath at my ear.

# 17

AS NOSTALGIC AS IT IS TO FALL ASLEEP CURLED UP WITH your big sister, the way you did as kids, waking up mere inches away from a fully alert set of beady brown eyes staring you down is a terror all its own.

"Hi," she says, once I'm finished screaming.

"Jesus, Zo," I gasp, clutching my heart as it kick-starts itself back to life.

Zola's unbothered by my near-death experience and wastes no time. "So have you guys talked since you got home?"

"Good morning to you too," I say, but she just stares back at me, waiting. "A little. Before I passed out," I tell her. "But nothing to warrant that look on your face. I can promise you that."

"No need for promises," she says, reaching a hand out, expectantly. "Let me see."

I could fight her on this, refuse to show her my phone, but it might actually be good for her to see with her own eyes that there's nothing going—

"Oh my god, Kaia. What is this?"

"What's what?" I ask, grabbing for my phone, but Zola pulls it out of reach, and begins to read aloud.

**1:59am**

**Ro:** Hey, thanks again for coming. I hope you had as much fun as I did.

**Me:** so glad I got to go

**Ro:** Me too.

**Me:** Thanks for the invite. It was exactly what I needed.

**Ro:** Oh yeah?

**Me:** Yeah! before the next round of Zola's torture.

**Ro:** Ah. Right.

When Zola finishes reading, she's wide-eyed. Her jaw slack, and dangling.

"What?" I ask, retrieving my phone from her now limp hand.

"You cannot be serious. Did you hear what I just read?"

"I don't need to hear it," I remind her. "I lived it."

"Then how don't you get it?"

Whatever suspense she's hoping to create with this dramatic pause is only building frustration.

"Fine," she says, when it's clear I'm not going to fill the silence. "I'll spell it out for you then: Ro. Is. Into you."

"That's just Ro," I say, rolling over, so she won't see the questions written all over my face. "If you would've seen him yesterday, you'd get it. He left all of Manhattan feeling like they were the main character. He's like that with everyone."

This conversation and Zola's insinuations need to end. I don't know where I'll be or what I'll be doing in a matter of weeks, but I do know that I'd like for Ro and me to not have blocked each other by then. *That's* what matters to me—not decoding a glance, or a vibe, or a text. And definitely not trying to convince Zola that Ro and I are *friends*—nothing messier, nothing more.

"Kaia," she says, reaching out for my phone once more. But this time, I'm quicker.

I leap up from the bed. Out of reach of Zo's greedy hand and her judgments. Unfortunately, in my rush to put distance between us, my comforter tangles around my foot, so now I'm fighting gravity for my life, and doing it all in white cotton booty shorts.

That look on Zola's face and the embarrassment of my near fall ignites emotions in me that I didn't see coming. When I open my mouth, I'm shouting.

"Enough! Zola, I'm exhausted. Ro is my friend."

The word sounds wrong, even to me, but I'll be damned if Zola sees me hesitate.

She's still in bed as I retreat to the bathroom, but she's also not above yelling this early in the morning. "Well, at least stop telling him what a good friend he is! You're just twisting the knife!"

Alone, finally, Zo's words bounce off the bathroom tile along with the thoughts of Ro that she's sparked—memories, strobing and dizzying in my mind. The tight dip of his dimple, the curve of his hand, his shirt, damp with sweat, clinging to his body under the studio lights.

*No,* I insist, even just to myself now, forcing Ro's blinding light to go black. Because the truth is I do care about him. More than I'd meant to.

So, I'd rather keep him just out of reach, if it means I get to keep him at all.

# 18

TURNS OUT THE OLD ADAGE IS TRUE: THE BEST WAY TO get over one guy really is to get under another. But after a week of faking interest in Zo's mystery bachelor number two to distract *her* from her Ro fixation, *I'm* the one left staring at another questionnaire, with Ro Jackson on the brain.

His popcorn should already be buttered, as his rapid-fire pre-date texts hit my phone, but my notifications have been disturbingly silent for days.

I hadn't even wanted time away from him like this. I'd just meant to gently walk us back to the friend zone.

But walk gently, I did not:

**Monday, 9:17am**

**Ro:** E! What's up?

**Me:** Life is life-ing as usual.

**Ro:** lmk when you're ready to escape again 😉

**Me:** I wish. Zo's keeping me booked and busy with these dates.

**Ro:** Ah, I see.

**Ro:** Let her know I'm almost done with the site.

**Me:** I can't wait to see!

**Ro:** Come through. I'll give you a preview.

**Me:** She'd kill me if I saw it first.

**Ro:** come anyway

**Me:** Ha I can't today. But good luck finishing up.

**Me:** I'll hit you later.

But of course, I didn't. And neither did he.

What I *did* do is reread the exchange so many times this week that I've nearly memorized it. But being able to recite every word forward and back still hasn't helped me figure out which of us is avoiding the other. And after so many days, our silence is starting to feel more and more like a final word.

I'm actively trying to pretend that prospect isn't eating me up inside when a knock at my door saves me from my thoughts.

"Ready to go again?" Zola says, like the madam she is.

"Round two," I say, monotone. "Bring it on."

But then I realize we're down a man. "Where's your sidekick? I thought collecting my dowry was a two-person job."

"Mom left while you were in the shower."

"With who?" I say, the words so sharp on my tongue that I taste copper in their wake.

Zola shakes her head. "Honestly, I didn't even ask."

I'm mid eye roll, pushing past Zola, when she pulls a folder from behind her back. I'm not mad at *her,* but I am mad that we're back here again. Even if I shouldn't be.

"Don't you want to see his picture?" she asks, attempting to breathe some levity into the moment, with a half-hearted shoulder shimmy.

"Oh," I say, not really caring either way. "Sure."

Seeing a stranger's face and learning that he'd want the ability to rewind time if he could isn't going to change today's outcome, but when your sister does a little dance, you read the file anyway.

There are no signs of life at the café Zola's directions have led me to, so without my permission, my brain does its *Dateline* thing: *Death at the Diner, Café Crimes, Lured to the Luncheonette.* I'm texting Zo to confirm the address when the front door swings open, and a very tall, very dark, *very* handsome man steps from the restaurant's interior.

I lock my doors immediately.

"Kaia?" he asks, shielding his eyes from the glare of the evening sun.

I nod and roll down the window, but I keep my phone in hand. Just in case. "James?"

He smiles his confirmation.

"It looks like this place is closed," I say, ignoring the fact that having come from inside, he's very likely already aware. "Do you know anywhere else nearby?"

James stuffs his hands in the front pockets of his jeans so completely that his shoulders round and slump. "It *is* closed," he says, smiling wide enough to reveal the slight gap between his front teeth. "But not for us."

Oh yay. The first date of every girl's dreams—all alone with a total stranger at an abandoned location with a Sub-Zero walk-in freezer.

As I commit James's features to memory for a possible future police sketch (early to mid-twenties, Black male, five foot ten, brown eyes, tight fade), he pulls a hand out of his pocket to grab the cloth apron slung over his shoulder. He unfolds it, displaying the embroidered word that mirrors the one scrawled across the café's green awning: *Josephine's.*

"You work here?"

"Yeah. It's my spot actually. I own it."

Slightly comforted knowing this guy's legal name is on the deed, I open the car door fully. "So it would be a really bad business model to bring women to your own restaurant to—ya know."

I make a knife motion across my throat, but smile brightly as I do it. The two gestures balance each other out nicely, I think.

James's eyes go wide and his skin goes ashen. He spins to face the darkened dining room and SORRY, WE'RE CLOSED sign at his back. "Oh shit!"

Seeing the scene through my eyes draws quick beads of panicked sweat from the ridge at James's brow. His genuine horror at his misstep gives me the confidence I need to finally join him on the sidewalk. He's too squeamish for homicide.

"I just thought it'd be cool to do a private cooking lesson," James says, adjusting the thick black frames of his glasses. "Fuck, when did I get so bad at this? I wasn't thinking. I guess it's been a while."

I peer through the window at the purposefully mismatched chairs and the salvaged wooden tables dotted with yellow daisies. The whole place is giving hipster-farmer adorableness, same as the man before me.

"Well," I say, stepping back to meet the worry in his eyes, "for me, it's basically been forever, so why don't we go inside and be terrible at it together. But you should know that I shed like a dog and I'm gonna leave my fingerprints everywhere."

James pinches the spot under the bridge of his glasses before digging his hands back into his pockets with a shrug. "I don't know how to respond to that."

I nod decisively, smiling at how little this date feels like a date so far when I tell him, "That's fair."

•

"How's the wine?" James asks from behind the bar.

Working in this space where he's so obviously at home has given James a confidence he didn't have outside. Every movement is choreography, the entire café an extension of his lean body.

Watching James do his thing reminds me so much of seeing Ro in his element at the gallery—a person doing exactly what they were born to do. It's not the first time I've thought of Ro since I got here. My fingers itch to check for a missed text or call, but after a week of silence, I know I'll only be disappointed.

"It's delicious," I tell James from my reclaimed barstool, hands clasped together in my lap to keep them from my phone.

"I wasn't sure if we should start with white or red," he says, not knowing I would've been just as happy with fermented grape juice poured from a plastic bag. "My ex only drank white. But our first course tonight is heavier, so I wanted something that could stand up to it."

I add that little tidbit to my growing mental list of things I've learned about James's ex in the past twenty minutes. Like how she helped him source the furniture from local flea markets, convinced him to partner with a bee farm that offered the CBD honey she liked in her tea, and there was something else about the café's name being tied to her grandma, but that particular detail is fuzzy because I was too busy *not* checking my phone.

"Well, it's great," I tell him, taking another sip. "The whole place is. How long have you had it?"

James bites at the inside of his cheek. His full lips twisting to allow for the expression. "It'll be two years next week."

"I can see how much it means to you. I'm always jealous of people who've already found their passion."

It seems the *Ro honesty effect* is happening now even in his absence.

James pulls out the stool next to mine and sits facing me with bent knees spread casually wide. Though my body's still positioned ahead toward the bar, I'm acutely aware of how close James is at my side. I see the moment he realizes it too.

He rises from the seat he's only just taken, circling the bar to retrieve the wine bottle neither of us need. "Remind me what you do."

"Teaching, I guess. Or I should be."

"Should be?" he asks, needlessly replenishing the two small sips I've skimmed from my wineglass.

"I just graduated a couple months ago, so I should already have a teaching position lined up for the fall. But I've been watching openings get snatched up for months, and I can't make myself care. I don't really think I'm meant to teach."

This newfound emotional promiscuity is absolutely Ro's fault, but James isn't helping. He's doing that bartender-therapist thing—wiping the same spot of nothingness from the wood between us. The hypnotic motion of his towel keeps me talking.

"Eventually I'm sure I'll just do it anyway. It's not like any other overnight passions have dropped into my lap lately. Maybe teaching's as close as I'll get."

James's hand pauses mid-circle. "What's the rush? Is there a deadline on passion?"

"You ask that as someone who's already found theirs. That's what *Josephine's* is, right?"

James considers my question, but from the look on his face something's not fitting quite right. "I don't know. I gave up so much for this place, so I need it to do well. And I've been lucky so far. But sometimes it feels like spite's driving me more than passion. Like I gotta prove it was all worth it."

I return his smile, easily. "Well, I for one will always drink to spite. And to these little cheese crisps," I say reaching into the snack bowl beside my glass. "These are ridiculous."

James melts at the compliment. "I can't take credit. It was my ex's idea to serve a signature bite with every bar order. I would've been good with peanuts."

My chewing slows as James's ex makes yet another appearance.

And another:

"Her tolerance was basically zero. If she had a sip of wine, I had to feed her. Probably why she thought everyone needed a snack with their drinks." He plucks a crisp from the bowl. "There's actually no cheese in 'em if you can believe it."

"Oh?"

"Yeah, my ex was lactose intolerant—"

"Oh."

"So I did a cashew cheese instead."

I nod and drop the crisp back into the bowl, feeling like I've just been caught eating someone else's food from the break room. I rinse the evidence from my mouth with a swig of the wine James's ex didn't care much for, as he continues.

"She used to—Riley. That's her name. Feels like I'm saying *she, she, she.*"

"I hadn't noticed."

"Riley used to come in and steal entire to-go boxes of these things."

He's smiling again, but it's becoming painfully clear that his smiles, like his cheese crisps, belong to *her.*

"Well, they're great," I say, unhooking my purse from beneath the bar. "Will you excuse me for a minute? I'm gonna run to the bathroom."

•

"Where. Is. Zola?"

James isn't likely to hear me over the pots he's banging around in the kitchen, but I still cup a hand around my mouth as I whisper-scream the question into the receiver. Squatting down into the small open space beside the toilet, for good measure.

"What's going on?" Mom asks, matching my volume. "Why are we whispering?"

"*I'm* whispering, because your daughter set me up with a guy who's very clearly in love with his ex-girlfriend—oh, I'm sorry. Riley. That's her name, Mom. Why do I know her name?"

Mom's shuffling around on the other end of the line but is quiet for a few beats until she sighs. "You're making this call from a date you're still on with a guy you're still with?"

This is so not the energy I need right now. I need her to find Zola. I need a plan to get out of this. I need action.

In muted exasperation, I pull the phone from my ear to put some distance between myself and the woman I'm irrationally angry at. "He can't hear me," I whisper-bark this time.

I leave out the part about being curled into the fetal position inches from the toilet bowl brush.

"Where is he now?" she asks.

"Starting dinner."

"Oh. So, he's cooking for you? And you're hiding. Talking to your mom. About his ex. You sure he's the problem?" Before I can argue my point, she continues. "People have exes, Kai. I'd rather a guy who's comfortable mentioning them respectfully than one who swears they're all crazy."

The banging in the kitchen has quieted.

I'm running out of time.

"I know people have exes," I say in a rush. "But do they bring them along on first dates?"

"She's *there*?" Mom says, finally as horrified as I need her.

"Metaphorically."

"So, not literally."

"No, but—"

"Kaia, is the guy decent? Are you safe?"

"Well, yeah."

"Then why are you calling me? If you're asking for permission to leave, no. I think you gotta ride it out. It's an hour of your life, sweetie. Get back out there. And be nice!"

*Are mothers even allowed to hang up on their daughters?*

I stand, mouth agape, pride wounded, snarling at my reflection. "I'm always fucking nice."

But I clamp my lips shut at the knock on the door.

"Hey," James says through the solid oak dividing us. "I gotta run downstairs for more sauce." He hesitates but hasn't walked away. Waiting for an answer I can't seem to conjure up.

I consider the prospect that I may now have to live and die in this bathroom to avoid ever facing James again, but when the aromas from the kitchen waft in from the slit at the doorframe, I know I won't last five minutes.

I square my shoulders and open the door, prepared to give James my best breezy bathroom exit, but he's gone. The hallway is empty. So, instead, I follow my nose to find my heartsick personal chef.

Compared to the rustic dining room that could've been built right into a French hillside, the kitchen, with its sleek steel and hard edges, is straight from outer space. Glistening and pristine as if it's never been touched.

The only hint of warmth is at the center of a long silver countertop in the middle of the room. It's covered in white linen, with the same preloved vases and dainty daisies from the front of the house. Only this table isn't set for dinner, it's covered in already prepped ingredients, waiting to be made into the meal they'll become.

*A private cooking class.* It actually would've been cute, if only I weren't on someone else's date with someone else's man.

The intensity of my internal conflict, and the fact that I'm most definitely running out of time, is enough to make me do The Thing™.

**7:14pm**

**Me:** Would you stay for dinner if your date was in love with someone else?

After minutes of silence that feel like a lifetime, it's official—we're not avoiding each other. *Ro* is avoiding *me.* I'm about to send a follow-up message claiming the previous text had been a misfire, when:

**7:19pm**

**Ro:** I'm lost.

**Me:** Zo sent me out with a guy who's in love with his ex.

**Me:** Like LOVE love.

**Ro:** Have you considered the possibility that Zola's fucking with you?

**Me:** Every day.

I'm still smiling at the first semi-normal exchange Ro and I have had all week, when a wineglass appears on the tablecloth before me.

"You left this out there," James says as he begins unloading thin silver trays from a rolling cart. "I made sheets of ravioli before you got here. I thought we'd cut and fill them together, but—"

I hold the sip I've just taken on my tongue in anticipation.

"Is everything okay?" he finishes finally. "I get the vibe you might not be staying."

The wine goes down like gravel. "What? Why?" I screech, but at the earnestness in his eyes, I try again. "What makes you say that?"

James points down the hall. "The whispering in the bathroom. And you've been staring at your phone all night." He shoves his hands into his pockets.

I hate that I'm the reason he's this uncomfortable in his own kitchen.

"You don't have to stay if you'd rather go."

I swallow hard. I guess we're doing this. "I actually got a similar vibe from you."

James's eyebrows shoot up his forehead before folding in on themselves in confusion.

I smile to soften the next part. "Riley. It seems like maybe you'd rather be making ravioli with her."

James's face falls at the mention of her name. "You're not the first person to say something like that. It's why I stopped dating. I told you I was bad at this."

"You're not bad at all," I say honestly. "You're actually doing pretty good. But I bet you'd be even better if you were doing it with her."

James places both his palms on the table and drops his head with a sigh. "I don't even remember any stories that aren't about her. But we've been done for a long time."

This is the closest I've been to one of these declarations in real life, so I'm not sure I'm doing it right. But James looks so broken that I try anyway.

"Is there a deadline on passion?"

James lifts his head at hearing his own words mirrored back to him. And now he's smiling.

"Okay," I say, assessing the evening's damage and the deconstructed meal in front of us. We're completely off book now. "I still need food," I start. "And it seems like maybe you could use a friend? Maybe we just agree that's what we're doing tonight. Low stakes. High gluten. Friends."

He rolls his shoulders back, standing to his full height before extending his hand to shake mine.

"Deal."

# 19

ZOLA WATCHES ME GET UNREADY AS I TELL HER ABOUT the date-shaped thing she sent me on tonight. It's more of an oral recipe guide than a date recap. James's lobster ravioli deserves a little commotion.

"So, you ended the date," she says, once I've finished. "But you were honest and actually nice, and you still got dinner out of it. It all sounds very grown-up of you." She takes a belabored seat at the window bench. "Minus hiding in the bathroom, I'm calling it progress."

The smirk she wears is meant to look playful, but her eyes betray her. She's tired. And not just because she waited up for me again. For the first time since I walked in tonight, I realize how uncharacteristically quiet Zola's been. Even through my recap.

She drops her head to the glass at her back and her eyes close for a beat longer than a blink.

"What's wrong?" I ask, finally.

"Just ironic that I'm the one doling out advice right now," she barely whispers.

No words follow the heavy sigh that escapes her lips.

The silence between us remains—untouched and suffocating—but it isn't mine to fill.

"Look at me," she says, her hands framing her belly. "How did I let this become my life? How did I play house with Jason for so long without noticing I was the only one playing?"

"No," I say, rushing to defend her from herself. "None of us saw that coming. He was covert until he wasn't, and you were—"

Zola's already shaking her head as she cuts me off. "Things had been off for years. But I held on to us till there was nothing left. I was so scared to end up alone that I became the person I grew up resenting. And I didn't even notice." She doesn't flinch as she says it, but I do. "I didn't notice until it destroyed us."

Without permission, my eyes shift from my sister to the sky at her back. The light of the moon is as spectacular as it is unrelenting. I want to move Zola out from under its spotlight—tell her she doesn't have to perform this monologue. I want to suggest we do literally anything else in the world, but she *wants* to say it. I know she does. So, I listen.

"I haven't wanted to look at my stuff," she continues. "My part in all of it. That's probably why I jumped at this." She gestures toward me, before her hands fall to her lap, balling into fists as she pushes on.

When she meets my eyes again, she lets her tears fall freely. Finally.

"I'm so mad," she says, gasping through a sob that seems to catch her off guard. As if she's surprised by the strength of her own emotions. "All the time. And I don't even know who to be mad at. I think about what I'm bringing this kid into, and I wanna scream. And I don't even know what I want from Jason anymore," she says, answering the question I hadn't yet asked. "I don't think I want him at all, but the idea of my son growing up without one decent male figure in his life is almost enough for me to beg Jason to come back. Almost enough to make me beg *Dad* to—god, I don't even know! Fuck, I'm still doing it. Still running so scared, like there's somewhere left for me to go."

Zola's admission stuns me into silence. If she's waiting for a response, we're going to be here awhile. Here, in this same bedroom we've always known, looking out this same window, at those same stars—but we were never these people. At least I didn't think we were.

"I want this baby, you know I do . . ."

"You don't have to say that, Zo. I know."

Zola's face is hidden behind her hands now, but as she continues, I think I may be seeing my big sister for the first time.

"I might not be the person who should be telling you what to do, but let me show you what *not* to do and who not to become. I don't want you to be scared anymore, Kai. I don't want you to end up like me. I mean, it's a slightly better alternative to ending up like Mom, but still."

Her smile is barely there at all before she wipes it away along with her tears. She's trying so hard to be okay, but I'm just glad she's also finally admitting she's not.

"I just want you to be braver than me," she continues. "You always have been, but it's so easy to lose that and not even know when it happened. You have to fight to hold on to those parts of yourself. And fight for what you want, even if you don't think it's the thing you're *supposed* to want. Whether it's teaching or dating or anything else. It doesn't even have to make sense. Just do whatever feels right to you for as long as it feels right. Trust me, you'll regret it more one day if you don't."

Zola looks so sad when she finishes that it's physically impossible for me not to go to her. And we stay that way—backlit by the moon and silenced by finally hearing the quiet part said out loud.

# 20

THERE ARE COUNTLESS WORDS I'VE USED TO DESCRIBE Zola in my life, but until a few nights ago, *scared* had never been one of them. *Be braver,* she'd said. The implied "or else" left hanging. Sisterly advice, wrapped in a warning.

That warning is the same reason my Edjoin search still hasn't made it past the landing page this morning. I can't even fix my fingers to type my fucking zip code into the search bar without my pulse racing and my vision blurring.

I'm still staring at the computer, trying to figure out if *being braver* means I should finally be applying or if it's time to delete my account completely, when my phone lights up beside me.

**Tuesday, 9:43am**

**Liv:** I put you on the list for Saturday. Again.

**Liv:** I'm not going away. You WILL be meeting Travis at some point xx

**Me:** no need for threats

**Me:** Zola's next guy rescheduled, so I'm free

**Liv:** He canceled a first date and Zola let him live??

**Me:** LOL she was like he's a DOCTORRRRRR!!

**Liv:** If that logic frees you up for the concert, I'm here for it.

**Liv:** Sending show details now.

At six-fifteen on Saturday evening, my phone buzzes on the bathroom counter. I expect for it to be Ro making one last threat about joining me in the city in leather chaps. Why he believes that's what one wears to a rock concert is beyond me, but over the past week, his ignorance and my fear of tonight's events have brought us back to almost normal. I'll take it.

These incoming texts, though, are from Liv. MTA alerts I didn't ask for, listing all my potential train delays. She was serious about not going away.

So, I give myself one final mirror check to make sure my curls are behaving, which of course they're not, and I'm on my way.

On the platform at Grand Central, a swarm of bridge and tunnel weekend commuters sweep me up into an involuntary footrace toward the nearest exit. Liv's hyperspecific itinerary for the night named Union Square as our meeting place, so when I emerge from the Metro North tracks, I'm surprised to find her waiting for me this far uptown—bouncy and bubbly, despite her *I'm with the band* ensemble.

Her excitement flashes to disappointment when she sees me approaching.

"Uh, hi," I say, stooping to catch her eyes as they work their way up my black Levi's and hover at my gray knit tank. "I thought we were meeting downtown."

She's still studying me.

"Is that what you're wearing?"

*There it is.*

My hands lift in question—despite their sudden urge to flip her off.

"Well, obviously my *real* clothes are in here," I say, yanking at the chain of my itty-bitty leather crossbody. "Of course this is what I'm wearing. What's wrong with it?"

"Nothing, sorry," she says, finally bringing me in to hug her vinyl-and-lace-clad body. "It's just a little . . . meh."

"This is what you said to wear."

"I did say to wear black," she admits, eyeing me as she lifts my shirt up a few inches. "Actually, I can work with this."

We step onto the 6 train, and I raise my foot in the air, still pleading my case. "Look, I wore your favorite sandals even though they make my pinkie toe go rogue."

Liv smiles and bats my leg away. "Don't blame the shoes for your octopus toes." Then she unclasps a few of her layered necklaces. "Here, put these on. I'll fix your makeup."

I try not to protest too violently as Liv tucks my shirt into my bra until it's cropped into something resembling a bikini top. She swipes a final layer of deep brown eye shadow on my lid and recaps her mascara as the train lurches to a stop at Fourteenth Street.

"Better," is all she says.

"Gee, thanks," I say, scaling the stairs.

When we're finally aboveground, I catch sight of my reflection in a passing window.

"Liv!"

I'm still laughing at the little Black Rocker Barbie staring back at me as Liv yanks at my jeans so they sit even lower on my hips. Once she's satisfied, she links her arm through mine the way we did as kids, and I'm reminded of how she used to dress me up, even then.

"Fine," I concede, smiling and falling into step with my best friend, "if you like it, I love it."

Liv makes a catwalk of the few feet between the bar's heavy double doors and the guys checking IDs. I resist the urge to untuck my shirt and throw my hair into a high poof to make it more obvious that I'm here against my will and better judgment.

"Don't check anything," she says, ushering me past a girl working coat check. "It'll just get lost or stolen."

Comforting.

**8:42pm**

**Me:** Start the clock.

**Ro:** Already?

**Me:** Already.

Liv leads us toward the bar at the center of the venue, currently overflowing with bodies thrashing haphazardly to the blaring music. Pretty sure the last "venue" I was in was the Richard Rodgers Theatre for a matinee performance of *Hamilton*. This . . . is not that.

Liv watches me do a once-over of our surroundings. The laughter that spills out of her at the horrified look on my face makes her look a little more like the girl I grew up with.

And she's still smiling as she leans into me to shout at full volume: "Obviously, I'm buying."

I smile my appreciation but keep my response brief to minimize my own vocal strain. "Tequila!"

Liv nods. "Soda? Margarita?"

"Yes!"

She places our order and the bartender leans in close, using the deafening acoustics as an excuse to put his lips up against her ear. My fist is ready to educate him on the meaning of consent, but before I can get us escorted out of here, Liv throws her head back in laughter.

Not the reaction I'd expected, but actually, I have no clue who this man is to her.

Maybe they're friends. Maybe he's friends with her boyfriend. Because Liv has a boyfriend now. One that I'm only just now meeting.

A few years ago, she wouldn't have even been able to craft a text to a guy without screenshotting the conversations for my input, but here and now, *I'm* the odd man out. In this place, we're not the *Liv and Kaia* of years past. And if I'm being honest, we haven't been those girls for a long time.

"Travis left his tab open for us," Liv says, picking our shots up off the sticky metal bar. "Fritz here says he's been instructed to get us good and drunk."

"How sweet," I joke. But as the high-quality tequila spreads its warmth through my rattled insides, I realize Travis getting us shmammered tonight may, in fact, be the sweetest thing after all.

The bartender slams down two more and Liv screams her appreciation. She seems free in this new world that I know very little about. It's so easy for her to let go here, and in *that,* at least, I see the appeal.

Liv closes the small gap between us, grabbing both my shoulders to drag my body along with hers, as she does what can only be described as a full body thrashing. Her headbanging is new, but her smile is the same one I've known forever and draws one out of me the way it always has.

Fueled by the music, the liquor, and the promise of a much-needed night out with one of the great loves of my life, I join Liv—in the shot, the dance, and the ensuing scream. And this time, when I survey the club once more, my head finds the rhythm of this new song I've never heard before.

When Liv eyes Travis and his bandmates walking toward us, she runs into his arms like he's a soldier, returning from war. The two of them making out is a car wreck I cannot look away from, though I really, *really* wish I could. I'm still trying to figure out whose tongue is whose, when my phone vibrates in my bag.

**10:01pm**

**Ro:** Liv get you onstage yet?

**Ro:** Did you wear the chaps?

**Me:** I'm beginning to suspect you've never actually heard rock music.

**Ro:** No yeehaw?

**Me:** Remind me to bring you next time so we can update your visual.

**Ro:** You could've brought me tonight.

My conversation's interrupted by Liv making introductions. She's still wiping her lipstick from Travis's face when he acknowledges me for the first time.

"Hey," he says, his tone so casual it borders on bored. Luckily, I've seen enough of his online presence not to take it personally. "Thanks for coming out."

But before I can quip that my only act of free will tonight came in liquid form, Liv's shouting again. "I thought you guys would be getting ready to go on by now."

"Evan needed a few minutes in the greenroom," Travis says, dragging Liv toward him by her pants pockets. "He had to work something out with the manager."

The band laughs as someone says under their breath, "Yeah, he's working her out, all right."

"This place is packed." My attempt to move on from a joke clearly not meant for me is clumsy. "You guys play here a lot?"

"Every Saturday," one of the guys says. "Ev got us the gig."

"Nice," I say, trying to ignore the fact that Liv and Travis are going at it again. "This is my first real concert."

"I can tell," a husky voice says from behind me.

*Holy hot.*

"Evan!" Liv squeals, anchored by Travis's arm still wrapped around her waist. "This is the friend I was telling you about."

Liv pushes me forward like she's presenting Evan an offering. The fact that he doesn't reach out a hand or even say hello makes me feel even more like a human sacrifice, but I make no move to escape my fate. I'm locked in place by his hooded green eyes and the way my name comes out on his exhale, sweeping across my face as it does.

*"Kaia."*

His lips stay parted like he's breathing the word back in, and when Evan licks his lips, I swear the button on my jeans pops open to grant him easier access.

Liv swats my butt, cuing me to speak.

"Hi."

Under the heady intoxication of tequila and the *walking sex* of a man in front of me, *hi* is the best I can do.

And apparently that's all it takes. Evan reaches for my hand, guiding me away from our audience. I can't say for sure why I let him, but the answer probably lies somewhere in this view of Evan from behind. In the way he mindlessly rakes his fingers through the perfectly undone black waves covering his head. In the tattoos that snake across his upper body, following every defined muscle.

My eyes trace the intricate black and red ink that paints every bit of his exposed olive skin before disappearing under his loose black tank top.

When he's satisfied with the distance we've achieved, he turns his slightly stubbled face back to mine. I'm acutely aware of his hand on the newly exposed skin at the small of my back. It's not unpleasant, but it is foreign enough that I can't stop thinking about the weight of it on me. When Ro touched me there, I'd nearly forgotten to notice because of how familiar it felt. Like he belonged there. Like he'd always held me that way.

I step back until I'm just barely out of Evan's reach.

"Thought we could use some space to get to know each other," he says, stepping closer with his fingers at my back again. He taps out a rhythm on my skin, making his presence even more impossible to ignore.

He scans my face for recognition. "We haven't met before, right?"

My laughter eases a bit of the tension. Mine, anyway.

Evan's brow quirks in confusion, but it's just *too* fitting that he'd be the type of guy to forget women he ought to remember. I adjust my purse to form a buffer between us and shake my head, taking a couple big sips of my cocktail. "You guys any good?"

"Just wait," he practically purrs. "You're gonna see these people lose their fucking minds."

I try to regain the composure of my earlier sobriety, but my blinks are lazy now, and even I hear new warmth dripping from my words as I tease, "Okay, rock star." And it's only when I'm removing my hand from his chest that I realize I'd touched him at all.

*Thanks, tequila.*

"Fair warning, though, this isn't usually my thing."

"Don't knock it till you try it," he says. And I can't tell for sure if it's his breath or his tongue that makes contact with my ear when he leans in to whisper, "It's always the good girls." Evan grabs my hips to pull me into him.

"Whoa," I mutter, stumbling briefly before catching myself on his sculpted biceps.

"You were all the way over there," he says. He dips his head down so his mouth is in my ear again. Lip jutting out as he pouts. "I feel like I'm yelling."

Tipsy as I am, and tempting as he is, if this guy doesn't keep his hands to himself, he's going to need all his pretty muscles to defend himself against mine.

"I can hear you just fine."

I take another step back from a shocked-looking Evan, just as Liv, Travis, and the rest of the guys appear to retrieve him. Without another glance in my direction, Evan pushes through the newly formed group, and before he's completely out of earshot, I hear him yell to the guys, "I need a fucking drink."

"Come on," Liv says, grabbing my hand. "Let's go backstage."

There's just no fucking way.

But Liv looks drunk and happy and I'd like to keep it that way.

"Is it okay if we just stay out here?" I say, instead of telling her that her boyfriend sucks and his friend's a creep.

Liv's eyes follow Travis's retreating frame as a gaggle of *pick mes* materialize from thin air, closing in on the band as they reach the red curtain by the stage.

I sense Liv's silent debate.

"It's cool if you want to go," I offer, knowing she might be two seconds from choosing Travis anyway.

She shakes her head. "Just let me tell him. I'll be right back."

"I'll be in the bathroom," I yell to Liv's back as she sprints toward her man as fast as her four-inch heels will allow.

**10:58pm**

**Ro:** If you end up in the mosh pit, I'm gonna need a video.

**Me:** unlikely

**Ro:** You good?

Before I can respond, Liv barrels through the bathroom door with fresh drinks, oblivious to the dirty looks coming from the line of girls she shoulders out of the way.

"Okay," Liv says, breathless. "They're officially onstage and safe from the Irvine Place sharks."

"I don't know how you do it," I tell her, opening the camera on my phone to snap a selfie or ten.

My hair's wild from the humidity, and my already smoky eyes have gone even more sultry on my dewy skin. For no reason at all I send a picture to Ro.

"So, Evan?" Liv asks. "So cute, right?"

She holds up her tall glass to cheers her approval.

With a very different reaction to his name, I leave her drink hanging, to take a swig of mine. "He seems like kind of an asshole."

"No!" she shouts. And this time, it's the alcohol, not the music, responsible for her volume.

Liv's still insisting what a *great guy* Evan is, when I hand her my mostly empty drink and duck into an open stall.

I check my phone mid-pee, curious if Ro got my picture:

**Ro:** Fuck!

**Ro:** Sorry. But damn.

I stifle a private smile. And the urge to ask him to send one back. *Relax, tequila.* Though I can't blame the alcohol for the familiar tilt in my belly that I've come to expect around Ro.

The back half of the venue is nearly empty as the band begins their set. The audience, a giant mass of colliding bodies, inches their way toward the stage.

Evan might be one giant red flag offstage, but under the spotlights, he's transformed into something else. His hands, once wandering and brazen, are deliberate, intentional, and fucking killing it. He's doing his thing up there. All the guys are.

Beside me, Liv's ponytail whips around with each enthusiastic nod of her head. She's doing *her* thing too.

A waitress drops off two more drinks, pointing at Travis to let Liv know who sent them. *It's not a boom box hoisted overhead, but it'll do.* Even from this distance, Travis hasn't taken his eyes off her. Maybe I'd been too quick to judge.

Back here, away from the madness, and with another cocktail coursing through me with renewed strength, I follow Liv's lead—letting go and allowing the strobing lights to turn me into someone new for the night too. We're completely lost to each other and the music. Our own two-man mosh pit.

The alcohol and exertion leave my skin glistening. Rogue curls, slick with sweat, drape themselves across my face until I whip my head back to tousle them into the voluminous mess my hair has become. I don't know if it *looks* nearly as good as it feels—the movements aren't pretty or perfect. They're not meant to be. And that, the freedom to move this way, to just exist exactly as we are, is liberating as hell. And sexy as fuck.

Evan's eyes find me in the dark. The sight of him, shirtless and dripping, stirs something in me. Something I'd signed away months ago, contractually. But buoyed by the night's energy, none of the old rules matter.

The thought of breaking those rules—of breaking my *own*—both stops me cold and sets me on fire. Mine is the permission I didn't realize I'd been waiting for, and once it's granted, I can practically feel his skilled fingers digging into my flesh. Rough and hurried with need. His sweat and mine, painting us both in a sheen of desire.

I want that. I want him. And tonight, my brain is just foggy enough to let my body act on it. Tonight, that wanting is reason enough for me to have sex with—

Liv and I both go still. A tiny scoff-laugh escapes from my lips, glossy and agape.

It's my first time at one of these things, but by the way Liv's mouth also dangles wide, it's safe to assume the wannabe Instagram model running onstage to straddle Evan at his drum set isn't part of the band's usual programming.

She pushes her exposed cleavage against Evan's bare chest, and Evan, to his credit, continues to play expertly. The crowd's at a fever pitch at this show within the show.

The final cymbal is still reverberating through the club as she throws her head back, expectantly. Without missing a beat, Evan's tongue sets out on a path from her bra up to her awaiting mouth.

I'm flushed and a little breathless from my earlier thoughts and the overtly sexual energy shift in the room that's left me even more eager. All I can muster is a head tilt and an inquisitory, "Huh," as I continue staring at the stage.

Liv and I watch them go at it for a while before my hand finds my back pocket to order a lifeline out of this place where I'd only ever been a visitor. I try not to look too excited as I brave my next words.

"Will you kill me if I go?"

"That depends." Liv points a red manicured nail toward my phone. "Are you going home?"

When I quirk my brow suggestively, she swats me before pulling me into a sticky hug. "Finally! Go. Have fun."

"I love you, you know that?" And though I've said it to her countless times, it sounds like a revelation. I'm always going to love her.

Liv brings both her palms to her lips to blow all her love right back to me.

The guys start their next song as I make my way toward the exit shouting, "Thank Travis for the drinks. And Evan for the show."

And when I look back for the last time, everything is just as it should be—only one body behind the drum set, Liv already making her way backstage, and me, requesting what's sure to be the most expensive Lyft I've ever taken. All the way back to Connecticut.

Because it was never going to be Evan.

**Me:** Hey. What's your address?

# 21

I HAD AN ALMOST NINETY-MINUTE DRIVE FROM MANHATTAN to East Norwalk to change my mind. To tell him I hadn't been serious, that I'd ordered another drink and forgotten I'd sent the text at all.

But that's not what I do.

The Toyota Corolla (Plate #: YBX326) pulls into a familiar parking lot—but it's way past closing time and pitch-black inside. My driver catches my eye in the mirror, awaiting instructions I don't have to give. I'm just as confused why we ended up here as he is. And for the first time in my life I wonder if this guy's worried *I* might be the murderer.

I smile my reassurance with a quick apology, promising to reroute our destination toward home . . .

But then, I decide to be braver:

**Me:** You gave me the address to the garage?
**Ro:** Oh shit you really came!

A light flips on inside, illuminating a window over the lobby. My insides flutter and I roll my eyes at myself a little for it.

I beat Ro to the door, but after only a second or two, there's movement behind the glass. He hasn't turned on the lights, so he's still mostly shrouded in black, but I know the exact instant he sees me. I feel it before I see it—his smile, setting the world on fire.

We study each other through the door for too long. Each of us giving the other one last chance to back out, but our eyes are locked, unwavering, and our bodies are still. The shake of his head is almost imperceptible as he reaches a decision of his own, turning the dead bolt to open the door wide.

With nothing separating us now, I lose whatever calm I'd been channeling. I'd felt so sure before, and I am, but I'm also suddenly very aware that I don't know what to do with my hands.

Ro steps beside me to wave off the driver I hadn't noticed still waiting in the lot. My body trills with electricity. Awakening at how he's taken the lead with that simple act. There's no going back now—and that had been Ro's decision as much as it had been mine to come. When his hand falls, he rests it at my back, ushering me inside. His touch feels exactly the way I remember. Almost unremarkable in its easy belonging. Yet I'm certain that I could pick his prints out of a lineup for how his fingers brand me.

When he applies the tiniest whisper of pressure at my spine, I sink into his touch willingly.

"You coming?" he asks, his lips at my ear.

Tonight, Ro's voice is gravel on silk. It leaves a mark. I've known his voice, but not like this. I've known this man, but not like this. Everything about this moment is new and yet, when I pull back to really look at him, everything is exactly as it's always been.

My lips part as a breath bordering on obscene escapes them.

Ro's dimple pops, and my chest and heart find their rhythm. In sync with his as always. Because for all the ways we're new tonight, it's still Ro Jackson staring back at me.

"You sleep here?" I ask, stepping deeper into the lobby.

Bathed in comfortable silence and the moon's glow, this place feels even more magical than it does in the day. But my eyes are most impressed by the man locking the door in gray sweats and crisp white socks. He wears sleep well. Eyes and smile a bit lazier than usual, but no less radiant.

"Yeah," he says, stalking me, but keeping his distance. I wish he wouldn't. "There's an apartment upstairs. I've been crashing up there."

He nods upward, and my eyes follow till we're both watching the ceiling, like we can see the future playing out on its tiles. Ro breaks his gaze first, his eyes boring into me now with a smirk playing at his full lips.

He's going to make me say it.

I shake my head but fold like a paper crane. "Show me."

Neither of us even attempts to conceal the smiles those words bring. His silently claims victory, but as long as he takes me upstairs, I'm winning.

Usually, by the time I'm in view of a bed with a man at my side, we both already know what it is. I'd expected for Ro and me to be a tangle of breath and bodies by now, but he slinks away to pour a glass of water, and I'm left rooted to the ground at the threshold between the living space and his bedroom. Hands tucked at my sides, like I'm waiting to punch my ticket for entry.

The lamp I'd seen from outside still glows on the nightstand, bathing his rumpled sheets in a soft light that makes the bedroom feel more intimate. It's different than I'd imagined—softer. Everything's different with Ro.

I'm not entirely sure I know how to do this. And apparently, I'm not hiding it well.

"We're not having sex tonight, Kai."

I jump, spinning away from the bedroom, at the sound of his voice and the knockout blow his words deliver to my fragile ego. Ro's leaned against the kitchenette counter behind me, watching *me* watch his bed. Arms folded across his broad chest, the rigid planes of his torso barely concealed by his worn T-shirt.

"What?!" I screech. "No, I just—"

His eyebrow raises in an amused challenge. He knows why I'm here. We both do. And hard as I try, I can't find the words through my disappointment to pretend otherwise.

"Well, why not?" My question is an admission.

The muscled bands of his forearms flex as he pushes off the laminate countertop. He pads across the floor almost weightless, despite his strength and stature.

He doesn't stop coming for me until our toes are touching on the plush rug. "Because," he starts, and the whisper of his breath on my cheek tightens muscles in my core that I didn't even know I had. "I've waited this long to touch you. When I finally do, I need to know it's what you want too. So I don't have to wonder. So I don't have to go slow."

A gasp is the only way I can bring air into my shocked lungs.

"It's what I want," I beg. He's claiming he won't touch me, but already I feel him. Everywhere. "I'm telling you now, it's what I want."

He fingers the curl at my temple, tugging at it so his hand just grazes the length of my cheek. "You smell like tequila," he whispers, still eyeing the curl as it springs back into position.

Desperate and breathless, I ask, "Do you have mouthwash or something?"

Laughter explodes from his chest, breaking my trance. "No, Kaia. You don't need mouthwash. You smell fucking great," he says, stepping back from me. "But I don't wanna be a decision you make at night and regret in the morning."

He takes another step farther out of reach, and the chasm he creates between us is his decision made.

My face falls. My shoulders fall. My libido, though, remains firmly in place.

The T-shirt Ro gave me to sleep in smells like him. The pillow where my head currently rests smells like him. The bed, the room, this entire place smells like Ro.

*What a fucking tease.*

He's quiet beside me, breath coming so steadily that I'm sure he's long been asleep. But how am *I* supposed to sleep with the heat from his body crawling onto my side of the bed. Taunting me with his closeness.

My phone's at my nose, blinding me as I scroll in an otherwise dark room.

"What are you doing?" His voice is thick with sleep.

"Sorry," I say, locking my phone to bathe us in blackness again. I turn so we're knee to knee and nose to nose. "But for the record, it'd been like twenty minutes from my last drink to when I left the bar. Let's say seven minutes waiting for my ride. Then ninety in the car to get here, and you've been punishing me now for at least sixty or so . . . so that's what? A hundred and seventy-seven minutes."

He's quiet as he waits for me to connect the dots. I do it eagerly.

"According to Google I could safely operate a construction crane or small aircraft by now. Pretty sure it's safe for us to . . ." I trail off in hopes I've presented enough data for Ro's restraint to give way.

His hand finds my waist below the covers. I toe his foot with mine. He pulls me the tiniest bit closer, and I think I've got him. Until laughter rumbles from his chest.

"That's what you're doing right now? Looking up the metabolic rates of tequila? You order a Breathalyzer off Postmates too?"

"No," I say, poking his ribs till he squirms. "But I could totally pass a field test, you ass."

He gently removes my hands from his body and rolls onto his back. "Okay then," he says, pulling up on his elbows. "Let's see it."

I sit up, meeting his challenge eye to eye. "You want it straight up, or we doin' the *bump, bump* version with the kick-ball-change." I'm on my knees now, popping my hip like the drunk cowboy in question.

Ro stuffs the pillow behind his back to prop himself up and folds both arms behind his head to take in the show. "Actually," he says, "gimme the kick step."

I mirror his smirk before yanking his pillow away and smothering him with it. His muffled protests tangle with my laughter, but I don't let up until his fingers dig into my ribs, tickling me into submission.

When he finally relents, Ro's propped up on an elbow above me and we're both breathless. His face hovers above mine, so close that if I lifted my head even slightly, our lips would be touching. So that's what I do.

I take Ro's bottom lip into my mouth and bite down the same way I've watched him do it. It's velvety and so lush that even this nibble feels sinful. Gluttonous. A growl escapes him, and I swallow it whole. When he parts his mouth wider to allow my tongue entry, I explore every bit of him. This isn't just a kiss, I'm inhaling Ro. Taking him all the way in. And when our lips finally part, my greedy fingers find his damp mouth—tracing it, memorizing it, claiming it.

Ro watches me with an intensity I'd usually run from, but I'm here.

I wait for him to kiss me again, for his tongue to line the veins at my neck, for his fingers to seek out my nipples, budding beneath the thin fabric between us. Instead, he drops his head to the pillow with closed eyes and a heavy exhale.

The air that rushes to fill the space he'd just occupied is colder than it had been before he touched me. I want more of him, and when he was on me, I could feel that he wanted more too.

My chest rises and falls with unfulfilled want, but when his lips find my shoulder, I warm some. Settling into him with a sigh.

"Good night, Kaia," he says, without removing his mouth from my skin.

And he keeps it on me, all night, as we sleep.

# 22

I STILL ARGUE I WAS SOBER LAST NIGHT. SOBER*ISH* AT LEAST. Sober enough. But when the sun rises and snakes in through a crack in the blinds, I'd pay the universe a small fortune to extinguish it entirely.

I bury my head under the covers, but where my cocoon effectively blocks out the light, I've also inadvertently engulfed myself in Ro's uniquely clean scent. While his is a smell I've come to appreciate, right now it's a noseful of rejection that does little to unscramble my brain or calm my churning stomach.

*We're not having sex tonight.*

I wince at Ro's words, sharp in my memory. They stab at my aching brain, quite literally adding insult to injury. At least he had the decency to leave so I don't have to face him this morning. What was I thinking showing up here like that? Drunk and horny and shameless.

*We're not having sex tonight.*

Zola was right, I am a cautionary fucking tale. And *this* is why I stay on the apps. If it had been an *app* guy, expectations would've been set before we even bothered with hellos. I would've been fucked and back home in my own bed, without wondering or caring what he thought of me.

This is what I get for drinking half a bottle of Casamigos and letting my guard down around some real-life guy. This is what I deserve.

But even as I think the words, I know they don't fit—Ro's not *some guy* and he wasn't trying to embarrass me. At least I don't think so. Right now, though, my head's throbbing too badly to want to think much of anything at all.

I'm still attempting to recall the exact height of the garage, to determine if a jump from this second-story window will result in a scuff, a break, or certain death, when voices from the far side of the closed bedroom door invade my shame cocoon. I emerge from the covers in a flurry of matted curls and regret, with an ear turned to the door. Feet already primed to run as fast as last night's strappy stilettos will let me.

Before I can hurl my body through the double-paned glass, Ro's doorknob begins to turn. Out of time and options, I do what any adult woman would do in my situation; I fake sleep. Unfortunately, when I yank back the covers while flopping down to the mattress, they catch just enough air that they're still gently lofting down over me long after the door swings open. A useless parachute floating down to cover the lifeless body it betrayed thirty thousand feet ago.

Confronted with just how intensely the universe seems to hate me, I ready myself to face the consequences of my actions—this isn't my first awkward *morning after* and it won't be my last.

But when our eyes meet, I'm in so much deeper than I could've known.

"Oh. My. God," I say, relieved that when I palm my chest, all my bits are still concealed by Ro's T-shirt.

He doesn't speak, so I'm forced to fill our stunned silence.

"Hi, Mr. Jackson."

The apartment behind Ro's dad goes in and out of focus as

panic blurs my vision. My heart thunders, beating way too fast in my chest and between my ears. As if my situation wasn't already bleak enough, it's becoming increasingly clear that my adrenaline spiking this high against my hangover is about to result in vomit or—did I already mention certain death?

His face is scrunched in justified confusion and his next word leaves me looking much the same. "Claire?"

*Who the fuck is Claire?!*

"No," I say, wondering why the ground hasn't yet opened up to swallow me whole. "It's Kaia. Harper." As if it's my last name that's the source of his confusion.

Neither of us move for what I can only assume are multiple lifetimes.

At some point, Ro appears from behind Mr. Jackson, looking as horrified as I feel to not only have been caught half naked and hiding, but to be doing it in another woman's spot. *Claire's.*

"Shit, Pops," he says, already guiding his father out by his shoulders. "You can't be back here right now."

Ro closes the door behind them, without so much as acknowledging my presence, and the instinct to fight reorients my insides in a rush. All signs of my hangover gone in an instant.

I'm on my hands and knees now, grasping at every stray piece of clothing I can find to shield myself from the karmic joke that awaits me outside. Hidden beneath the makeshift armor that is my own shirt layered over Ro's T-shirt, all concealed under one of his discarded sweatshirts, my rage temporarily cools enough for me to make a plan.

I'm on the edge of the bed, with my phone in hand, when I hear a knock at the door. So soft, I may have imagined it.

*Please tell me I imagined it.*

The door cracks open, and this time it's Ro's head peeking in from behind it.

He takes my silence as permission to enter, hands raised in approach. "I am so sorry."

"You're *sorry*?" I bite back.

He visibly recoils. "I totally forgot they were coming."

"They?"

"My mom's here too. Sunday brunch." He says it with a shrug, but the words hit me like *shots fired*. "We've been doing it since I got back. But last night I was . . ." Ro gestures to me, and I'm suddenly acutely aware that I'm still on his bed. "Distracted. I forgot to cancel. Are you okay?"

If he keeps talking, I'm going to scream or read him for filth. Neither of which I want to do with an audience.

"I'm fine," I lie, and though I have no claim to this man, I can't keep the venom from my tone. But I'm the one who showed up uninvited and unannounced. I'm the one who should be sorry.

I force steady breaths as I stand, righting the borrowed sweatshirt, covering my frantically beating heart.

"It's my fault," I tell him. "Just give me a minute to get outta the way."

He doesn't go. He's watching me, tying his fingers in knots in front of his chest.

"Was there something else?" I ask.

"She's asking if you'll stay. For breakfast."

My neck goes slack and my head falls as if it's been severed from my body. Which may actually be a circumstance preferable to my own.

"Roooooo," I whine, staring into the exposed ductwork overhead.

He stuffs his hands in his pockets. "I know, I'm sorry. I'll tell 'em—"

"Fuck," I whisper, mostly to myself, but Ro pauses to hear

what's coming next. If the situation was reversed, I know Ro would do this for me and more. "Fine," I decide, finally. "It's fine. *Claire's* the one who should get to be mad, anyway, right?"

I practically spit the words at him, but even through my glare, I'm trying to discern if an admission or denial crosses Ro's face. All I find there is confusion.

"Wait, why will she—"

But I can't listen to any more. "Just tell them I'll be right out."

Mr. Jackson turns from his place at the stove when he hears me shuffling out of the bedroom.

"Ayye!" he says, with a ladle in one hand and a huge smile across his face like the last ten minutes never happened. "There she is."

He extends his fist to me and I meet it with my own, staring through our hands to avoid meeting his eyes. He turns back to his pot, but my relief evaporates when Mr. Jackson opens his mouth once more, hollering, "Claire, get in here!"

*The fuck?*

A woman who could *only* be Ro's mother emerges from a laundry room off the kitchen that I hadn't noticed last night. She's carrying a stack of cloth napkins while Ro trails dutifully behind her with other assorted linens.

I'm still looking expectantly behind Ro, for the woman in question, when his mom approaches me. "Morning, Kaia. I'm Mrs. Jackson, but with the way my husband's been hollering, you might as well just start out calling me Claire too."

"*Oh!*" I say, entirely too loudly. "Claire!" I enunciate it so dramatically, I turn her name's single syllable into two. She's kind enough to pretend not to notice any of it.

The furrow in Ro's brow deepens even more, with what I'm sure is a very real concern that I may be losing my mind. He shrugs in question, but since I will not be explaining, I wave him off instead. Bringing my focus back to his mom.

"What are we doing?" she continues. "Handshakes, hugs?"

"Mom," Ro complains.

I like her immediately for making him uncomfortable, while trying to spare me.

"What?" she says, standing beside me now. She turns so we're both facing Ro, like she and I are on the same team. "I'm trying to respect Kaia's space."

*If she only knew how hard I was working to get her son to disrespect my space just a few hours ago.*

"I went with a fist bump," Mr. Jackson says, still stirring his grits. "But I also didn't ask."

"Well, I'm just so glad you agreed to stay," Mrs. Jackson says, like I had a choice.

Before today, I would have sworn Ro was his dad's twin, but now I'm not so sure. His smile is Mr. Jackson, but the gleam in his eyes, his expressions, the way he carries himself? That's all his mom.

And she wraps her arms around me as she says, "I've been dying to meet you."

By the time we sit down to eat, the apartment smells like every family reunion I wish I'd had growing up. The morning's awkwardness has lifted enough that I'm now able to make direct eye contact with Ro's parents, but the smile in his mom's eyes remains. She hasn't forgotten.

Our brunch conversation is mostly *Kaia and Ro Trivia,* with his parents recounting everything they already know of our last couple months. It's more than I would've expected, though they seem to be missing a few key details from our time in the city. I'm more than happy to fill in the blanks for them, though they aren't nearly as surprised by Ro's dramatics over the oysters as they are by the prospective sale of his live installation.

His parents have provided a natural buffer between us all morning, but when I finally catch Ro's eye to make sure I haven't overstepped by sharing the good news, the rest of the room fades away. Only for a moment, but it's long enough. My face splits into an embarrassingly proud smile at the quiet contentedness tucked behind his eyes. And now that we're finally really seeing each other, it's impossible to look anywhere else.

My face heats when Ro's dad claps a hand on his shoulder in congratulations, reminding me of our very real audience. His mom beams, but from her knowing smile, it's safe to say Ro's art isn't the only thing on her mind.

A natural lull in the conversation brings out those standard *getting to know you* questions.

"My mom's in medical sales," I tell them. Which is partially true, though she's had to work less and less with each divorce settlement.

Mrs. Jackson nods. "And your dad?"

Ro seems to be debating whether or not he needs to bail me out, but I've had to answer this question more times than I can count. I do it easily. "He's a professor. But he's not really in the picture anymore."

"Oh, I didn't realize," Mrs. Jackson says. "I'm sorry to hear that."

"More of us with that story now than not," Mr. Jackson says, folding his napkin and leaning back from the table. "My mama raised us on her own too. All five of us. Divorce is a damn epidemic."

Well, that's *not* the standard response to my brush-off. I don't remember the last time I had to go off script like this.

"I see it as an adult, but when it first happened, I felt like I was the only one," I say, surprising myself. "My family fell apart overnight, but all my friends' parents were still together." I gesture to their interlocked hands resting on the table. "Case in point."

"Oh, this?" Mr. Jackson says, playfully pulling his hand away and flicking his napkin toward Mrs. Jackson for added effect. "Don't let this fool ya for a second."

"It's unnatural," Mrs. Jackson says, rolling her eyes playfully. "Two fully formed adults, havin' to make every decision and work through every little thing *together*?"

"Well, you're still doing it," I say, laughing at their bit.

Mr. Jackson sucks his teeth, more seriously. "Ain't nothing harder than staying together in a world that makes it easier to leave."

Mrs. Jackson's face is so warm when she says, "It's all in the picking."

And when she looks back to her husband, her eyes are soft, like there's never been a harsh word exchanged between them.

What she says next, though, tells a different story. "Sometimes, especially at the start, love's a feeling, but other times it's a choice. You gotta find someone who'll keep picking you every day. Even on the tough ones. And you gotta decide to do the same for them."

They smile at each other—a shared secret decades in the making—and say, in tandem, "And therapy." Without missing a beat.

I can't help notice the way their hands find each other again, as if drawn together by a force too powerful to resist.

"Now that's real," Mr. Jackson says, breaking the connection between himself and his wife to bring me and Ro back in. "And at two hundred dollars an hour, you better believe I'm dropping knowledge on y'all whether you wanna hear it or not. We 'bout to get our money's worth."

We're all still laughing when Mr. Jackson continues. This time, though, he gestures toward me as he speaks.

"Not like our folks did us when we were coming up," he says, losing himself in my eyes. "Ain't that right? Made us learn it all the hard way."

I look to Ro's mom to see if I've missed the joke, but her smile has fallen and for the first time, there's a tinge of sadness in her eyes, where before there'd only been joy.

Mr. Jackson's laugh is sharper this time. It pulls my eyes away from his wife, and when I turn back to him, I realize he hasn't stopped looking at me.

"Tell 'em bout that time your daddy was sleeping out on the . . . shit. He was out on the . . ."

"Mr. Jackson?" I say, surprised by how small my voice sounds.

His words have trailed off, but he's still searching. Rushing now to fill the space and the silence between us. Growing more agitated with each passing moment. Fear ghosting his usually proud face.

"On the porch." He says it like it's a guess. His eyes still tuned only to me. "Isn't that right, Claire? He was on the porch."

Seeing Mr. Jackson this way, frazzled and undone, is an unsettling departure from the larger-than-life character I've only ever known to be at the helm. Anxiety pricks at my skin as he watches me, expectantly—desperate for a lifeline. But it's his wife who lifts him from the storm.

Mrs. Jackson wraps both her hands around her husband's. His eyes fall to where they connect like he can't quite make sense of her touch, and when he looks up this time, there's a distance I hadn't noticed before.

Mrs. Jackson is solid as she speaks only to him. Steady enough for the both of them. "They always did think they had us fooled," she says simply.

Then she raises their interlocked hands to kiss his weathered flesh. And I know, just now, I've watched her choose this version of her husband, all over again.

Ro's parents leave in a rush. An easy morning turned dark, and Ro's mood turned right along with it. He hardly said a word as he helped them into their car. Speaking only enough to promise his mom he'd be by later to check in.

When it's just the two of us upstairs again, I leave space for him the same way he's done for me so many times. He's folded onto the edge of the couch, elbows at his knees, palms steepled around his nose and mouth like an oxygen mask.

I should leave too. He never asked me to come in the first place, and he certainly hasn't asked me to stay. But I can't find the words to suggest it, and I can't make my body move from this spot beside him.

Ro's hands scrub at his face, until the pads of both palms settle over his eyes. And though he's not making a sound, I know he's crying.

"This is his," he says finally, pinching back tears he never let fall. "All of it. This apartment, this garage."

Ro's long legs sprawl wide as he sinks deeper into the couch cushions.

"When I was little, we couldn't get him outta here. That's where Sunday brunch came from. Pops would work straight through the weekend if my mom didn't force him to stop for a meal."

A small laugh escapes at a passing memory, but just as quickly as it comes, it's gone again.

"Now when he's here, I gotta damn near babysit so he doesn't get hurt. Or hurt somebody else. How fucked-up is that?"

For the first time since he started speaking, Ro looks at me, and the pain on his beautiful face is so out of place, so wrong, I can hardly make sense of it. I have to stop myself from turning away.

I hate seeing him like this. But I won't abandon him.

His arms fall wide onto the back of the couch, and though he's not touching me, I feel the heat of his arm at my back.

"Dementia?" I ask, finally speaking the word that's been running through my mind for the past hour.

Ro nods. "It's better when he's working. Keeping his hands busy, being in the garage. It helps, I think." His lips press into a harsh line like he's trying to hold himself together when he says, "Fifty-six years old."

I want to yell about how unfair it is—about how none of them deserve any of this, but I'm too busy putting the pieces in place.

"That's why you came back."

It's not a question, it's an understanding. Ro didn't have to do it. He has a whole life in the city—I've seen it—but his family needed him home. So he came.

Ro's fingers draw a lazy path along the length of my neck. Barely skimming my curls, before returning to the fabric at my back. I stifle my shiver, but can't calm the goosebumps that bloom in his wake.

"Just till we get somebody to help out full-time. It's too much for my mom to manage the garage and him. But even with their insurance, home care is expensive as hell. And he's not ready to have somebody in his business like that anyway." Ro's smile is sad when he looks at me. I can feel how much effort the gesture requires. "How's he supposed to go from being everybody's *Pops* to being . . ."

"I get it," I say, to save him from having to say it out loud. If only I could save him from having to live it. "I can't even imagine."

My words don't begin to express what I feel for Ro, for this family that deserves so much better. I want to tell Ro that it's okay, that it *will* be okay, but those words are even emptier. They're lies. And I won't lie to him now—not after he trusted me with his truth.

My hand finds Ro's leg, and I mean for it to be a show of support, of comfort, but this is also the first time we've been alone since last night. The first time we've touched since our kiss. And it's the first time I've felt brave enough to lean into Ro and kiss him again.

Last night, we'd been hurried. Greedy. Now, when our lips touch, it's feather-light, but it's everything. All the things we haven't said, all the times we didn't touch, all the promises we haven't made. Everything's here now. Another question awaiting its answer.

# 23

MY LIPS SWEEP AGAINST RO'S. TENDER AND TEASING until his lavish mouth awakens, parting wide against mine. Heavy with dormant want. Our tongues entangle and desire shoots down my core. Tearing through me like a flaming wick—igniting my body and singeing every nerve ending in its path. Exposing me till there's nothing left but *feeling.* Nothing left but Ro.

Heat and electricity thrum in my veins and spark in the air between us. I exhale Ro's name into our kiss and he buries his fingers in my hair to deepen our connection. The pads of his thumbs massage the supple skin at my temples before Ro breaks away to study me.

I rest my head in his strong hand, turning to press a kiss into his palm for safe keeping. When I face him again, we're bound only by the tips of our noses and the whisper of each panting breath as our heaving chests find air. A moan escapes with my contented sigh, and when a single finger grazes my mouth, my eyes flutter closed. Ro traces my lips, plump from pressure and glistening in anticipation. He's mapping me the way I did with him last night. I would've expected to be embarrassed by the tenderness, but I can't be. Not with him.

My lids part lazily, as if waking from a dream. But then Ro tugs at the heft of my bottom lip and I come alive—nipples pebbling at the tinge of smarting pain that accompanies the promise of ecstasy. I suck his thick fingers into my mouth, trapping them in my warmth. Licking and taming them with my lust. It earns me a pleased smirk and that fucking lip bite.

*I. Cannot. Take it.*

In a rush, I move to straddle him, knees digging into the couch at Ro's sides. Thighs heavy on his lap to feel his bulge at my center. My hips roll and wind in primal response as he begins to swell beneath me. The satisfied sigh I'd meant to exhale turns to a whimper, and Ro drags my face to his, just as hungry. Licking into my mouth, hot and wicked. Loose curls tumble over us. A privacy curtain—bed mussed and finger tousled—where only Ro and I exist.

He's so distractingly hard at my ass that I barely notice him yanking at the hem of my borrowed sweatshirt. He's asking permission and I give it eagerly. Our mouths don't part as he peels off the heavy layer, but when he notices that there are still three more in its place, he pulls back, quirking a brow.

"Are you wearing *all* our clothes?"

I lift off his chest so I'm balanced mostly on my knees and Ro's straining zipper. I tear my crop-top T-shirt combo off in a single urgent movement, like maybe the clothing's to blame for the blaze engulfing me. Ro's full attention is on the peaks of my breasts, spilling out of my black lace bra. His lust, anchored only by his tight grip on my ass.

My words are a purr. My gaze, something feline. "Do you really want to be funny right now?"

Ro shakes his head with renewed focus. "Not even a little."

I'm desperate for his lips to find mine again, but as his large palms splay across my back, Ro's mouth slides to the cup of my bra instead. Licking the garment's outline against my dewy skin. His tongue is sharp—a sinful blade of torture, jutting through lace. Teasing each nipple before his teeth clamp down with an ownership I've not seen from him before. I gasp at the blissful anguish of his intensity and the pleasure it sends rippling through me.

His teeth abandon my breasts to yank at the bra itself. Dragging the material down to free me from my cage. His velvet tongue circles and soothes the spots he's nipped and my head falls—chest arching into Ro, sending me deeper into the awaiting trap of wet heat that he's set. His mouth ensnares me and I moan shamelessly. My core constricting at the easy control he has over my body.

"This isn't fair," I whine. My rebellious hips rocking on his lap. "I want you inside me."

The rush of air that accompanies Ro's laugh is warm at my chest, but against the skin he's licked clean, a chill follows. The contradiction is heady. Intoxicating. I want him out of those clothes, but with each touch and suck and bite, I lose all composure. Writhing and pleading as Ro swallows my protests like they're his to keep.

He unclasps my bra, and when my breasts spring free, Ro palms their weight. The sting of his pinch at my nipple is all wrong and so right against the relentless dusting of his featherlight kisses lavishing me.

We could keep going like this, but I refuse to miss out again the way I did last night. I'd only *wanted* him then. I need him now.

I free myself from his grasp, standing just long enough to shimmy out of my jeans and let my black panties fall. I'm bared to him now, ready and wanton. I prowl back to my spot on Ro's lap and bounce a little to reclaim some control. He clutches my ass to find his own.

We tear at his T-shirt together and before he can even discard it, I find the ridges of his taut stomach. My fingernails claw at his firm chest, rising and falling with labored breaths. My touch, drawing shivers, as it trails down his sculpted abs toward the hem of his jeans.

When my forefinger dips below his denim, Ro's lips curl at my invitation. He unzips, finally. Mercifully freeing the thick length of his impossibly hard dick and reaching for it reflexively. I stop him—if I had to wait, so does he. He's steel, growing harder still as I slide his hand down my heaving chest and below my belly. He skims my opening to check my arousal. I'm so hot for him, drenched in need. My greedy hips tilt to urge him inside, but his slickened fingers seek out my clit, circling till I press into him. Begging for the pressure I need. He gives it to me before dipping inside. Pumping into me with one finger and stretching me with a second. His cock twitches and strains between us.

"Shit, Kai," he rasps. "I could come like this." He growls when we hear just how wet I am for him.

I still his hand with my own. "Don't you dare."

I'm the one who guides Ro back to himself, but still, I whimper at the loss. Before my pout can form fully at my lips, he taps my pulsing entrance with the silky head of his dick and I scream. Dizzy at the unexpected torture of his teasing.

"Ro," I gasp, nails clawing into the plush fabric of the sofa.

He strokes himself from base to tip before gripping tight around his ridge. Sheathing himself in my remaining wetness that coats his palm. My feral eyes drink him in, but my touch is restrained. Exploring my own body instead of his. Because even more than I want to touch Ro, I want to see him touch himself. To study the pressure and pace he uses, so when it's my turn, I'll also have the keys to his undoing.

He's slick with our shared arousal now, and when he crests

his tip again, I grab his wrist. Lifting his hand to my mouth to lick a wicked path from the center of his palm to the end of his middle finger. Bringing him into my mouth once more. Ro watches me, eyes wild, as I savor every drop of us.

I reach out to stroke Ro the way I now know he likes. Eager to feel him. Dying to taste him. But when his eyes roll back at my touch, he chokes out a curse and growls. "You told me not to come."

His forehead presses into mine as he palms my thighs to lift us both. Flipping us so I'm on my back on the couch beneath him. Ro holds himself taut above me as our ravenous mouths consume each other, and when he finally kicks all the way out of his jeans and boxer briefs, there's nothing left between us.

His mouth leaves mine to paint kisses down my neck, my breasts, my stomach. My entire body is singed red-hot by his tongue and left chilled by the air that rushes in at its absence. When he kisses my thighs and his face settles between them, I splay my knees to watch this beautiful man.

His brown eyes are midnight and warring when he looks up at me. Obvious in their craving, but patient still. Ro lifts my plump ass to angle me how he wants me, licking his thumb to part me wide. When it skims just the right spot, I buck and nod my approval. In a single thrashing heartbeat, his mouth is on me. Hot suction from his lips alternating with the firm pressure of his tongue. When he stumbles onto the right rhythm, my hips match it enthusiastically.

His mouth is open for me and I use it as I please. Hips swirling against him as he draws every drop of pleasure from my build. In my final moments, when everything is tight and hard, frozen solid and blazing hot, Ro brings one finger to join his lips and I careen over the edge. Eyes blurring, pussy throbbing, and inhibitions shattering as I reach for him. Fingernails at his fade, till I'm slack and breathless. Dripping where we're still connected as Ro takes a final taste.

His mouth is on mine before I even recover. Our tongues laving filthy kisses while I cling to Ro with a desperation I don't interrogate. Wrapping my legs around him, pinning his glistening body to mine. Fighting for purchase, like if I slip even a little further, I may fall for real this time. My fingers dig into his flesh like I'm trying to climb inside him, like maybe I could be safe there.

His chest vibrates with a deep laugh of understanding, and he whispers one word in my ear: "More?"

"More," I pant. "Everything."

He rolls a condom on and circles my entrance, using my wetness to ease his entry as he sinks into me slowly. Inch by precious inch. There's a newness as my body stretches to take in his ample size, but his fit is also familiar, somehow. Like this is where he belongs. Gem and setting. Lock and key.

Ro holds me, deep and unmoving, and my eyes water at the fullness. I claw at my hair, the couch, his back. Desperate for him to start thrusting, but just as decided that he should stay this still forever. When I can't take it any longer, I let my waist swivel in barely perceptible circles. Ro's hips round, too, and when he rocks even farther inside, my body tightens to hold him there. Waves of electric pleasure crest over me, and my breath hitches at feeling him this way. Finally close enough.

But when I open my eyes, Ro's watching me with an intention that matches his movements, and I moan at the way he holds my gaze, commanding me without saying a word. A smile lifts the corners of his mouth at how hungry I am for him, but this time, when Ro's teeth sink into the pillow-soft flesh of his lip, I see vigilance there. Caution. He's holding back. Keeping quiet, when right now, I want him free and loud.

"Say it," I beg. "Tell me."

His thrust threatens to tear me apart as his voice breaks free. "Shit." The word sounds like an admission. A curse wrapped in a plea. "You feel so good. So fucking good, Kai. I want you."

"You have me," I rasp. My body shaking and screaming that it's his.

And if he hadn't buried himself inside me again right then, I might've noticed how those words tasted on my tongue. Bitingly harsh in their truth. Brutally sharp in their honesty. But as our bodies move together, pleasure rips through me and my mind blurs. Mouth nipping and sucking at Ro's neck till all I taste is him. Salty and sweet.

Ro's rhythm mounts as he unabashedly chases his own release and I relinquish all control. He pulls out one last time before thrusting all the way back in. His body stutters as he splinters apart.

There are no screams or sounds between us anymore. What had been violent crests earlier are now slow rolling tremors. Silent intensity that our mouths devour whole as our breath, deep and ragged and shared, races past the rawness in my throat. Ro's still filling me and my body is still pulsing for him, with him. His subtle twitches inside me ushering my aftershocks.

And, I realize I'd been wrong just moments before: We hadn't been close enough then, because we hadn't been *this* close.

Until now.

# 24

MY MIND IS RACING. LITTERED WITH SCENES FROM MY afternoon with Ro, as I Uber home on autopilot. As soon as our sex fog lifted, I knew I'd made a mistake. Not the sex necessarily. Being with Ro had felt so right in the moment. It was everything that came after that left me racing for the door.

The way I'd nuzzled into the nook under his arm like I could belong there. The way my body fit so perfectly against his, like maybe I already did. The comfort I took, listening to the steady beating of his heart, how it had lulled me back to sleep. The peace I'd felt hours later when I woke in his arms.

But that peace had been short-lived.

I'd woken to the sound of his breathing—his chest rising and falling under my cheek—and I hadn't moved. I hadn't wanted to. Instead, I listened. I listened to his fucking *breathing.*

And then, lying there with him, our naked bodies tangled under a gauzy blanket, smiling at the sound of this man's lungs exchanging vital gases, I'd let my heavy eyelids close again. I'd let myself *want* to stay.

So I knew I had to go. Instead of memorizing one more beat of his heart or waiting for one more exhale. Instead of letting him wake to find me naked and happy and powerless against this thing I've seen play out too many times for too many women, I left.

Because I'm not ready to start the clock on when he'll pull back the mask to unleash whatever fresh hell men inevitably subject their partners to after days, months, years. I'm not ready to see the inevitable truth of him.

Right now, I still believe in Ro. So, just this once, I don't want to know how the scary story ends.

**4:48pm**

**Ro:** You left?

**Me:** Had to help Zola w/ some baby stuff. Didn't want to wake you!

My fingers hover over the keyboard after deleting my fifth attempt at a follow-up text. I'd meant for the lie to sound vague enough to be an easy out. To release him from having to say all the right things to prove he's *not like other guys.* Ro doesn't need to promise me the world. He doesn't need to promise anything at all.

But standing in my driveway, staring into the phone screen so hard my eyes actually water, I quietly allow myself to admit that maybe that's exactly what a not-so-small part of me is hoping he'll do. I don't need the three dots appearing and disappearing from our exchange to mean everything, but maybe they can mean something.

**Ro:** No worries.

Or maybe not.

# 25

OVER THE NEXT FEW DAYS, I REREAD THAT BRIEF CONversation with Ro more times than I'd ever admit. Didn't want to wake you! doesn't even read like an actual sentence anymore. The words have lost all meaning.

I wish I'd said anything else. I wish I hadn't left that day at all. I wish I'd never gone over there in the first place. But no matter how many times I return to our thread to fix things, it's Ro's No worries message that leaves me at a loss.

Right now, though, I've got more pressing matters to attend to anyway. Like my extremely pregnant sister, who's currently gnawing a pen cap and pacing the length of the living room, while she barks orders at me and Mom like a drill sergeant.

By their ninth month, most moms-to-be are deep in their nesting phase, but my big sister has always been the exception to every rule. Her focus is still on world domination.

Zola's emergency call for an *all-hands-on-deck* company launch has made this past week an incessant onslaught of round-the-clock planning. I'm indebted to her for minimizing the free brain space I have to dissect Ro's notable absence, but if *I'm* struggling to keep up this pace, I have to wonder how she's handling it all. Unfortunately, after one too many days of checking in with Zo about the dark circles under her eyes, Mom and I have been warned off the topic entirely.

At this point, though, they're distracting. As is the way Zola keeps wincing and clutching her lower back as she speaks. My eyes dart to catch Mom's, but she's already looking at me. I raise my eyebrows, silently prompting her to take the lead on this one.

Mom clears her throat. "Zola, honey. Do you want to sit down maybe?"

She's trying to sound as unconcerned as possible but fails miserably because she *is* concerned. We both are.

"I'm not the first woman in history to have a baby," Zola seethes, her head volleying from Mom to me, like she's caught us mid-coup. "If Serena can win a Grand Slam pregnant, pretty sure I can plan a party."

Zola doesn't sit as she refocuses on the steno pad that's become an extension of her hand.

"Another week's not a lot of time," she continues. "But we've already got a decent-size group committed."

She turns her laptop around, so it's facing Mom and me from its spot on the coffee table. My heart trips over itself at the sight of her website. The site Ro built for her.

"Ro added an events feature, so any time I enter the details of an in-person mixer here, it auto-blasts to subscribers and everyone following our socials."

Hearing Ro's name outside of my own head is dizzying. My personal boogeyman, stepping out from his shadowy dimension and into a world that's meant to be mine.

Zola clicks the link for next weekend's mixer, and my face flushes with pride. It's my first time having this reaction to Ro's designs in front of an audience, but it's far from my first time. Since leaving his place a week ago, I've become overly, intimately, *stalkerishly* familiar with every detail of Ro's online presence. When he added Zola's branding to his portfolio, let's just say I got my clicks in.

"Everything's tracked here," she continues. "He set it up to generate shareable graphics, so we can leverage each attendee's contacts to fill in gaps in the guest list like a pyramid."

This is what I mean—Zola's building a new business *and* a tiny human from scratch, and she's still way ahead of me somehow. I look to Mom again to see if she's tracking, but she's lost too.

I raise my hand a little as I speak: "Meaning . . ."

Zola pauses her pacing only long enough to huff dramatically before she explains her plan. "If everyone sends it to a friend who sends it to a friend, and so on, the guest list grows exponentially without us having to do any legwork. And we build out our own contact list in the process."

I scrunch my face. "Isn't that a little too close for comfort? Sounds borderline incestuous."

Zola gently pushes on her belly to shift the baby. Like that's a completely normal thing to do and not an alien scene from a sci-fi movie. But when relief washes over her face, I'm ready to volunteer my own two hands to prop the baby up until he makes his exit.

"I don't care if we end up with a beach full of second cousins," Zola says. "As long as I get some content."

"Got it."

It's all I have a chance to say before Zo continues.

"Can you get Liv and Ro to help out with that part?"

"With what part?" I ask, doing my best to ignore the way my heart rate spikes at the promise and threat of having to contact the man who, prior to this meeting, I'd only successfully gone two minutes without thinking about.

Zola's less than impressed by my inability to keep up. At this point in her pregnancy though, an eye roll is basically her resting face.

"You said Liv's dating a rock band—"

"Just one of them," I correct.

"And of course Ro should be there. Because I owe him, but also because he's hot and single and local."

All valid points.

"He acted funny when I invited him, but his circle and Liv's would probably account for the most photoworthy attendees. I need them both there."

I don't know what's more horrifying—the thought of Liv's world converging with my real life, or the prospect of Zola classifying Ro as *hot and single* at her dating mixer. I open my mouth to argue, but Zo silences me with a raised hand.

"Now if you'll excuse me," she says, chin lifted as she pridefully waddle-limps toward the stairs. "If I don't get this kid off my sciatic nerve, I'm gonna tear it out."

When she hears her words out loud, Zola turns back to face our horrified expressions. "Tear the nerve out," she clarifies. "Not the baby."

Her abrupt exit leaves us with a weighty silence and our marching orders. I text Liv first, who commits the entire band and their entourage without pausing to check their schedules. But I know she's good for it. Liv's as impossible to deny as Zola.

As much as I don't love the thought of Ro at a beach mixer with a bunch of bikinied women, I'm glad to have a script and a purpose for the first text I'm sending him in days. Once I do, though, I worry he might be offended that this is how I'm popping back up after the way we left things. I wouldn't blame him.

But when my phone pings in my hand, a smile finally breaks free as I read the text that's just so impossibly *Ro.*

**Ro:** Now why am I in it?

# 26

RO AND I HAVE BEEN TEXTING SEMI-REGULARLY AGAIN since he agreed to come to Zola's launch with a plus one, but by the night of the bonfire, we're still a million miles from where we'd been. Our conversations used to flow, languid and easy. Now they're clunky. Staccato. We trip into each other, stumbling and fumbling for the proper cadence until the conversation fizzles. Again, and again, and again. But if I'm being honest, it's more than just his easy conversation that I miss.

In the quiet stillness of my room each night, my thoughts drift back to the pillowy touch of Ro's lips on mine, the warm length of his tongue, claiming a path that could only ever be his to follow. His kisses lapping up my screams, until he owned every sound his body drew from mine. I feel the weight of him, pinning me down as we moved together. I see my pink fingernails digging into the dark flesh at his back. And every night when I think of him, my own hand wanders the curves of my body when what it really wants is to reach out for his.

*But mostly it's the conversation.* I lie to myself, as I spend an inordinately long time setting the lone curl Ro loves to tug.

"Oh, you look pretty!" Mom says.

The sound of her voice is an ice bath on my daydreams. I whip around to face her like a twelve-year-old boy hiding porn behind his back.

"Mom," I whine, sounding equally prepubescent. "Can you knock?"

"Why? You got a guy up here?" She pretends to look around before laughing at her own joke and joining me at the mirror.

I study her reflection. The signs are all there—fresh cut, fresh color, fresh fit. Her eyes are clearer, and her face is brighter than it's been in months. Just once, though, I wish the light I saw shining was her own.

She picks her hair out with her fingers, as she speaks. "Zola ran up to the beach to supervise the bar staff. I told her we'd be two minutes behind. I'll be glad when this thing is over. She's pushing too hard. It's not good for the baby."

"It's not good for *her.*"

Mom nods her agreement. "I was the same way before I had Zo."

"Manic?"

Mom laughs, but she doesn't deny it. "And terrified. When you get this close to becoming a mom, it feels like there's a clock ticking over your head. Like everything is either now or never. Nobody warns you about that part." She sucks her teeth. "Nobody warns you about a lot of it, but I remember that one being really scary. You're counting down to baby, but you're also counting down to a free fall into the unknown. To losing yourself without knowing if it'll be weeks or months or ever before you get you back."

"How long did it take you to get back to yourself?" I ask, certain Zola can beat it.

But Mom's smile is small. "I'll let you know when I do."

I finish tying up the sides of my crochet cover-up dress, not wanting to leave Zola waiting any longer. "We should go. You know how Zo is. She's probably already unloading everything on her own."

Mom's side-eye is vicious. "Like you're any better. Both of you always try to do everything on your own." She points to the laptop, closed on the desk behind us. "Summer's almost over and I still don't know what's going on with you over there. But I know you won't let me help."

"Is this you trying to kick me out?" I ask, half joking and fully deflecting.

Mom laughs. "I'd keep you here forever if I could. I just worry about my girls." Then she sits on the bed. "And I know you worry about me too," she continues. "But I wouldn't want that to be the reason you stay if you'd rather leave. Lately, I've been wondering if I might've been the reason you came back in the first place."

"Did you think I was gonna stay in Kansas? Permanently?"

"I wouldn't have blamed you." The smile Mom wears is so fake, it might as well be painted on. "There are a lot of things I wish I would've done differently when you girls were young. So, once you got out . . ."

She shrugs like, *you know,* but I don't. So I wait for her to tell me.

"You used to be your dad's shadow. Whenever I needed to find you, I'd just look for him. He'd be on the phone, or working in the yard, watching a game—and you'd be right there."

Mom hasn't talked about Dad this casually in years. Even after everything, there's still a softness for him in her voice.

"I used to feel so proud that I'd found that for you girls. Someone worth idolizing. But then he left."

I expect her tone to sharpen when she says it, but it doesn't.

"And then you left. And it made sense to me—the two of you back together."

"Mom," I say, feeling guilty though she hasn't once asked me to. "We weren't together. It wasn't like that."

"It would've been okay if it was. He's your dad. You're allowed to want him. To need him."

I hadn't realized just how long it'd been since Mom and I sat together like this. Her, the adult, and me, finally allowed to be the thing I was meant to be all along—the child.

"I haven't applied for any jobs," I say, setting the words free before I can think better of it.

Mom nods but doesn't appear shocked by the subject change or the admission.

"Not one. I've tried. But whenever I think about walking into a classroom, and doing it again the next day, and the next day, forever . . ." Even explaining the thought brings a wave of dread, same as it always does. "It just feels like someone else's life."

"Maybe when you chose it, that'd been part of the appeal."

"What, Dad? You think I wanted his life? Because I gotta tell ya, it leaves something to be desired."

Mom smiles at my gentle ribbing. "Fine then, not his life, but his approval maybe. His respect, his love. Any of it would've made sense. And it makes just as much sense to want something different now. Something that's yours."

Mom pats the mattress beside her, and I join her. "Kai, I see the ways you're stuck right now. And I get it, I've been there. Too many times to count. But you've gotta believe you're exactly where you're supposed to be."

"Completely lost?"

"Sure," she says easily. "Why not? I'm fifty-two and just now figuring out what I wanna be when I grow up. And you know what it is? Happy. That's it, that's all I want. And it's all I want for my girls too." She wraps me into her arms as she says it, and

I let her. "This life is long, baby. You're gonna fall backward and start over more times than you ever imagined. And the only thing that changes each time is how quickly you learn to give yourself the grace to do it. It's the only thing we get a say in. Might as well start practicing that part now."

# 27

BY THE TIME THE SUN DROPS INTO LONG ISLAND SOUND, Zola's flitting across the beach, converting contacts to clients. I, on the other hand, am still nursing my drink from the makeshift bar. Someone's got to make use of these rented boho beach cushions Zola maxed her credit cards out on—and Zo has no plans of getting off her feet and onto one. She's made that much clear. Firmly. A few times.

I'm scanning the beach, *just taking in the view, like everyone else.* But when Liv spears me with the base of a fallen tiki torch, I know I'm caught.

"Why don't you just text him?"

"Who?" I ask, pretending not to be startled by her presence.

When I last saw Liv, she was mid-water fight with her motley crew at the shoreline. I was so busy *not* watching the entrance, I hadn't noticed she'd made her way inland.

"Whoever's got you glaring holes through Zola's welcome signs," she says, dropping onto the cushion beside me.

Liv adjusts the cutout of her one-piece so there's more Liv peeking *out* from the *cut.* Against her skin, kissed golden by the sun, and her hair creeping closer to platinum as we reach the height of the season, Liv's green eyes glow neon. "You think once he gets here, we can start having fun?"

"I am having fun," I insist.

But her eyes flashing *LIAR* leave me more exposed than the slinky string bikini under this cover-up.

"Fine," I say, relenting. "But I'm only checking for him because he doesn't know anybody here. I'm being a good hostess per Zola's threateningly specific orders."

"While I'd love to hear more about your hosting prowess at a party you've yet to speak to anyone at," Liv says, rising from our sandy love seat, "seems like our guest of honor is making his way over."

My head whips around just in time to catch Ro's entrance. His tongue wets his lips when he sees me, and despite the cool ocean breeze, my skin sizzles. Ro's white beach shirt catches the wind as he elbows the guy at his right, exposing the tan shorts slung low across his hips. They both do that little head nod in my direction.

"Quick," I say to Liv. "Gimme the tiki so I don't look like an outcast at my own party."

"Not a chance," she says, yanking the torch out of reach. "But I promise not to tell him you've been stalking the—"

"Hey!" I say, cutting Liv off as Ro crosses the torched perimeter. "You found us."

"Yeah," he says, reaching around my waist for a hug that's over as soon as it starts. "This place is hard to miss."

He looks back toward the borrowed beach house where a steady stream of waitstaff exit, hoisting themed hors d'oeuvres overhead.

"If this is Zola's idea of a start-up launch, I need to pick her brain more than I have."

"She roped our mom into sponsoring a good chunk of it," I

tell him. "And convinced Liv's dad to let her use his beach house."

"Well, my dad loves you guys," Liv says, turning to Ro for the rest. "And if you've ever met Zola, you wouldn't have expected anything less. I'm Liv by the way." She extends a hand to shake Ro's. "I didn't even realize we were waiting on anyone else to join us."

She raises an eyebrow at me to say, *I couldn't help myself,* and I show her the full whites of my eyes, so she knows better than to play with me right now.

Oblivious to our silent battle, Ro shakes Liv's hand. "Ro," he says, smiling. "And yes, I've met Zola, so I'm not surprised. But I am impressed." Ro puts a hand on his friend's shoulders, bringing him closer to our little group until his arm and mine are touching. "This is my boy Matt. I promised him an open bar and at least one phone number tonight in exchange for padding the guest list."

We all laugh, but my smile falls a bit when I see the way Matt's watching me.

"I think we can make good on both of those," I say, my eyes shifting from Matt back to Ro. I tilt my plastic cup toward the bar. "Should we start with the easy one?"

Liv shakes the ice in her mostly empty cup. "To the bar?"

Ro holds his arm out for Liv to lead the way. "To the bar."

With the fire raging in the background, Liv and I sit huddled under a blanket, while Ro and Matt stand, staring off at the ocean. Liv empties her drink first and heads off to get another round.

She's only gone a few feet before Ro starts moving in her direction. "I'll see if she needs hands on the way back."

I watch Ro jog after her till Matt's voice calls for my attention. "I was wondering how long that'd take."

"How long what would take?" I ask, wrapping the blanket tighter to block out the slight chill wafting in off the water.

"Ro figuring out how to give us a minute alone," he says, before draining his cup.

The idea of Ro strategizing his exit makes me want to vomit all over a tiki.

"Oh, no," I say, careful to keep the bite from my tone. "I think he's just being nice."

I do a quick once-over of the beach, hoping, for the first time, that Travis will appear to join us. Or join Liv, rather, forcing Ro to make his return. But the darkened beach is so crowded now that it's impossible to make out anyone who's not immediately beside a torch or lit by the bistro lights overhead. Except Zola. I've been watching her little clipboard flashlight buzzing around all night.

Someday when *Forbes* calls me for a quote about the early days of XO by Zo, I'll think back on how my sister single-handedly saw this night through from conception to execution. And how she did it all with pregnancy-induced sciatica.

I smile at the thought until Zola's tiny light disappears into another crowd of prospective clients. I'm about to suggest Matt and I relocate to the bar, too, when he joins me on my cushion.

"No, I didn't mean it like that," he says, without explaining how he *did* mean it. "Man, it's such a nice night. A little chilly though." He eyes the side of the blanket Liv left abandoned. "You mind if I steal some?"

"Go for it," I tell him. "This thing's huge."

At least when I was under here with Liv it had seemed huge. With Matt beside me, it's like trying to share a hand towel with a giant. A handsome giant, with natural, lived-in balayage, but a giant nonetheless.

Objectively speaking, Matt's working that L.A., white boy, skater vibe, but I'd still very much like him to get his Avril Lavigne ass out of my bubble. Respectfully. The last thing I need tonight is another random guy spitting mediocre game my way. And even on the off chance his game is superb, I'm still too focused on reading Ro's lips from across the beach to notice.

"Ro thought it would be good for us to get to know each other." He says it casually, like that sentence isn't a punch to the gut.

"Oh?"

I'm afraid if I say anything more, disappointment would literally drip from my words onto the sand.

"Yeah," Matt says, smiling now. "Sounds like we have a lot in common."

The plot twist I hadn't seen coming: *Ro brought me a date.*

I tell myself the bile rising in my throat is just annoyance at yet another person meddling in my life, but when acid hits the back of my tongue, I know it's more than that.

"What the fuck is taking so long with the drinks?" I say, yanking off the blanket that's suddenly suffocating me.

Matt's eyes widen briefly at my abruptness, but he's quick on the recovery.

"This place is packed," he says, stating the obvious. "Bar's gotta be slammed."

"Yes, I know how bars work," I say, relieved to finally see Travis and Evan a couple hundred yards out.

Even if Evan hasn't spoken two words to me all night, and Travis hasn't stopped complaining about the lack of vegan options among all the free food, right now, I'd still prefer their company to Matt's.

Travis yells a single word I can't make out, which Liv responds to immediately. She leans into Ro, smiling, before running to Travis and jumping into his arms. I watch to see if Ro has any reaction to their dramatic embrace, but he just laughs and loads the four drinks into his hands. He turns to me, still smiling, but his brows crease when he sees my face. I must not wear betrayal well.

I'm standing now, so when Matt *uhhh's* to my insult about the bar, it doesn't help that I'm also *physically* looking down on him.

He stands to his full height. "So, like I was saying, Ro thought we should talk."

This time, though, before I can tell him that *yes, Matt, I got that!,* he continues.

"I was over at Winston Prep for a couple years after graduation, but ended up leaving pretty quick. I loved the kids, but teaching wasn't really for me. Ro said you might be in a similar spot?"

Ro's still stalking toward us, brows furrowed in question, but I finally break eye contact with him to look back toward Matt.

"Wait, what?" I start, tripping over myself to catch up. "You came to give me career advice? I thought you were trying to hook up."

"Wait, what?" Matt echoes.

Just as Ro reaches us.

His eyes ping-pong between us. Matt's do the same with me and Ro, and mine with Ro and Matt. So now we're all just looking at one another, waiting for someone to make sense of something.

Finally, Ro says, "I see you two are getting along," and he holds up the cocktails he apparently had to ferment at the bar himself. "Drinks?"

Even with legs nearly twice as long as mine, Ro struggles to keep up as an inexplicable rage fuels my march down the beach.

"Hold up," he calls from just behind me. "I don't get why you're mad. What'd I do?"

He jogs in front of me to block my path. His face is awash with concern and something bordering on panic. If his body hadn't just physically stopped me in my tracks, that look might've done it.

Ro's hands are still holding my arms in place, and without registering it, I've let myself just barely lean into his touch. I'm quick to right my posture before attempting an explanation I don't have yet.

"Well, first you basically go ghost—"

"You think *I* ghosted *you*?"

But I don't slow down to address his incredibly sound argument. "And then you bring that *guy* to try to—I don't even know what. Coach me? Fix me?"

"Fix you?" Ro echoes, swiping his hands across the air like he's attempting a hard reset. "I thought talking to Matt might *help* you."

He hadn't meant for his words to hurt, but they leave me hollowed. My heart in free fall with nothing left to catch it. He thought Matt could *help* me. Because even Ro knows something's wrong. That no one should be this stuck for this long.

"And that's you, right?" I need to remove myself from this conversation and this beach. "Always there to help."

His nod is sharp as he digests my words. I pray he somehow also hears the ones I leave unspoken: *I wanted you to see me differently. Better.*

But Ro releases his hold on my arms. I miss his touch instantly.

"My bad. I forgot, you don't do *help.* You don't need anything or anyone."

Hurt rushes from my body like the ocean retreating from the sand. Resignation taking its place.

He says my name on a sigh. "Kai, I've never thought you needed fixing, but damn. You could stand to change the approach up a little. For everyone's sake."

"What does that mean?"

"It means I've been watching you hide from everything real in your life for months. Even with me. I've been trying like hell just to know you. And you won't let me."

"You *do* know me," I say, throwing my hands up. "This is me—a fucking mess. Hi, it's nice to meet you."

Ro surrenders and clears my path. "Look, I shouldn't have brought Matt without talking to you first. That's on me. I just thought it'd be easier for you to be real with someone who didn't have any skin in the game."

My laugh is small and cold, but the sound is quickly lost to the waves gently crashing at our feet. When I move down the beach this time, Ro falls into step beside me.

"It's fine," I say, praying the waves swallow that lie up too.

None of this is Ro's fault. Not really. *He just wanted to help.*

I toe the wet sand, drawing shapes and erasing them. Ro watches me work. So still and silent, I'm not even sure he's breathing until I steal a glance. He knows a stiff breeze or one misplaced word could end our flimsy truce. So, like always, he lets me go first.

"Maybe I should just start teaching," I say, surprising us both. And I turn to face him dead-on when I finish. "I have the degree, it makes sense, and it would save everyone around me from having to help me fix my life."

The moon is bright enough tonight that I see a million emotions play out on Ro's face, before he settles on annoyance.

"No," he says, and the single word is a declaration. "That's not what this was."

The steady crashing of waves fills the silence between us, but all I hear is Ro. "I'm not trying to fix you. Look at you," he says, grabbing my face in both hands. "Right now, even when you think you're a mess, you're fucking perfect."

I'm relieved when he releases his hold on me, because I will never be prepared to face a compliment that direct.

"I don't care what you do or don't do, but telling people what you want shouldn't be this fucking hard."

And that tone, I'm more comfortable with.

"If you'd just say it," he continues. "You might be surprised. Not everyone's gonna let you down. You don't have to expect the worst of people, just so you can act like you're not fucking crushed when they prove you right. I think trying *not* to have expectations is actually what's fucking killing you." He shrugs, and I hold my breath to fortify myself against the way he sees me. "Because, when it comes down to it Kai, you care *more* than most people. You're just better at hiding it than the rest of us."

The ocean takes pity on me, sending waves up the beach to kiss my toes, before they retreat back to the depths. Ro settles into stillness beside me, standing so close his knuckles graze my arm. But with so much between us now, he might as well be a world away.

And when I step back, arms wrapped around myself protectively, Ro steps away too. Still following my lead, like always. But for the first time, I wish he wouldn't.

Whatever emotions haunted Ro and me on the walk back evaporate into nothing when we see the commotion on Zola's roped-off section of beach. I run ahead, pushing through the crowd to see what's happening.

Zola's at the center of the circle, and she's finally sitting—

which would be great, if she wasn't also clutching her belly and grimacing in pain.

When I run to reach her, a little sand sprays onto her lap, and I'm momentarily comforted that she's still capable of rolling her eyes at me.

"Jesus," she says, dramatically spitting out the one or two grains that make it into her mouth.

But I don't know whether to laugh or cry when she clasps my hand in hers, her eyes locked onto mine with a fear I've never seen.

"What happened?" I ask, panic, a vise at my chest.

She shakes her head, tears springing to her eyes as she whispers, so only I can hear, "Something's wrong."

Before I can ask anything more, headlights illuminate the beach and Mom's horn blares.

Ro's at my side in an instant, draping Zola's arm over his broad shoulders. He maneuvers her easily, rendering me useless. Which is fine, because mentally, I'm still playing catch-up. *Zola's hurt. She's scared. Something's happening with the baby.*

Ro looks directly into Zola's eyes, and I'm relieved to know what she'll find there—it's the same thing I've come to know over the last couple months—safety.

"I've got you," he says, his voice steady and sure. "Lean on me."

Ro all but carries Zola the short distance from the beach to Mom's awaiting car, and I follow. He releases Zo gently into the passenger seat and reaches over to buckle her in.

I pause for half a beat when he closes her door, unsure what to say about how we left things or how to thank him for his help.

He opens my door now, too, waking me from my stupor when he says, "Later. Go."

It's the final word I needed.

And when Zola groans in discomfort, I'm back and focused, not wasting another fraction of another second before I shut the door behind me.

Nothing else exists outside of this car right now. Nothing else matters.

# 28

"IF YOU DON'T FIND THAT FUCKING CLIPBOARD, I SWEAR TO god."

Welp. Zola's feeling better.

They're keeping her at the hospital overnight as a precaution, but I think that's mostly because when they said the words *bed rest,* Zola literally laughed. The doctor has since made her promise that for the next few weeks, she won't be on her feet for more than thirty minutes a day. She was somewhat placated by the doctor's suggestion that Zo get a little bell to ring when she needs our help. Mom and I were less amused.

"I mean it," Zola continues, barking orders like she's in a three-piece suit, not an open-back hospital gown and grippy socks. "I need to sign at least three clients from that party just to break even. I'm sitting in the red right now and I'm almost out of time."

"I already texted Ro," I remind her. "I'm sure he has it."

Even connected to a bag of fluids, Zola doesn't miss an opportunity. "You texted Ro?" she asks, eyebrows raised and mouth downturned with suspicion. "Not Liv?"

I smile because it's further proof she's feeling better.

"I like him for you," Mom says, emerging from the attached bathroom at exactly the wrong moment.

"You saw us together for like two seconds," I say, ignoring the pang I feel at the thought of him.

"I like him too," Zola says, as if I haven't spoken a word. "He seems like a really good guy."

"*A really good guy,*" I repeat, testing the words in my mouth. "I think I read about those once."

Mom steals a cafeteria french fry from Zola's discarded tray at her bedside. "You don't think he's a good guy?"

"I mean, sure," I say, collapsing onto the most uncomfortable little couch in the world. If Zola asks me to stay the night, we're drawing straws for the bed. "So far. They all seem good at first. But it's death, taxes, and guys going Hyde. Or Jekyll. Whichever the bad one was."

Neither Mom or Zola says a word, so I continue with a shrug. "The things in life you can count on."

Now Zola's the one who looks unamused. "Is this seriously how your brain works or are you just trying to get a reaction out of us?"

"If I wanted a reaction, I'd tell you guys I had sex with Ro two weeks ago."

"WHAT?" they both shout in unison.

"See?"

"Talk about burying the lead," Zola says, smiling. "Though professionally speaking, I can't condone it. As your sister, though . . ."

Zola pops her shoulders in approval.

Mom holds her hands out to reclaim the floor. "Okay, we *will* be revisiting that, but let's try to stay focused for a minute. Kai, you can't really be ready to write off every guy because there's a possibility they'll let you down at some point in the future."

She joins me on the couch and I laugh when she looks down at the lumpy cushion like it's stabbed her.

She ignores me. "Relationships aren't that simple. Life's never that simple. It's messy and awful and it gets really ugly sometimes—"

Zola's face twists into a knot. "What side of this are you arguing?"

"*And,*" Mom says, to hush me and Zola. "It's impossible to protect yourself from it. Honey, you're gonna make yourself miserable trying."

"Seriously," Zola deadpans. "Mom. What are you doing?"

"There's no point in lying to you girls. You're gonna get hurt."

"Shocker," I say out the side of my mouth.

Mom rolls her eyes. "But if your only focus is how or when something will end, or all the things that might go wrong, you're gonna miss out on the good stuff. And there's so much *good* stuff." She enunciates the word so I can't miss it. "Even when things end in that bone-deep hurt that makes you so sick to your stomach, you can't stand up straight—"

I don't have to ask what comes to mind for her when she says it. It was only ever really my dad.

"Even *that's* temporary. There will always come a time when you stand back up and walk again. And when you do, what you take with you is everything else. All the things you learned. Stupid inside jokes that still make you smile. The long nights with sick babies, where neither of you wanted to be anywhere else in the world." Her voice cracks on the word. "Him holding you girls in that goddamn recliner."

I rest my hand on Mom's. She turns hers over in mine. And squeezes.

"That's not the consolation prize," she whispers. "That's all of it. That's life."

The room is a mess of unshed tears, and when Mom clears her throat, I'm prepared for her next life lesson to send them spilling over.

"So . . ." she begins. "You fucked Ro?"

Zola and I turn to each other and scream. The tension in the room splintering to give way to laughter, as Zo and I shout, "LANGUAGE!"

And it's that same laughter that brings a new wash of tears, because my little family is as whole right now as it's ever been.

I survive the Ro interrogation that follows, and once she's convinced she's bled me dry of intel, Mom leaves to make a call.

"So, what are you gonna do?" Zo asks. Her eyelids are heavy after our eventful day.

"Who knows," I say, standing to adjust the pillow she's struggling to reposition. "Maybe nothing. Don't even worry about Ro right now. You need to rest."

"It's my job to worry about it," she says, a lazy smile at her lips. "We signed a contract, remember?"

I'd been hoping that somewhere between the bonfire and the baby, Zola would've been the one to forget, but I don't tell her that. "You want me to stay while you sleep?"

"No," she says, through a yawn. "Mom said she would."

I'm collecting my things to leave, when I see the awaiting messages from Ro. Zola will want to know if he's found the clipboard, but I think better of checking now. XO by Zo can wait a day.

And there's one thing I can't wait to ask any longer. I nod toward the open door leading to the hallway. "Who do you think Mom's out there calling?"

Zola shrugs. "Your guess is as good as mine. My services are for paying customers only."

"You say that now," I sing.

"I mean it. This kid's coming any day now. I won't have time for anyone else's drama unless they're cutting me a check."

I'm about to argue the likelihood of that, but Zo cuts me off.

"If Mom can learn how to date without making it our problem, I'm happy to let her."

Even if I don't believe either of them are capable of that kind of change, I appreciate the sentiment—and for tonight, that'll have to be good enough. Even with Mom's sweater over my beach getup, I haven't stopped shivering since we got here. I need clothes and Zo needs sleep.

I lean down to hug my sister, but Zola's tired eyes are still working on something. She's still got something on her mind.

"Listen," she starts. "I think we can all agree I got dumped pretty fucking hard. But if what happened to me is the big, bad thing you're so afraid of, I just want you to know, I'm okay. And even if I'd like to think I could've learned these same lessons a little more gently, in some ways, I'm better for what happened to me." She rubs her belly as she finishes. "You can only really walk things back so far anyway. I'd never wish my relationship with Jason away. It got me to this moment with this little boy."

I hate myself for even caring enough to ask this next question, but I do. "You think Dad would say the same thing? About not wishing us all away."

Zola smiles in a way that reminds me so much of how Mom used to look at me. Like if she couldn't stop my hurt, at least she'd hold my hand through it.

"What I think," Zola says, finally, "is that trying to forget us is the only way Dad could stand being gone. He loved us, Kaia. I remember. Love doesn't just go away."

I place a hand on her belly and try to force a smile too. Then I feel my nephew moving below my palm, and my smile comes a little easier.

**8:59pm**

**Me:** She was just dehydrated. They put her on bedrest for a few weeks but other than that she's ok.

**Ro:** Bedrest? Zola?

**Me:** Ha, Mom and I are gonna have to take shifts holding her down.

**Me:** Thanks again for your help.

**Ro:** All I did was grab a clipboard. Liv handled everything else.

I near the hospital exit, watching Ro's typing bubbles appear and disappear. As much as I want him to clear the air about what happened between us on the beach tonight, I also kind of don't. I'm too tired for a reckoning.

"Kaia?"

At the sound of my name, I turn to see a face I'd expected to leave buried in the pages of my old yearbooks. *#28*. The boy I'd once branded my cheek for. Asher *freaking* Hall.

His laugh sounds the same as I remember. It takes me back to a time when life was so much less complicated.

"Oh my god," I say, smiling genuinely, despite the night's events. "What are you doing here?"

He pulls me into a hug, and it feels good to let somebody else hold me up for a minute.

"I work here," he says, into my hair. "What are *you* doing here? Everything good with Zola?"

I pull back. "How'd you know I was here for Zola?"

"We ran into each other here a couple months back." Asher looks like he's been caught doing something he shouldn't as he says, "Actually, she was supposed to be setting me up. With you."

"Oh" is all I say.

But I'm not disappointed exactly. Which may have something to do with how adorably uncomfortable he looks right now. Or it might be that he's Asher *freaking* Hall, standing in front of me all these years later, with a stethoscope at his neck, asking about a date.

"My schedule's been impossible this month," Ash continues. "I thought Zola was gonna come escort me outta the OR when I had to cancel a couple weeks back."

We both laugh, because, well, *Zola*.

"I can't believe you were the date."

"Were? Does that mean I shouldn't ask if you're free now?" He checks his phone. "I could sneak out for coffee or dinner, or—I don't know. You got any errands to run?"

I get lost in his golden eyes for a beat too long, and I'm back in the student section on those hard metal bleachers.

"I can't believe you're here," I say, finally.

He doesn't try to hide his smile. "I was just thinking the same thing about you. You look—"

"A mess," I say, suddenly remembering my current state of *mid-beach-bonfire-emergency* dress.

"Really good," Asher corrects.

And the way he says it, I almost believe him.

"So," he continues, "you wanna catch up over dinner?"

Even though I'm half dressed and bone-tired, when Asher asks, I say yes. Because, while I may not be up for a reckoning, a girl's gotta eat.

I sent Zo a text about the universe's assist when I stopped to do a quick change at the house. I'm halfway back to Asher when she finally responds.

**Zola:** Damnit! I wanted to do the reveal.
**Zola:** He looks exactly the same right?

I've only got a few seconds left at this red light to hammer out my response. I waste one or two biting the inside of my cheek at the thought of Asher's bright eyes and warm brown skin, before typing:

**Me:** Same old Ash.

The pause before Zola's next text is longer than I would've expected for someone getting everything they want.

**Zola:** You sure you wanna do this?
**Me:** WHAT?! Isn't this what you've been plotting all along? saving Ash for last. Your big finish.
**Zola:** That was before you told us about Ro.

Earlier, rushed by the night's relentlessness, I'd skipped right past Ro's missed texts. But with Zola's reminder I open them now, and my heart sinks at his words on my screen.

**Ro:** You want this stuff tonight?

**Ro:** I can swing by before I go see my parents. Drop everything off.

**Ro:** Have you guys eaten?

**Ro:** ??

Shit.

# 29

NOTHING SCREAMS *TODAY WAS FUCKED* LIKE A MASSIVE chicken parm, so when Ash asked for my vote back at the hospital, the site of my first Zola date was the restaurant that came to mind. It's not like I made any particularly fond memories at Antonio's the first time around that demanded preserving. But as I cross the parking lot, I realize that that's not entirely true.

Ro's everywhere out here. His phantom truck might as well be parked at the curb, waiting for my mezcal-laden ass to teeter out in need of a getaway driver. He didn't have to volunteer for the role, but he did. Because he's Ro.

*Shit,* I think, for the second time since leaving him on read. *This is bad.*

And suddenly my little black romper that had felt simple and effortless is too short and too tight and too everything.

*Any shot that's a good enough excuse to cancel on Ash?*

No. I'm being stupid. I'm not doing anything wrong. Ro and I aren't together. With the exception of tonight, we'd barely even spoken these past couple weeks. And he knows I agreed to these dates.

It's all completely true.

It also does absolutely nothing to assuage the solid brick of guilt lodged firmly in my gut as I walk inside.

"So," Ash says as we wait for a table, "this place as good as the old Pizza Shoppe?"

"Oh my god," I say, relieved that my smile makes it momentarily impossible to continue gnawing the inside of my lip raw. "I forgot about the Pizza Shoppe! That weird mayonnaise they called salad dressing."

Ash's grimace is entirely appropriate when he says, "The pink stuff."

"The pink stuff! God, that place was amazing."

I'd imagine there are likely entire textbooks devoted to the physiological effects of ingesting mayo-slathered pepperoni "salads" biweekly for four years, but Ash's face is still shifting to consider it.

Finally, he lands on a smile and says, "I'd still fuck it up."

We're both laughing when the hostess returns, beaming at the happy couple, before leading us through the familiar candlelit dining room. There's still a *Ro* echo from the last time I was here, but when the hostess stops short at our table, I step back to avoid a collision and my shoulder sinks briefly into Asher's chest. My skin flushes at the contact, and the echo gets a little bit fainter.

"What are you smiling about over there?" Ash asks, unfolding his napkin. I follow suit.

"I just did not see this coming," I admit. "Being out with you like this."

"Why not?"

I wasn't prepared to have to defend my statement. I'd assumed it was a given, but apparently, I'd assumed wrong.

"You were like Mr. High School, and back then, I was still slurping spit through my palate separator."

Asher winces, but he doesn't deny the graphic picture I've painted.

"Do you still talk to anybody from back then? Michelle?" I'm not sure why I ask it or if I even care to know the answer, but once it's out there, I shovel an entire baguette into my mouth so I can't make it worse.

"That was a million years ago," he says, sidestepping the question.

"Eight, for you," I correct from behind a fist to minimize the breadcrumb spray.

"Well, it feels like a million. We were kids."

"So that's a no?"

Ash laughs and shakes his head. "No, I haven't talked to her. And before you ask about any other ancient history, since Zola set this up," he says, referring to the two of us, "I haven't talked to anyone else either. I've just been waiting for you. Like always."

"Why do guys do that?" I ask, genuinely curious. "You hardly knew I existed and that's okay. It was a million years ago, right?"

"Well, I always thought you were cute."

"Asher," I warn. "Don't make me box up a perfectly good chicken parm."

His fork clinks the plate when he drops it in mock offense. "Fine, I was too dumb to be checking for you back then, but I am now." He retrieves his fork but doesn't bring his bite of linguine to his lips until after he says, "You're beautiful."

I sip my wine to hide the heat creeping up my face, but watch him with the same quiet fascination I did when we were kids. It really doesn't seem fair that some people are genetically blessed to be hot all their lives, while the rest of us had to wait for modern technology and karma to take pity on us.

Eventually, the screaming thirteen-year-old girl inside my head quiets, and I lean back in my chair. "I can't figure out if it feels like it's been forever or—"

"Like no time has passed at all?"

"Yes! What is that?"

"I was thinking the same thing a few minutes ago," he agrees. "But then I remembered we reconnected because Zola's having a kid and I feel my age again."

"Right? Who decided any of us are grown enough to raise a whole human person?" I'm laughing, but I know in my bones she's ready.

"Is she still with the same guy she was dating when I left? Jason something?"

"Nope" is all I offer. "But she's got this."

"What about your parents? How are they doing?"

"My mom's good. I think she enjoys embarrassing me with these dates almost as much as Zola."

"I can't be mad at that. Saved me from having to work up the nerve to ask you out myself."

On the outside I'm rolling my eyes like *shut up,* but inside, the screaming teen is back.

"And your dad? How's he feel about all this?"

"You'd have to find him to ask," I say without thinking. I'm as surprised as Ash looks by the words tumbling out of my mouth, but I'm even more surprised that I don't immediately want to shove them back in. They're true.

"Your parents split up?"

"They did," I confirm. And though my admission doesn't feel as heavy as usual, tonight I'm also fine to leave it at that.

"So, what about you," I say, buoyed by how relaxed I feel. "Last year of med school, right?"

•

Dinner with Ash is like pulling an old dress out from the back of the closet. It's fun to try on and you're kind of proud it still fits, as if that's some great accomplishment. But even if it looks good—and it does, it looks good as hell—I'd rather be in sweats.

Which is the next step on the night's itinerary as Asher and I say our goodbyes outside.

"I don't want to seem too eager or anything," he says, shifting his weight. "But this was fun."

"It was," I say easily. "I'm really glad we did it."

He moves to join me, and I notice how nice it is not to have to crane my neck quite as much to meet Asher's eyes the way I do with Ro. I also notice that this is far from the first time tonight I've compared these two men who have little in common outside of me.

"So, how'd I do? You gonna give me another shot sometime?"

He really does look the same. Like he's been waiting for me in a time capsule buried under the football field. Along with my wire retainer and training bra.

Ash's tongue darts out to wet his lips, and a not-so-small part of me is tempted to satisfy an old curiosity about kissing the quarterback, but I can name a million reasons the hug I actually give him makes so much more sense.

I'm still wrapped in his arms, when Ash repeats his unanswered question. "You're gonna give me another shot sometime. Right?"

When I tilt my face up to respond, we're closer than I'd expected. The biggest, goofiest smile spreads across Ash's face at our nearness.

I hope he doesn't notice when my own smile falters, just a little, as I dodge the question with a gentle, "I'll text you later."

For all the reasons I don't kiss Asher Hall, his final smile is the reason I know we won't, in fact, be doing this again sometime.

Because no matter how perfect or pearly or kind, his smile doesn't have Ro's dimple.

# 30

I WATCH ASHER WALK THE ENTIRE DISTANCE TO HIS CAR, AND when he turns to see me in the same spot he left me, I'm glad I stayed. He waves across the lot, and I commit the scene to memory for a new time capsule. Filed away for safekeeping. But now, I file it away with everything *Ro.* Because even in Ro's absence, he's been with me all night.

The memory of his phantom truck, the exact details of his smile, the tone of his voice when—*wait.*

His voice.

"Kaia?" he says again, more forcefully this time.

This isn't phantom. When I turn to follow the sound, he's there. Here. In the flesh.

And he is . . . snarling.

"Hey," I say, and even the single syllable feels like a lie. "I thought you were with your parents."

I scan the parking lot in search of them, and as an excuse to break contact with the daggers shooting from Ro's narrowed eyes.

I'm still looking anywhere but at him, when he laughs. At least that's what I'm choosing to call it, though it's never sounded this sharp before.

"Oh, nice," he says. "So, you *did* get my texts."

"Shit," I say, realizing I've caught myself up. "I'm sorry. I've just been—"

He doesn't give me a chance to finish the thought, which is fine, since I don't know what I would've said.

"Busy," he says, nodding toward the empty spot where Asher's car was moments ago. "Yeah, I see that. Who was that guy?"

"Ro," I say, braving his eyes again.

This time in addition to his rage, I see hurt when he repeats himself. More slowly, like maybe I'd missed it. "Who was that, Kaia?"

I shrug, because what else can I do? "He's a friend. A friend of Zola's, really. That was the last date I agreed to. Forever ago."

Even to me, the excuse sounds weak, but I hadn't expected it to also be funny.

Ro pivots, so he's briefly facing away from me. In one hand, he holds a take-out bag similar to the one I'm carrying. He brings his free hand to his mouth in a fist, stifling his maniacal laughter before his palm squeezes the back of his neck. He releases it and turns back to me once more.

"Fuck," he says, smiling in a way that makes me want to throw up a little. And cry a lot.

"Ro, it was a hug."

"Kaia, it was a date. You weren't answering my texts because you were on a date."

When he says it like that, so simply, my eyes burn.

"I should've been the one you called," he continues. "I should've been the one sitting across the table tonight."

"Stop," I say, shaking my head, because if he doesn't, I'm going to break.

"Stop what? We can't talk about the fact that you only wanna see me by accident?"

"Ro—"

"I don't wanna find you on the side of the road anymore. Or save you from some shit guy who shouldn't have gotten a chance with you in the first place. I don't wanna run into you on a fucking sidewalk, while your leftovers gets cold," he says, and the words knock me back. "Let me take you out. A real date, where we both know why we're there. You and me. On purpose."

He's looking at me like he expects something from me. Like he wants something from me, needs it even.

It makes me want to run.

So that's what I do—emotionally speaking.

"What are you even doing here?" I say, like that's what matters after everything Ro's just told me.

"What am I doing here?" he parrots, and for the first time ever I wish he'd stop smiling. "What a great question, Kai. What *am* I doing here? Why am I standing here with a bag of food for *you* thinking you and Zo might be hungry, while *you're* out here on a date. That's a great fucking question."

He's not yelling when he says it, but that almost makes it worse.

"Can you stop? I get it, you're mad I went out with him. But you've known the whole time that I was doing this for Zola. I agreed to these dates before we even met! And it's not like this"—I wave my hands between us—"is even a thing. You've hardly talked to me in weeks."

"I've been chasing you around like an idiot since the day we met. Trying to figure out what you wanted, how slow you needed me to go. I stopped for a few days, to see if you'd come to me for once. Which you didn't, by the way. But I'm still here tonight, because I can't stay away from you. Even when I try, I can't."

I am so not in the right headspace for a grand fucking gesture right now.

"Ro, I can't do this."

"Well, maybe if you'd ever just let go instead of trying to predict every worst-case scenario, you'd have time to *do this.* Or at least to return a fucking text."

And apparently there's more he needs to get off his chest.

"God, you're so scared."

My body recoils like he's hit me.

"I thought you put up all these walls to keep the bad guys out, but that's not it, is it? You build 'em to lock yourself *in*. So you don't even have to try. You'd rather be right and alone than admit you don't have all the answers."

I take a step forward on unsteady feet, shaky from the verbal assault I'm withstanding, but my next steps are surer. Into the parking lot, and away from Ro.

"You know what your problem is?" he says, like he's finally solved the riddle.

"Oh, there's more?" I say, walking away from him still. "Don't stop on my account. Tell me exactly who I am and everything that's wrong with me."

"Careful, Kai, you might mess around and trip into your first ever honest conversation."

"Well," I say, turning to face him, finally. "Let's get into it."

He shakes his head, like he's trying to decide if it's even worth his time.

"You're not doing any of this for Zola."

His tone is too calm again. And I hate myself for the way I lean into the sound of his voice.

"It never had to be you. And it sure as fuck didn't have to be you tonight. You spend all your time talking about what you don't want, but you'll do almost anything to avoid having to decide what you *do.* Because as long as you're wrapped up in whatever this is"—he gestures between the restaurant and Asher's long-abandoned parking spot—"you don't have to deal with anything real. Make any decisions about your own life. Nah, this way it happens *to* you. Right? And since you didn't *choose* any of it, when it all goes to shit, you get to say, it's somebody else's fault. That you're living a life you hate, because Zola needed you. Or your mom. Or shit, this might even be my fault now."

"Fuck you," I say, practically spitting the word in his face. "I chose to be here with Asher tonight, didn't I? *I* chose that."

I hate myself for saying it and I expect Ro to hate me too. I expect him to leave.

"Ah. Asher." He says the name like it's a punch line. "From my bed to the next guy. Sounds familiar. And all this time you had me convinced your dad was the bad guy."

I rush past his words like being compared to my mom hasn't stolen the air from my lungs. "Nobody's forcing you to be here. If I'm so pathetic, then go."

"You're not pathetic." For the first time since he got here, Ro touches me. Grabbing my wrist and spinning me around to face him. "You're terrified."

My hands on his chest stop the movement, but it's not until I release my hold on him, so I no longer feel his heart raging under my palms, that my world stops spinning.

"I get it," he continues. "I understand feeling stuck. Fucking frozen, like whichever step you take next will be the one that hurls you off the cliff. You think I knew it was the right decision to come back here? Working at the fucking garage and watching my dad fade away a day at a time? That shit kills me, Kaia. I'll never know what my life would have been like if I'd decided to stay gone. But making the half-assed decision to come home is the only reason I met you."

I take a shaky step back. If he wanted to, Ro could close the space between us in an instant. He could force his way in, he could stop me.

But his voice is sad and he doesn't come any closer when he says, "If you're so broken, Kai, then why does it feel like you're putting me back together?"

And I understand why Ro didn't cross the physical line between us—he didn't need to touch me to reach me.

I need space to think—to breathe—but each step I take farther from Ro is like sloughing through quicksand.

"I wish you'd let yourself try." He's practically pleading. "I wish you'd let yourself choose. A job, a life. At least figure out how to choose yourself."

He pauses for so long that when I reach Mom's car, I turn to see if he's gone. He's not. He's there—real and solid and unwavering as ever. He digs his wallet out of his back pocket and walks to me, holding out a folded paper. My shaky hands reach for it instinctively.

"Or choose me," he says. "I wish you'd choose me."

His voice is smaller than I've ever heard it. So I hold his words gently, in case they're the last I ever hear him say.

But he's right that I'm a coward, because I still can't meet his eyes when I say, "I don't wanna do this."

Yet I know he's looking right at me when he tells me, "I know."

My insides are screaming out for Ro, as I drive away. I can't tear my eyes from his reflection in the rearview, and he doesn't turn his back on me as I go either. Not once.

And it's the quiet realization that he never has that chokes me until I'm barely breathing.

My hands tremble violently as I pull onto the nearest side street, unfolding Ro's note that's so worn, it's nearly torn along its creases. When his narrow scrawl comes into focus, my hand is at my lips. Covering a gasp as my heart thunders in my chest. Because this isn't just a note. It's everything.

**Describe your perfect date:** *We already had it. Being in the city with Kaia was perfect. Bringing her into my world made it new again. But it wasn't the show. It's never just the big stuff with her. It's the nothing moments in between. The way she mouths the words on highway signs. Knowing she's always going to burn her mouth on that first bite, because she's too impatient to let a slice cool down. The way her hand twitches when she wants to reach out for mine, even if she won't let herself.*

**I want a partner who _____:** *tells you what she thinks, even when it's not what you want to hear. Someone who isn't trying to be what other people want or expect. She's unapologetically herself. I want a partner who will call me on my shit. Someone who sings along to old-school music, orders pepperoni on her pizza only to pick it off, spills her guts when she's tipsy. Someone who can have a good time anywhere, even stuck in two hours of traffic. Someone who considers murder documentaries educational programming. A fiercely loyal daughter, sister, and friend. And someone who pretends to like nasty-ass oysters just to make me look bad.*

**I don't want a partner who _____:** *isn't kaia harper*

# 31

I'D GIVEN RO ACCESS TO MY SOFTEST SPOTS, TRUSTING HIM not to poke too hard, but it feels like he'd been collecting my faults like ammunition. And last night, he unloaded on me.

I'd thought he might be able to know me without holding it against me. I'd let myself want that. But when I wake the next morning, eyes swollen and head throbbing with the emotional hangover of our purge, I'm so angry with myself for wanting anything at all.

"And then you just left?" Zo says, once she's home and settled with her new favorite accessory—that fucking bell.

I hadn't planned to tell her and Mom about my fight with Ro so soon, but when Zola walked in, still wearing her hospital socks and bracelet, everything that happened yesterday washed over me. I opened my mouth to say hello, but a scream sob escaped in its place.

Her first bed rest demand is that I let her dissect every detail, since I, as she puts it, am "not to be trusted."

"Oh, I'm sorry," I say, handing Zola a bowl of Ben & Jerry's before sinking into the recliner with my own. "Should I have stayed for round two?"

Mom kisses the top of my head as she joins us in the living room. A night spent at the hospital on a leather-clad pile of rocks has accentuated the bags under her eyes and every usually subtle line on her face. She's exhausted, as further evidenced by the second or third cup of coffee she carries.

*All this time you had me convinced your dad was the bad guy.* Ro's words continue to hit their mark, as Mom lifts Zola's leg with her free hand, nestling into her spot at the foot of the couch like she's done since we were kids. Because she's been right here with us every day.

Dad's the one who left, and everything left broken in this house is nothing more than a ripple of his selfishness. He *is* the bad guy, and Ro's anger doesn't change what I know is real.

"Kai, he said he wanted you to *choose* him. He wasn't trying to go another round. He was trying to get you to hear him."

"Well, I definitely did," I say, losing my appetite as I recall the rise and fall of Ro's every inflection last night.

I'd dissected each word he launched at me and held my breath through every pause. I was up all night, reading between every line, desperate to find comfort in the things he left unsaid—in the parking lot, but also on his questionnaire. Those words, upstairs now. Stuffed into the corner of my nightstand and branded into my flesh, my mind, my heart.

But I still haven't been able to admit that part to Zola.

"No," she says, and I wish I was more surprised that she's not on my side. "Some of the words might've gotten in, but you didn't *hear* him. When I collapsed on the beach, it was *Ro* who picked me up," she reminds me, as if I could forget. Her voice is rising now. "But no matter how many times he shows up, I don't think you see him. And no matter how loud he got last night, no, I don't think you heard him either."

"Y'all good?" Mom asks, before either Zola or I can keep this thing going. "'Cause what we're not gonna do is anything else that puts my grandbaby at risk." She says this in a tone made infinitely more effective by that look she's giving us. "Zola, you need to calm down. And Kai . . ." She searches for a directive but comes up short. Something tells me it's not for lack of options, but an inability to choose just one. "Hand me the damn remote."

By Zo's second week of bed rest, I'm daydreaming about all the places I could shove her bell, while she peppers me with demands for everything I should be doing for XO by Zo while she's immobilized.

"How many times do we need to go through this?" I raise my fingers to count off my running checklist. "Address books are updated, the mailings you drafted are out, new client profiles are already in the system, images from the bonfire are doing numbers on social, engagement and followers are up tenfold, and the click-through rates on your newsletters are surprisingly impressive. I thought we'd all collectively agreed to send those things to spam."

Zola almost narrows her eyes at me when I say the last part but thinks better of it. Likely when she remembers that I am now her legs, her right hand, and a pretty hefty chunk of that baby brain she's working with. She needs me.

I'm still waiting for a *thank you* when Liv breezes through the front door I hadn't realized was unlocked.

"Hi, Harpers," she announces, like the breath of fresh air that she is.

"Oh, thank god," I say, collapsing back onto the couch. "Someone else for Zola to talk to."

"Hey," Zola says, tossing a pillow I catch easily.

But I don't smile or backtrack when I say, "Zo." Because she knows it's true.

"Happy to buffer," Liv says, handing Zola a box of the good macarons from the city.

"Liv, you're an angel," Zola says, already opening her dainty box. "Unlike your friend over here, who can't even make it through a ten-minute status update without throwing a tantrum."

I raise my hand in protest. "A status update is something a boss can demand from their employee. Maybe it's time for you to get one of those."

Liv laughs. "Oh my god, can you imagine if the two of you went into business together? You'd take over the world. Or at least the Tri-State."

Zola's eyes ignite as the seed of Liv's idea takes root. I won't admit it without a negotiated title, but I wouldn't mind padding my résumé by helping Zo out for a few more months.

My phone pings from its spot on the coffee table, and with Zola otherwise entertained for once, I can actually check it.

**Thursday, 3:17pm**

**Ash:** When can I take you out again?

"Ro?" Liv guesses, because she's the last of us left with any hope for that reunion.

It's been thirteen days and I still have exactly zero missed texts from Ro. Not that I'm counting.

I shake my head, returning my phone to the table. Face down. "Asher."

Zola adjusts herself, and I already know she's about to start with me, so I cut her off at the pass. "You think I could get like two hours off? No nurse duty, no Ro talk. Just silence?"

Liv braces herself, but Zola doesn't say another word about it. I'm counting it as a win.

•

An hour later, we're playing Netflix roulette. Shuffling through categories with our eyes closed, letting the chips fall where they may. On Zola's turn, we get stuck with a low-budget horror movie that looks more like an art school project than a feature film. The writing's horrendous, the special effects are laughable, and for some reason every character ends up shirtless in the woods at one point or another. But everyone knows, the only thing better than a scary movie is a bad scary movie.

We throw popcorn at the screen every time someone falls over a strategically placed twig or untied shoelace. We boo at the couples illogically making out when they should be trying not to die. And we pretend not to jump every time a chain saw tears through the paper-thin walls.

But it's still not enough to keep me from incessantly checking my phone to see if I've missed anything from Ro.

"Okay," Zola says, turning off the TV mid-dismemberment scene. "If you check your phone one more time, I'm gonna scream. And I'm not entirely sure that's great for the baby."

"Well, why are you watching me and not this cinematic masterpiece?" I try to deflect, and when that doesn't work, I lie. "I haven't even been checking it that much."

I look to Liv for backup, but she's suddenly engrossed in the blank TV screen on the wall. Her forced silence is all the agreement Zola needs to continue.

"Why don't you just call him?"

"Zo, I'm saying this calmly for the baby. But you are officially fired from being my matchmaker." I say it with a smile, so I'm pretty sure it's allowed. "It's time to give up on your Ro fantasies. He already said everything he wanted to say to me."

Of course this is the moment Liv chooses to find her voice again. "And what about you? Anything you wanna say to him?"

*Judas.*

I close my eyes in exasperation. "I've been busy," I say, as if I didn't just spend the last couple hours watching shit TV. "Zola's ice cream bowl doesn't refill itself."

Zola gasps in offense. "Don't put this on me. You're free to make a call or take a drive any time you want. I have delivery apps, and look—I even have Liv to keep me company now."

"He doesn't wanna talk to me," I say, standing to collect dishes that have been piling up for days, yet now seem to demand urgent tidying. "And he's got enough going on with the garage, and his dad—"

Zola's meddling radar fires. "Wait, what's happening with his dad?"

I tell them about Mr. Jackson's dementia and seeing him lose himself that morning at brunch.

I expect the conversation to stay on this more serious track, at least briefly, so I'm caught off guard when Zola says, "Are you kidding me?"

I look to Liv, who's waiting for Zola to continue, same as I am. And continue, she does.

"At this point, it doesn't even matter if you're into him or not. Now you're just being kind of a shit friend."

"Zo, we're not even speaking right now. You want me to show up at his doorstep and demand he cry on my shoulder?"

I leave out the fact that Ro recently did, in fact, cry on my shoulder.

"Yes," Zola says, without missing a beat. "It's really not that complicated, as much as I know you love making things as difficult as possible. You show up for people who have shown up for you. It's just what you do."

I open my mouth to argue, but she cuts me off.

"You're over here acting like it's still a choice whether or not to let him in, but he's already in. And he needs you. Now. Not when you're finished pretending he's just some nothing guy you kinda know."

"He doesn't need me," I say in a rush. "He needs someone who isn't adding their own shit to his plate. He needs someone solid, and I don't even know if I'll be here in a month or two. I don't know anything."

"Who does?" Zo says at a volume that can't be good for her blood pressure. "Nobody has their shit figured out. But if you're this committed to watching life go by until it magically starts making sense, maybe you're right to stay out of Ro's way."

I drag my hands over my face, hoping the sheer force of the movement will scrape off a few layers of my guilt. "Zola, you have to stop. My life isn't yours to fix."

"Well, who the fuck else is gonna do it?"

I look to Liv again, not so much for support this time, but to gauge her silent reaction to the argument unfolding before her. She's looking right at me, brow furrowed in pity. She agrees with Zola.

I'm drowning in everyone's disappointment in me. I'm drowning in my disappointment in myself. I have to get out of here.

But when I stand, Liv's voice is still so full of love that it stops me in my tracks. "Kai, walking out isn't gonna fix this."

"There's no point," Zola says, her voice ice by comparison. "Let her go. She's just like our dad."

She said it to hurt me and it worked. Zola's words echo in my head as I drive aimlessly until I'm parked at the beach, trying to remember how I got here.

Not even the expanse of endless glittering ocean can lift my spirits today. I curl my toes into the sand, warm from the afternoon sun even as it sets, and think back on the past few months. Or years, really. All the times I've left the room, deaded a conversation, ended the thing before it even became a *thing.*

*I'm not our dad,* I assure myself, behind closed eyelids, breathing in the salt-soaked air. Zola's not right about me. But maybe she's not exactly wrong either.

All this time, I'd wanted to protect myself, because if I don't, who will? But somewhere along the way, I forgot about the people on the other side of the shield I was hiding behind. I never stopped to consider who'd been protecting them from me.

Mom's car has joined Liv's in the driveway by the time I finally return home. Zola will most definitely be asleep now, but I stopped to pick up her favorite burgers just the same.

Inside, three bodies litter the living room in various states of consciousness. Liv's knocked all the way out on the floor in a makeshift bed of throw pillows and blankets. Mom's asleep in the recliner, but still tosses and turns. Restless. Zola, I realize, is the only one who's actually awake. Though she doesn't look particularly happy to be.

I kneel at her side to extend my greasy bacon and BBQ-sauce-slathered olive branch, but before I can offer it, she groans.

"Hey," I say on a whisper. "You okay?"

She pushes out a heavy rush of air but doesn't respond for a few beats. When she looks at me, I see the hint of perspiration beading on her upper lip. She nods, taking deep meditative inhales to catch her breath. I've attended enough birthing classes to recognize them.

"How far apart?" I ask, trading the burgers out for my phone to time her contractions.

"I don't know," she says. "I didn't want to wake anyone in case it's false labor again."

"How long ago do you think they started?"

But before she can respond, another contraction hits, and this time she moans loudly enough that Mom stirs in her chair. Her eyes flutter open, taking only a moment to focus before she too assesses what's happening.

Mom doesn't even try to whisper as she hops up out of her chair. "Is it time?"

Zola's smile is tinged in uncertainty. "Maybe?"

By now, Liv is up, too, her eyes wide as saucers as she watches Mom and me help Zola up. She battles through her next contraction with a grimace and blows out a breath so forcefully, I'm shocked it doesn't knock the whole house down.

Liv covers her smile, which is fine, because I'm ignoring her completely as I time how quickly Zola's contractions are hitting. When Mom rushes ahead of us to grab her keys, Zola leans her body into mine and we hobble toward the garage.

Before the door shuts behind us, I call out to Liv that I'll text her from the hospital, to which she responds with her usual *POP! POP!* "We're having a baby!"

# 32

I PARK THE CAR WHILE MOM AND ZOLA MAKE THEIR WAY INTO the hospital. By the time I finally reach Zola's room, I'm half expecting to be welcomed by a new baby's cries, but there's laughter bubbling out instead.

Zola beams at me with a dopey grin as she bounces on her yoga ball.

"Well, you seem better," I tell her.

"Right?" she says, framing her chin with her hands. "Turns out having a kid is actually kind of easy."

Mom laughs from her spot on the couch. "That may have something to do with the epidural."

Our jokes taper off when Dr. Nazim comes to update Zola on her progress.

"Well, my dear, things are moving along," she says. "I'd say you'll probably be ready to start pushing within the hour. What do you think? Ready to have this baby?"

Zola nods, looking so happy, and to her credit, only slightly terrified. "Let's do it."

The doctor smiles. "I'm gonna go get cleaned up. You have any last questions for me?"

"Has anyone heard from Jason?"

The question goes out to the room, but Mom's the only one with information. "He was in the city when I called, but he's coming. He'll be here."

Zola nods and takes a deep breath. "Then I'm good."

When Dr. Nazim excuses herself, I ask Zola a question I'm not sure I'm allowed to ask.

"Jason's coming?"

"It's his son too."

"Even after you've seen who he really is? What he's capable of? You're just gonna welcome him back in here?"

"I let you come, didn't I?"

"Zo, I'm serious. You've done everything on your own, and now he gets to show up and play Father of the Year?"

Zola takes a deep breath and I can't tell if it's a response to my inquiry or another contraction.

"First of all, I haven't been alone." She reaches out for my hand. "And as far as Jason goes, he's family. He's always gonna be family. Making a mistake—"

Zola changes her wording when she sees the look on my face.

"Okay, making a lot of really bad decisions, back-to-back-to-back, doesn't change his role in all this. And right now, I don't want to waste energy being mad at anybody. Least of all him. He's the father of my child, and in that way, I'm always gonna have love for him."

"All right," I say as soon as she finishes. "I get it."

"You do?" Zola stops bouncing and tilts her head suspiciously. "Damn, what kinda drugs did they shoot me up with?"

"Shut up," I say, gently hip-checking her shoulder. "You're right. I can't forgive him, but for your sake I can play nice. I don't want to waste any more energy being mad either."

She shakes her head in disbelief. "Who knew becoming an auntie would make you so soft?"

"Oh my god. You guys, I'm gonna be somebody's auntie."

From there, things move quickly. Dr. Nazim comes back in with the delivery nurses, and Mom and I take our places beside Zola. When she's in pain, she looks at Mom to help her through, but any time she gets scared, Zola looks right at me. Right into my eyes, and I tell her in that silent sister way: *I'm right here with you and always will be.*

Just before she starts pushing, the door opens and a nurse ushers Jason inside. Even though we said it wouldn't be, for the quickest moment it's awkward that he's here with us.

He hangs back by the door, looking unsure of his place, until Zola and I squeeze each other's hands one last time before releasing our grip. I step back when she reaches out for him, relinquishing my spot next to my big sister. It doesn't matter that he's the one holding her hand now, she knows I'm here. Always.

So many things are happening all at once, and when Dr. Nazim calls for one last push, I worry Zola might not have anything left. But then a first cry cuts through the chaos, and the whole world is forever changed. With his single breath and that single cry, this pointy-headed little baby leaves us all forever changed too.

A mother, a father, a grandma, an auntie. He did that.

Love did that.

"Are they always this cute?" I ask Zola when it's my turn to hold baby Zane.

Jason and Mom excused themselves to call everyone with the good news, so it's just the two of us—the three of us.

Zola's smile is sunshine. I've never seen her this happy or this in love.

"I don't think so," she says, reaching for the tiny toes that have just escaped their swaddle. "I think I got a really good one."

"Yeah," I tell her. "I think so."

"Hey," she says, waiting until I meet her eyes. "I'm really sorry about what I said earlier. That wasn't fair. You're not like Dad."

I shrug, because right now, that fight and everything else feels so far away and so unimportant. "It's okay. You've got a lot going on," I say, smiling down at Zane again.

"But you do too," Zola says, reaching up to take the baby. "You saved me these last months, you know that? I wouldn't have a job to go back to if it weren't for you—let alone my own company. Tiny as it may be."

I pull up XO by Zo's Instagram account and turn my phone to face her. "But still growing."

Zola laughs, but she hardly looks at the numbers before her eyes lock back on Zane.

"I'm just excited I finally get to do it my way." And she's still looking at the baby when she says, "Even though Auntie Kaia probably thinks Mommy's just the worst matchmaker in the world, yes she does."

"Is this where you finally fill me in on your master plan?"

"I'm just fixing the things Eliza always got wrong."

Zola leans down to place Zane into his bassinet. She keeps a hand on him, but she's looking up at me now.

"She'd ask people what they wanted, and then she'd give it to 'em. If it was that easy though, nobody would've needed us in the first place. But she didn't care if it worked out or not. Her check cleared the same either way. I don't wanna do it like that. Giving people what they *want* doesn't help them figure out what they need."

Her eyes glint under the fluorescent lights overhead, and even though I know she's wearing an adult diaper under her hospital gown, Zola's still as commanding as ever. And she's finally ready to show me the wizard pulling the controls behind the curtain.

"And what you needed was to let yourself sit in the mess and the discomfort of not having any control over what comes next. So you could stop looking so far ahead and finally let yourself be exactly who you already are. This has never been about making you believe in love. It's only ever been about reminding you how to believe in yourself."

I'm tempted to applaud when she finishes, but I don't want to wake the baby. So instead, I lean over him and whisper, "You're in trouble, little guy. Your mommy's a fucking genius."

And from somewhere behind me, my own mother walks in smiling and whispers, "Language," but it doesn't carry its usual bite.

Zola laughs, and when she looks out the open hospital door to where Jason's still making calls, her smile remains. "All I know is that you're allowed to do whatever it takes to be happy. Even if it means diving headfirst into the unknown." And she's only got eyes for Zane again when she finishes. "That's where all the best stuff happens anyway."

# 33

WHEN JASON RETURNS WITH THE PROMISE OF OVERbearing would-be in-laws, I excuse myself. I could use a shower, and Zola and Jason are too busy watching baby Zane to miss me.

I swear when I got behind the wheel, I really did try to head home. But this car has its own muscle memory, and before I know it, I'm outside Ro's shop. I just need to see if his truck is in the lot. Catch a glimpse of him to make sure he's okay. But the pull of being back here sucks me in deeper than I'd meant to go.

When I yank the lobby door wide, back in this space that's so Ro in its hard lines and soft beauty, this place that was ours for a single day, my insides physically ache for him.

I wasn't sure what kind of greeting I'd receive, or if I'd be received at all, but the dimple that pops from behind the counter makes me feel as at home here as ever.

"There she is," Mr. Jackson says, in his signature greeting.

The kindness and grace shown in those three words is the last thing I was prepared to hear. It's more than I deserve. It reminds me so much of the undeniable goodness of his son.

When I ask about him, my words are muffled by tears I

hadn't meant to put on public display. My embarrassment is cut short by the force of steady arms comforting me. Holding on to me in a way that makes me sure nothing bad can touch me. In that way only a father can.

It's a feeling I've gone years without. One I've spent so long trying to forget. But standing with Ro's dad this way, I remember.

"Ro knew you'd come when you were ready."

"He said that?"

Mr. Jackson nods, but my relief is short-lived when he continues. "Unfortunately, timing's working against you two. Last I heard, he was heading back today."

"To the city?"

"Got talked into a show real last minute." Ro's dad nods toward a youngish man talking to Mrs. Jackson on the far side of the garage doors. "And with my new aide settling in, Ro can finally come and go as he pleases again."

"Oh," I say, choking on the word. "That's great."

The words are sour in my mouth, but no more than the accompanying realization: Ro's gone. He was a temporary fixture here, and now he's gone. I don't even try to fix my face for Mr. Jackson's benefit.

He nods again like things are falling into place, but for me, nothing has ever made less sense than Ro Jackson being truly out of reach.

"I didn't get it at first," he says. "When Ro told me about your sister settin' you up. You didn't strike me as someone who needed help findin' your people. But when I heard you talk about your dad, it made sense. Being left behind like that—I know what it does to a person. My own dad leaving changed me in ways I'm still figuring out. Even as an old man." He looks so much like Ro when he smiles like that. "Once I knew what that kinda loss felt like, I didn't wanna depend on anybody. Didn't wanna get used to needing somebody who could leave. And there was a time where being good on my own felt like a superpower. It meant I was untouchable."

Mr. Jackson looks back to the garage, where his wife's face is framed by the plexiglass window. She laughs at whatever was just said on the other side of the door, and Mr. Jackson smiles right along with her.

"But thirty years ago, Ro's mama decided she was gonna know me whether I wanted her to or not," he says, laughing. "I didn't always like learning how to let her in, but I'm so grateful I didn't waste too much time fightin' her on it." He's still watching Mrs. Jackson as he continues. "She knows me better than I know myself now. And even if I forget everything else, some part of me will always know her. I'm certain of that."

He turns back to me as he finishes, his eyes wet with tears, and it takes everything I've got not to turn away from the kindness Mr. Jackson offers so freely. It takes everything I've got not to run anymore.

"You make it sound so easy," I say, blinking past the sting in my eyes.

His laugh surprises me, but as he catches a fallen tear, the emotions playing on his face aren't warring. He welcomes them all.

"Ain't nothing easy about livin'. But how lucky are we that for today, at least, we get to do it anyway?"

# 34

THE DRIVE HOME FROM THE GARAGE IS AS FAMILIAR AS it is excruciating. Which is, ironically, also how I'd describe the sound of Ro's voice emanating through the car's speakers. The distance I hear in his tone makes him nearly unrecognizable to me. A stranger. Still, I let the entire voicemail greeting play. It's torture to hear him this way, but it's also the most I've had of him in too long. I can't hang up.

I search Ro's deep timbre for a hint of the warmth I remember. Pause to hear a smile alter the shape of his words the way it always does. Neither comes. Because this recording isn't my Ro. And the truth is, he was never really mine at all. I don't blame him for ignoring my calls while he goes back into his real life.

*Ro's real life.*

For as close as he'd felt to being *mine,* Ro's real life is one I know very little about. I can't begin to guess how he'll spend his first day back in the city, or who he might spend it with. When we walked those streets together, they felt like they belonged only to us. The thought of him stepping in our footprints with someone else leaves me sick with regret.

I shift into park in the driveway and reach for my phone, but

I don't know who to call. Ro's gone. Liv's with Travis. And me feeling sorry for myself isn't a good enough reason to pop Zola's newborn bubble.

I'll pop Mom's instead.

**1:37pm**

**Me:** How's it going up there?

**Mom:** Hi! I actually left right after you did. I'm exhausted.

If she'd been on her way home, she would've said so. Mom's going to get her rest in a bed that's not her own.

I wait the requisite beat or two it usually takes to feel the way I always have with the confirmation that Mom's chosen a new guy to fall into—disappointed, abandoned, angry. Even after my conversation with Zola, I'd expected it, but my indignation doesn't come.

This pang in my chest actually feels closer to envy. Jealousy that after the night we just had, there's someone waiting to wrap Mom up in their arms. Jealousy that no matter how many times she's been hurt by the fall, she remains unbroken by it. That her heart is just as open now as it's ever been.

In a week or a month, there could be leopard slippers and red wine—she's got to know that as well as I do, but she's not scared of it. Not enough to build up walls to hide behind. And for the first time in my life, I don't know that it makes her wrong or reckless. It might just make her brave.

**Me:** Get some sleep. I love you.

**Mom:** I love you too.

Eventually, I'll go back up to the hospital, but for all the ways my world has shifted, I think I've earned a few hours of rest, too—my bed, my sweats, and my favorite guilty pleasure.

•

Ten minutes into one of my forever top five *Dateline* episodes, I'm shifting in the bed like this mattress is to blame for my discomfort. The police tape, the body bag, the grieving friend reflecting on how the dearly departed lit up a room. My stomach churns and I'm no closer to finding the thing I'd been so desperately craving—that comfort that comes with the absolute certainty of a sad story's sad ending.

The dreams they shared, the plans they made. The finality of words left unsaid and love left with no place to go. None of it feels like entertainment anymore. It's a tragedy.

A voiceover plays as the scene cuts to a backdrop of a staged morgue. I rip out my AirPods, fumbling to lock the screen before the next heartbreaking scene can be set.

My eyes, reflected in the screen's total blackness, are red-rimmed. My skin, clammy from a smattering of tears I hadn't even felt fall. I hardly recognize the person staring back at me.

*Losing Ro is one thing, but when did I lose myself?*

I want to unthink the words as they form, to deny them, but the truth is I *am* lost. I've *been* lost, trading out one mess for another, and it's not working anymore.

I can't keep my own life at arm's length forever. And it's not a matter of knowing or deciding what comes next, because life is happening in real time, all the time, without warning. That's the design. A constant series of terrible and beautiful moments butted right up against each other. And I can't escape that. I don't want to anymore.

But right now—in this moment when I *do* get to choose—why would I pick anything other than a happy ending?

I switch over to Zola's Netflix account, and I'm greeted by British baking shows and shiny plastic real estate moguls posed under waxy palm trees. There are no boogeymen on her landing page. It's bright and beautiful and all the things I've been too scared to admit to wanting.

Until now.

I click the first title in her watch list, and I'm transported into the big emotional swell of whatever romance Zola probably fell asleep to last night. Even without knowing anything about who these characters are, or how they got to this moment, I can't look away. Every word of their declarations draws me in, and before I know it, I'm rooting for complete strangers to find their way back to each other.

It's not just their words, though, it's the way they *see* each other. It's how he seems to know all the reasons she's hard to love, but he wants to do it anyway.

And when they kiss, a spark of something vaguely familiar ignites in my chest. My breath hitches at the memory of when I'd last felt that spark—with Ro. When I was undeniably, inexplicably happy.

The credits roll. But it's not enough.

I start the next movie in the queue. Another romance where I don't want to know what these characters had to endure to earn their happily ever after. I just want to feel what they feel when they get it.

*More. I need more.*

So that's what I give myself, jumping from sweeping romance to sweeping romance. And when my eyes finally give in to the exhaustion of my sleepless night at the hospital, it's long-awaited first kisses, second chances, and forgiveness that play out behind my eyelids.

Love: shiny and happy, and just within reach.

•

In my dreams, I find him, but when I wake a few hours later, the sun still high overhead, Ro exists only in my memory again. I'm not ready to leave him there.

I call one more time to tell him how wrong I'd been. How sorry I am that it's taken me too long to see what he seemed to always know, but again there's no answer.

I don't pause to make a plan or to contemplate exactly what I'm racing toward as I trip over myself to get out of this house. There's no more time to waste. I have to get to him. I have to make things right, to see if we can be all right.

I'm one foot from the door when my shaking hands, clumsy with adrenaline, swipe at my purse and spill its contents onto the kitchen island. I curse the mess delaying me by even these few seconds.

But then I see the business card. Life delivering something beautiful, even in the mess.

**5:14pm**

**Me:** Hi, this is Ro's friend, Kaia.

**Me:** You said to text if I ever needed anything.

# 35

THE THRASHING OF MY HEART BETWEEN MY EARS IS SO deafening that I hardly register Paul's hello as I enter the gallery.

A few people are still milling around the main room in the Greenpoint art space, but Paul leads me past them to the live instruction studio off the back. He pulls a heavy black curtain aside, and the room comes into view—what little I can see of it from behind the swell of the standing-room-only crowd.

Bodies shift, angling to get a better view of the stage, and the propulsive energy of the last two hours drains from my body. My hands are slack at my sides, my body anchored to its spot on the ground, and when I see Ro before me, the whole world stops spinning. It takes all my strength just to stay standing. But it's not Ro's eyes or smile that come into view. It's his heart.

A freshly painted mural is revealed to me, precious inch by precious inch. It drapes the walls in countless shades of calming blues and grays, melting into one another like notes of the sweetest song. Swirling together in a way that's so haphazard and so intentional all at once. I follow the movement of each line, hear the rhythm of every brushstroke, and I can feel him. Everywhere. Like he's standing behind me, holding on to me.

And then, I see *him*. Paint splattered and breathless. Pulsating muscles beaded in sweat.

I'd thought I'd memorized his every feature, but for the first time, when I see Ro, I *see* Ro, and the sheer force of him consumes me, inside and out. My breath comes in quick bursts, squeezing past the weight at my chest. I need to get to him now. I've needed to get to him always.

The audience responds to a cue I've missed, some raising plastic cups of prosecco, while those with two free hands break into applause. I'd join them, if not for the look on Ro's face when he spots me. His smile newly hesitant, but no less spectacular than ever.

Even from this distance, my body heats in his presence. I fight my way between bodies to get to him, ignoring how faces twist in judgment and question as I pass. I can't wait another moment to tell Ro the only thing that's ever mattered.

I'm only halfway through the room, when the crowd before me parts, and the only person I owe an explanation to emerges.

"Hi," I say, aware that we have a curious audience but unwilling to retreat from him. Not again. "I called you."

Ro takes a tentative step closer. "I didn't see it. My hands were full."

My gaze shifts to his paint-smeared fingers, open at his side, palming the air the same way they had that night under the streetlamp. I've cherished that memory as something nearly perfect, but looking back I see it differently now. I see how terrified I'd been to reach out for him then, and how much we almost lost because of it.

"I have something for you," I say, and his eyes drop to the paper dangling from my hand. His face ignites when he sees the questionnaire, and though he doesn't speak, I'm grounded by the steady support of his smile.

"This was always the deal, right?" I say with a shrug, laying the page bare along with my heart. It still feels impossible, but I do it anyway. "You show me yours. I show you mine."

I force a shaky step in his direction, swallowing past the worry playing at the back of my throat, ignoring the fear teasing the base of my neck. Ro doesn't have to bridge the gap between us—I don't deserve for him to make this easy on me—but because he's Ro, he does.

He takes my hand, and when he squeezes, I pray his fingers paint mine. I want him to leave his mark.

The crowd around us thinned some once it became clear the artist wouldn't be sticking around for a Q&A, but Ro still leads me to a sculpture courtyard I hadn't noticed on my way in.

Even in this world that Ro's built for himself—visually stunning and bathed in the glow of the setting sun—it's Ro, himself, that commands my gaze.

"That piece in there," I say, pointing back the way we came. "It's beautiful."

Ro joins me where I stand. "It's for you," he says, but when he sees the confusion on my face, he continues, "Well, the baby."

He studies my reaction with such gentleness that I can hardly remember why I'd ever been running from him, when now, all I want in the world is to go to him. But for all Ro's given me, there's something I still owe him. It's my turn.

I look to my questionnaire.

"You were only half right about that day in the city," I say, unsure where to begin. "Since I don't think it was technically a date. At least I wasn't sure at the time. Maybe that's why I didn't ruin it."

I only realize I'm bending the page back and forth when a corner rips off in my hand.

"For me, our best night was at that pizza place. Which is odd because I distinctly remember humiliating myself. But I also remember how you never looked away. Because for some reason, none of my stuff scares you. But you were right—it scares me. Being called out on my bullshit, the fact that you never let me hide . . . it scares me. I kinda hate it." I smile now. "But I don't hate the way you do it."

Ro would probably let me leave it there, but he deserves so much more.

I don't want to say this next part. I don't want to remind Ro of our worst day, but if we're really going to do this, I have to. "I'm so sorry I hurt you."

"Kai," he says, trying to spare me. "I'm not even worried about all that."

But even if I want him—and I do—I still don't want him to save me.

"How? How do you keep believing in me when I give you nothing to hold on to?"

"Because whether you like it or not, I get you. I know you. And you may be scared of this, but I'm not scared of you."

"You should be with someone so much better than me," I say, not caring how it makes me look. His kindness is a gift I've never had to ask for. One I may never deserve. "You should be with someone *good*."

"Kaia, I could stand here and tell you every good thing about you, and I will, but I also need you to know that what I feel for you isn't something you gotta earn by being 'good.' I want every part of you. Every version of you. I want *this* version of you." And we're so close now that I feel the warmth of his breath on my lips as they part for him slightly. "But only if you can stop trying to break up with me before we even go out."

My own laughter catches me off guard, and I know that's exactly the reason he said it.

"You know I can't stand you, right?" But when I say it, finally, I fill the empty space Ro's been saving for me all along, and the weight of his hand in mine grounds me.

Ro studies our interlaced fingers like they're a puzzle, solved. Our amusement is snuffed out by the warmth of our touch as he guides our hands to rest at my back. My body arches into his, and I couldn't run now even if I wanted to. But where was I ever really going?

Ro pulls me into him even closer, and my stomach drops in anticipation of the kiss he doesn't make me wait for. Raw and honest, finally. Ro and me, on purpose. He palms my face and my lips part wider to meet his urgency as I climb up onto my toes to get that much closer. But I'll never be close enough to Ro Jackson.

I pull back till my lips just graze his as I whisper, "Thank you for not hating me."

Like always, when Ro smiles, I don't have to see it. I *feel* it.

"I could never hate you," he says. "I'm too busy falling in love with you."

So many unanswered questions remain—for me. For us. So many things I can't even begin to know. But here, with Ro, *not knowing* doesn't feel like something to run from. It's a promise I want to run toward. A promise that there's so much still to come.

I'd stand with Ro in this not knowing forever, if I could.

I'll stand with him now, in our beginning.

# Acknowledgments

In some ways, this story's been taking shape forever. This *book,* though, took shape during a very particular season of life for me. And while writing and publishing a novel is always a challenge, doing it through times of personal upheaval can feel impossible. These are the people who, in one way or another, whether they know it or not, made getting here possible.

Melanie Figueroa, I sincerely hope this isn't your first time realizing how much I love working with you. You've been such an incredible partner to me in every sense of the word. I trust, respect, and value your opinion so much—and not *just* because we always agree, LOL. You are a joy to work with but, more than that, a joy to know. Let's keep going! And to the rest of the team at Root Literary, thank you for the many ways you empower your staff and client roster through endless collaboration and care.

Emma Caruso, you've shown so much enthusiasm for this story and such unwavering trust in me from the very beginning. You guided me through this debut experience with your expertise while also teaching me to follow my own instincts. You sent me into every revision feeling prepared, capable, and excited—

which is all any author can ask for in an editor. I'm so glad we get to do this again.

Talia Cieslinski, you stepped in while Emma was otherwise (and adorably) occupied. Thank you for all the juggling I know you did—though I never actually felt it. You showed up round after round and email after email without missing a single beat. I couldn't have asked for a more present or competent partner to help me cross the finish line. You're already a superstar, but I'm so excited to see all you'll do in this industry.

And to Whitney Frick and the rest of the editorial team at Dial, thank you for making me feel so welcomed, so valued, and so safe in your supremely capable hands.

There are many more skilled professionals who help steward a story to pub day. Thank you also to Dial's marketing and publicity team, sales, design, production, and Sarah Horgan for the cover design.

Over these past few years, people have shown up for me like never before. Thank you to Lauren, Lenore, Haley, Ruth, Amy, Maurade, Shae, Birukti, and so many more incredible women whose friendship got me through.

And to the many talented writers who offered me steadfast community in various groups and discords, thank you for being a safe space to talk fiction *and* to get real.

Niccole, thank you for your excitement and belief along the way!

Taylor—I'd rather be saying this over margaritas, but thank you so much for your support and your friendship. If I ever need someone to go to war on my behalf, I know exactly who to call.

Ana, thank you for all of it. Our ridiculously long phone calls about everything and nothing. Voice notes that turn into podcast episodes. The shared experiences and brutal honesty. The feedback and genre expertise. The girl's girl energy of my literal dreams.

Alex, your friendship has meant more to me these last fifteen or so years than I could ever put into words. I'm forever grateful for the love you've shown me throughout every life stage, every hard-earned win, and every painful loss. Your friendship is *home* for me—somewhere I never have to be too strong and am never made to feel too weak. I love you. Craigslist forever!

Monica—my Zola—I'm not even gonna try to get into it here, because I've hardly typed anything and I'm already crying. But thank you for every time you've lent me your strength, your insight, and your calm. For every conversation that probably should've ended in tears, but instead ended in laughter. Thank you, sister.

Mom, I don't know if you'll read the book (kidding), but I *do* know you'll read this—and honestly, it's the most important part anyway, because you've been everything for me these past few years. So, thank you. Just thank you. And three squeezes (because I love you . . . more than my lips can say).

Lyra, by the time you read this book, you likely won't remember what life was like for us while Mommy was writing it. But even as we defined our new normal again and again, this period of life has been magic. Because *every* day with you is magic. You are the best person I've ever known, and I'm so grateful that I get to be your mama. Everything I am and everything I do is for you, sweet girl. This book included.

And to the readers, librarians, booksellers, book influencers, and all other *bookish people*—none of this would be possible without you. Thank you for always proving the limitless power and impact of a good story well told. And thank you for reading mine.

# Don't Tell Me How It Ends

Adrienne Thurman

DIAL DELIGHTS

**Love Stories for the Open-Hearted**

# XO by Zo

## New Client Intake Questionnaire
## Instructions

Below, you'll find a series of thirty-six targeted questions that will help lead our efforts together.

But these aren't dating-site prompts to skim past. And they aren't meant to be easy.

This questionnaire has been strategically designed to fast-track the vulnerability and intimacy required for lasting connections that will take you from first date to forever.

The answers you provide here will not only help our team find your best match, they'll help you begin to tell your story as only you can.

Congratulations on being one step closer to your happily ever after!

We're so happy you're here.

xo, Zo

1. If being rich meant you had to be famous, too, would you want it?
2. What's your favorite solo dinner/girl dinner/struggle meal—either now or from childhood?
3. Describe your "perfect" day. If it hasn't happened already, explain what's stopping you from making it happen.
4. What's something you were taught in childhood that you've had to unlearn as an adult?
5. Do you rehearse what you'll say on phone calls before making them?
6. What was the last song you sang to yourself? When was the last time someone else heard you sing?
7. At the age of ninety, would you rather still have the mind or body of a thirty-year-old?
8. Name three things you'd like to have in common with your partner. Name something you *don't* want to have in common with your partner.
9. Do you think most heavily in pictures or words?
10. What are you most grateful for in your life? How do you show or acknowledge it?
11. If you had to pay your most recent ex a compliment, what would it be?
12. What's something you wish you would've been told as a child?
13. What do you love about the way you were raised? What would you change about the way you were raised?
14. Is there anyone who has impacted your life without them knowing it? Why haven't you told them?
15. What is a hobby from childhood that you miss? Would you ever pick it back up?
16. Which is most damaging to a romantic partnership?
    a. undelivered communications

b. unmet expectations
c. broken promises

17. If a crystal ball could show you anything—what would you want to see/know?
18. Fill in the blank: The person whose death will hit me hardest is . . .
19. What's a mistake you've made in past friendships or past romantic relationships that you hope to never make again?
20. What do you value most in a friendship? Is it the same as or different from what you value most in a romantic partnership?
21. Would you rather live like you'll die tomorrow or live like you were born yesterday?
22. Do you prefer your vacations to be:
    a. active and adventurous
    b. culturally stimulating
    c. restful and relaxing
23. In a single word, describe:
    a. how you hope someone feels with you on a first date
    b. how you hope friends feel in your presence
    c. how you hope your long-term partner will feel in your presence
24. If you had one year left to live, what would you change about your life? What's stopping you from making that change right now?
25. Fill in the blank: "I wish I had someone with whom I could share . . ."
26. What does money mean to/for you?
27. If you died tonight, what would you regret not having told someone? Bonus points if you tell them now.
28. Is there anything your friends know about you that you'd struggle to share with a romantic partner?

29. What's the best compliment you could ever receive about yourself?
30. Describe the ideal body type for your romantic partner. What nonphysical quality are you drawn to in others?
31. When was the last time you cried in front of another person? By yourself?
32. What's one thing people get wrong about you?
33. If your next long-term relationship could have either *novelty and desire* OR *stability and security,* which would you choose and why?
34. Would you rather choose how you'll die but have to also know the exact date and time it's going to happen, or would you rather live without knowing any of it?
35. Have you ever felt jealous of a romantic partner? Did you tell them?
36. For better or worse, who in your life has taught you the most about love?

*Keep reading for an exclusive sneak peek*
*at the first chapter from*
*Adrienne Thurman's next book,*

**Better in Real Life**

# 1

I BLINK HARD THROUGH A FIZZY VEIL OF PROSECCO, BUT THE numbers on my banking app remain unchanged—more commas and zeros than anyone in my position has a right to. This moment may not be picket-fence-wrapped or sealed at an altar with a kiss, but it's a dream come true nonetheless, and it's mine. As are all those zeros.

For the first time in almost three years, I let myself acknowledge my own audacity for dreaming any of this. For wanting this impossible thing that had felt too fragile to even name aloud. Like if I'd let the universe know how badly I wanted it, it might not have let me have it at all.

*But fuck I wanted this.*

At the first prickle of tears behind my eyes, I close the app, grinning back at the matching smiles on the phone's lock screen. My vision clouds with emotion again when I see us—when I see *him* and that little smile that has always been a sort of full-body undertaking. Every muscle contracting to split not only his face wide open but the entire world. My son has split *my* entire world wide open. And that's been even more than a dream come true—it's my happily ever after.

I swipe up and into my photo album to reveal another memory—a rubber band–armed Zane mid-belly laugh. I know the tune of it so exactly that I could swear I hear it now, echoing out of the screen and filling the room as I speak to the image aloud. "We did it, baby."

Unfortunately, the response I get in return isn't sentimental coos or phantom giggles. It's a violent banging that pulls me from my reverie, drop-kicking me back to this dank and too-dim East Village bathroom stall.

When the next round of pounding comes, I don't know if it's the second or maybe third assault on the heavy metal door separating me from the bar outside. But before I can figure that out, a woman's frantic voice cuts through my cloudy Korbel haze.

"What the fuck? I've been waiting for like twenty minutes!"

I yank at the toilet paper, as if she'll be able to sense and appreciate that I'm hurrying now, and though I also don't remember if I actually peed or if I've just been sitting here this whole time, I still use the entire giant ball of tissue to wipe as I yell back, "Coming!"

At the sink, I cringe a conspiratorial *oops* at my reflection as the woman outside continues her complaints. Quieter now. With less banging.

The brief moment of calm gives me just enough time to forget *again* that I'm supposed to be rushing—*thanks, champagne!* I'm too distracted now by the girl in the mirror. Boho braids tossed to the left, reminding me of my long-forgotten side-part superiority. The freckled brown skin of my cheeks flushed a tipsy pink, and my eyes, that are usually piercingly dark, now unfocused and slightly hidden under lazy lids at half-mast. It's not *Zola the mom* staring back at me or even *Zola the CEO,* whose matchmaking company was recently acquired in a landmark deal for Black female entrepreneurs. It's just Zo. It's just me.

When the heavily New York–accented "I swear to god" snakes into my consciousness, I briefly consider texting my sister for backup. Sure, making drunken friends in line for the ladies' room is a thing, but so is getting jumped.

Kaia's never been known to de-escalate a situation in her life, though, so I leave my phone pocketed—already starting a genuine, if not slightly slurred, apology as I open the door.

"Girl, I'm so sorry. I think I actually got drunker in there. I forgot I was in the bathroom."

The woman raises one perfectly sculpted brow and I can't tell if that means I'm making it better or worse. But now that I'm standing, my buzz has floated directly to my brain, so I can't stop myself. "I never go out. And I *never* drink like this. I'm a mommy. *Mamacita!*"

Shockingly, loosely quoting that old Love Island meme hasn't immediately made this person want to be my best friend, but she doesn't shoulder-check me as she shuffles into the bathroom either. *A win is a win.*

An email notification buzzes in the pocket of my too-tight jeans as I vibe through packed bodies bopping to the opening bars of a song coming through the speakers. Kaia, still sidling up to the bar with our nearly empty bottle of cheap champagne, starts talking shit as soon as she sees me.

I ignore her *I literally almost left* as I *bing-bop-boom-boom-boom-bop-BAM* along with Kendrick Lamar. Flipping my now-unlocked phone on the *BAM*, so only Kaia can see the pending and life-altering deposit that just hit my business account.

And together, we yell, "The type a shit I'm on you wouldn't understand ayyyye!"

•

Kaia's been too drunk since our second celebratory tequila shot to notice that I've switched to water. And right back into work mode. Multitasking is more than just my secret weapon—as a single mom, it's a necessity.

As Kaia regales a group of fintech bros with our elevator pitch for XO by Zo, the matchmaking company she helped me launch when I was pregnant, I open the email that hit my inbox earlier. The official welcome note from my new boss at The Playbook—New York's premier dating app for young creatives of color. Technically, the deal happened months ago, but we couldn't really get started until contracts were signed and checks cleared. Which, by my foggy new-mom-alcohol-tolerance math was a whole two hours ago. Yvette is as hungry for this as I am.

*From: YvetteMorris@theplaybook.com*
*To: Zola.Harper@gmail.com*
*Today at 10:58 p.m.*
*Subject: Welcome to The Playbook!*

*Zola,*

*You don't know how eager I've been to send this email. When I started this company a decade ago, it was already a "risky investment" for a Black woman to enter the "saturated market" of dating apps. But I had a feeling about The Playbook. I have that same feeling now—about you and XO by Zo.*

*What you've managed to do in just three years without any major capital is astounding. You've built a space of authenticity and connection that tens of thousands of people have already discovered through your grassroots efforts and word-of-mouth success rates. But with The Playbook's data-driven expertise and financial backing, your usership and impact will scale from tens of thousands to millions. Overnight.*

*This acquisition, though, is about more than your company. It's about you. Your instincts, your North Star. You've followed them this far and The Playbook won't reroute you. We'll stand behind you and beside you as we all continue to march toward the future of romance in this digital age together.*

*An invite will follow for first thing Monday morning. Protected time to plan your introduction to our board and existing platform. But as you can probably tell from the timestamp on this email, I'm available any time you want to ideate.*

*More soon! Welcome aboard.*

*Y.*

The phone vibrates in my hands as I read, but this time, the buzzing doesn't indicate another incoming message. It's coming from my fingertips. From the adrenaline coursing through my veins—excitement and nerves, in equal measure, buzzing just beneath the skin's surface.

I hadn't intended to start brainstorming here, but Yvette's note is a subliminal starter pistol, signaling the race is on. As I look around the bar, my head snaps the scene into jagged bits and pieces like a puzzle. The windows, fogged by the heat of too many well-dressed bodies pressed together, though nobody's actually dancing. The heady bass bumping through the speakers as liquor and mocktails flow freely through the crowd.

Once my brain chops and screws a thing, it never comes back together the same way, and I smile at the new image taking shape now. Because for all the things that are right about this Friday-night scene, I also see what's wrong. My fingers start tapping out a reply to Yvette before I've even consciously decided to do it.

*To: Yvette*
*From: Zola*
*Today at 11:18 p.m.*
*Subject: Re: Welcome to The Playbook!*

*Yvette,*

*Thank you for your note. And apologies for diving right in, but I don't want to lose the spark I feel right now.*

*There's no doubt that online dating has changed the contemporary landscape—both for good and bad. But the thing I love most about matchmaking is that it's part of a person's real life. Their whole life. Not just the performative fraction of a "self" they can curate online. Not something that's separate from who they are and how they move through their actual world.*

*You spoke of the future of romance in our digital age, but it's exactly those concepts that so often seem to be in conflict. Romance is not digital. It's tactile. It's multidimensional.*

*Yet, right now, I'm sitting in a bar, watching groups of beautiful young people speaking only to the friends they came with. No mixing. No mingling. And most of them will likely return home alone tonight, swiping right and left until they fall asleep.*

*You've made The Playbook a leader in the online dating space, but we've got to get people offline again too. They need more integrated experiences. Something that feels more real. But in order to do that, we have to teach them how to look up again. How to flirt, how to banter, how to have fun. In the real world. We've got to give them a new "playbook" so to speak. The X's and O's. By Zo.*

"Okay, period," Kaia says when she gives the email her obligatory read before I send. And she says it with so much confidence that I ignore the fact that I'm trusting her with my next business plan when I wouldn't even trust her to operate a City Bike at her current level of sobriety. "And will *you* also be rejoining the real world or naw?"

I snatch my phone back, already exhausted by the conversation she's trying to have. It's the same one she's been initiating since Zane stopped nursing a year ago and started doing overnights with his dad. "I'm in the real world now, aren't I?"

"You're working," she says, unimpressed.

"In a bar!" I yell, genuinely offended that she's doing this.

I know Kaia means well. She's seen me through some dark days since we moved to the city together. Two sisters and a baby living in a one-bedroom Greenpoint walk-up is not for the faint of heart. But we've come so far these last two years here—like a three-bedroom *Manhattan* walk-up far. And for all the things we've accomplished, yes, we've also had to sacrifice a lot. My social life included. But I refuse to defend any of that right now. Not when I'm finally fucking winning for once.

"In forty-eight hours I'll be back on mom duty, so apologies if I'm distracted by—ya know—trying to create a legacy for my son. My job is to help other people and I do it well. The day I start getting paid to go outside myself is the day I'll start prioritizing it. For now, though, just be grateful I squeezed my MILF ass into these pre-baby jeans to buy you alcohol you can't afford."

Kaia, who's also now switched to water, raises her glass to her lips, muttering into it as she speaks. "And that zero to a hundred transition is why no one should go four years without getting laid."

"Zane was only born *three* years ago."

She tilts her head, resting her chin on a fist in mock contemplation and genuine challenge. "And how long before that had it been since Jason fucked you?"

*Damn.* But also fair. My relationship with Jason, my ex–high school sweetheart and baby daddy, was over long before our son came. What we had ended slowly and took way longer than it should've for all the good stuff to seep out, little by little, through a hole we couldn't patch. Like a two-week-old helium balloon. We hadn't been whole for a long time, and when he finally admitted that starting a family with me wasn't what he "signed up for," there was nothing left holding us up at all. And exactly zero fucking.

Kaia knows all this and more. She knows how hard it was for me to admit that while I'd loved Jason in a familial way, I'd never *loved him* loved him. Not like I needed to for us to last. She knows all the ways I broke and had to be put back together once he left—once I realized I'd be living the single-mom life of my literal nightmares. And she knows how wrong I was about all of it, because nothing about life after Jason was a nightmare at all. It's been the opposite, really.

I signal the bartender for our check and steal another glance at my inbox to see if Yvette's tunnel vision is as bad as mine.

Kaia's voice and her words demand my full attention as she says, "You're an incredible mom."

I'd be happy for her to leave it at that, but she continues.

"And your bank account is a testimony to what happens when you throw your back into something. But you did it. You're doing it—the deal is done, your baby's happy, and Jason's finally stepping up. I'm not suggesting you take your foot all the way off the gas, but look around. You're not treading water anymore. Maybe now's the right time to catch your breath a little. Even if breathing doesn't come with a paycheck."

The low buzz on my lap briefly pulls my attention back to my phone as the bartender returns with the bill. I skim Yvette's response that simply says, *"I LOVE everything about this. Give me tangibles Monday and we'll get the campaign into action immediately."*

And just like that I'm shaking again. Because I can do this. Kaia's right—I'm already doing it.

And suddenly I don't feel like closing out anymore. Not yet. I want one more bottle of champagne. I want one more hour to be the girl I saw in the mirror earlier. One more hour to be Zo.

PHOTO: © VICTORIA GLORIA

ADRIENNE THURMAN writes romance and commercial fiction where gloriously unlikable women get the happily ever afters—or revenge plots—of their dreams. As a BIPOC creator, she writes stories with a diverse cast of characters that make her readers feel seen. *Don't Tell Me How It Ends* is her debut novel.

To learn more and get updates, visit adriennethurman.com.